Alejandra Olivera

HC SVNT DRACONS

(HERE BE DRAGONS)

To Danny, Mickey and Luis

Rising moon
Geese in flight
She to the west
They to the sea

He had been adrift all night, unsure whether ocean or sky parted and fell away before his eyes. In the first blues of dawn, he took the gleam of waves for that of stars and Milky Way murmurs for salt and surf.

Sextant in hand, Tanaka Hikaru-san[1] could hear a faraway bell chiming a quarter past five. Useless to know, unless he could find a point to fix on and establish his position. But the world lay shrouded in fog. Sky would not separate from water; dawn would not yet break. So on and on, through hours so thick they barely moved, through time that slid by without a trace, he waited. To port, a glowing space began to unveil it, until he could finally see it, majestically anchored in the translucent immensity, inhabited by mooning wide-eyed fishes weaving through towers of coral and snoozing anemones. There it was, just as he remembered it from so many other dreams: the Great Wall.

---

[1] Honorary suffix used to refer to people of both sexes; its meaning is close to 'Mr' or 'Ms'.

To starboard must lie Qinhuangdao, where the Dragon[2] was said to dip its head in the warm waters of the Bohai Sea. He had the coordinates by heart: 39° 24' north, 118° 33' east. He thought that, if he managed to drop anchor on the far end of the rock, then just maybe... but he has lost his way. He cannot remember... the solution slips from his grasp as the problem itself seems to dissolve.

Now, as the bell rings half past five, he struggles to recall the shipwrecked words and cannot reel them back. In his head an aquarium of weightless amœbæ are drifting away, just as he is.

'Hey!' he hears. 'Let's go, Tana-chan!'[3] Slowly he finds himself floating back. But... where to? Trapped in a limbo between two worlds, something is calling out his name. The voice's vibrations make his body shudder. Through the cracks in his eyes Tanaka can just make out his friend Oshima-san rocking him awake.

'I've been calling you since five,' he complains. 'It's twenty to six!'

Tanaka cannot shake the feeling of being on the verge of a momentous discovery. In vain he strives to recover the last shreds of his visions even as the dream-gates begin to close. How often this happened when he was little! His mother would wake him early for school and he would dream of getting up. In these 'real' dreams he registered every step to the bathroom, brushed his teeth and even pulled on his clothes. On he would dream until, realizing they'd be late, his mother yanked on his socks unceremoniously and crammed his breakfast down him while he was still half-asleep.

---

[2] *Laolongtou*, 'the Old Dragon's Head', is where the Great Wall of China meets the sea.

[3] Diminutive suffix indicating affection, generally reserved for adolescent females or children of either sex. It can also express warmth of feeling, as when addressing friends or pets.

Wrapped in his yukata,[4] Tanaka has successfully packed his futon,[5] folded his quilt and stowed the bundle in four minutes flat. Now a whirlwind of activity, he has gulped down his rice and his "Oriental Chef" soup, dressed and left the house, buttoning up his shirt as he goes, sweater between clenched teeth, coat slung under one arm, a couple of brown paper-backed books tucked under the other. By the time he reaches the station, he is almost running and out of breath, and just makes the train.

The carriage is packed, and he's soon sweltering beneath all those layers of clothing. Hemmed in on all sides by bureaucrats and young girls smelling of strawberry chewing gum, he can't move an inch. Some are reading manga[6] or the morning paper. Others are dozing in an alcoholic haze that gathered last night, in the company of other Company people, and lasted until three this morning.

Tanaka can tell immediately who will alight at the next stop: they study the electric signs intently, or fidget with their umbrellas or their briefcases, where their entire day is packed away. As the train stops, he joins the jostling press of commuters with a grim look of 'now or never' and struggles through the crowd: 'Sumimasen, sumimasen, sumimasen!'[7] They spill out of the carriages onto the platform like rice bursting from a sack, and search for names, numbers, signs. Tanaka charges up the escalator two steps at a time: 'Suimase, suimase!'[8] He walks through the tunnel, entangled in wafts of witch-hazel that fade and die as he boards the train to Shinjuku. At Hakone Yumoto, he changes

---

[4] A casual, light cotton kimono.

[5] A traditional bed consisting of a foldable mattress.

[6] Comics.

[7] 'Excuse me': a way of getting someone's attention.

[8] Colloquial for 'sumimasen'.

platform and completes his journey aboard the "Hakone Tozan".[9] He finds an empty seat, settles down and opens his book, breathes deeply and finds himself dreaming away... The small train climbs slowly through narrow, winding stretches of woodland where blackbirds sing love songs... where nothing has changed.

He had never been on holiday with his parents. Not in his wildest fancy could he imagine his otō-san[10] relaxing in a simple hammock or enjoying a quiet beer. It was his grandmother who took charge of the portion of his life that began at the end of the school term. He remembered his mother telling her 'Look after the boy for a few days,' perhaps fearing he would end up driving everyone to distraction with his unremitting boredom. But Tanaka positively relished retiring to a corner and getting bored. Other boys would call and try to lure him out to play, but he preferred to stay at home, bored and alone.

'Take him away across the sea, so he can see the world out there!'

Days later, from some faraway place, his grandmother would turn up on their doorstep. He had seen photos of that "place". It was very different from where he lived. She would come to fetch him and off they would set, across the sea, arriving at a port, negotiating a big city with railway stations, buildings, restaurants, bars... But they would soon be on the move again, back on what seemed their endless trail.

'Are we there yet?' Tanaka would ask. 'When will we be there?'

'Not long now, my child.'

---

[9] Hakone Tozan Railway's small train.

[10] Father.

'How long is "not long", Obā-san?'[11]

The landscape transformed abruptly as their train burrowed through valleys and barrelled across massive bridges hanging above rivers.

'I want to go to Mount Fuji! Can we go and see Fuji-san?'

Swaying gently, they ploughed on through fields of hardy late-summer hydrangeas and bored through tunnels in the bamboo drunk with early morning light on the hillsides.

'Not long to go now, my lad. Not long.'

'Mount Fuji's full of fire but doesn't burn. My mother has a calendar that shows Mount Fuji by some cherry tree branches. She has it hanging on the kitchen wall. Can we go and see the Fuji-san?'

Grandma was slightly built, like a little girl, and peered out at the world through wondering, smiling eyes. They would sit together and play at 'battles' – of dinosaurs or robots or warriors. But she couldn't always remember the plots of the stories Tanaka would make up. He would have to go over them again every now and then, from the beginning, only for her to forget. It wasn't her memory; no, but her attention, her gravitation towards the edges of things; the world around her was far too interesting to be stuck in one place at a time.

His mother had told him that, during the Meiji Restoration,[12] his obā-san had lived in China with her parents and fourteen siblings, including her twin brother. 'Out to the west, farther even than where the sun goes down,' she said, 'in the land of silk and gunpowder.' In those days her father worked for the Japanese government. She was still only

---

[11] Grandmother.

[12] The chain of events leading up to the restoration of imperial rule in Japan under Emperor Meiji in 1868.

little when war[13] loomed over the horizon. In a matter of days her family dismantled the entire house and packed up everything from the dinner service to the folding screens. They let the birds out of their cages and left at full tilt, returning to Japan aboard a Navy warship.

Amidst all these hasty preparations and with so many children to see to, they had scooped up the little girl's twin brother but somehow contrived to leave her behind. They were in the curious habit of counting the twins as a pair; add them together and they made one. This must have been the source of the confusion, for no one noticed the little girl's absence until dinnertime, when they were already far out at sea. The nanny had counted and recounted them. But every time she totted them up on her fingers, she couldn't work out where it was that she had gone wrong. So she lined them up, took the abacus out of her bag and counted one last time: the little girl was missing. In light of their daughter's inveterate penchant for hiding, the family held out the hope she might still be tucked away inside one of the travelling baskets. 'Could we have locked her in a trunk?' they asked themselves, racing to the cargo hold. They rifled through the luggage – other people's as well as their own – well into the small hours... but all to no avail. The little girl was nowhere to be found.

Communications were down due to bad weather; there was no way of contacting the Consulate. Still they tried and tried, regardless all journey long, beaming out a stream of telegraphs but receiving none in reply. All they could make out over the radio set, crackling strangely in sounds not of this world, were Russian voices, possibly officers aboard other ships. By the time they put in at Tokyo, they were worn ragged with desperation. The mere thought of having abandoned their child, of having left her in such dire straits,

---

[13] The First Sino-Japanese War, from 1st August 1894 to 17th April 1895.

triggered in them such shame that they agreed they would, in future, never own to having fifteen children, but fourteen. People were bound to forget, what with everything else that was going on... But, despite having only a vague notion of the exact numbers involved, their relatives remembered perfectly well there had been twins. So they set about pairing off the smallest girl and the remaining twin, they being the most alike. As they grew older, however, people began to suspect there was something 'wrong' with this impromptu sister, still a pint-sized dot next to her 'twin' brother. To make matters worse, as some of the children had been born in China – 'nikkeijin'[14] kids as they were known, a mildly derogatory epithet that they never quite succeeded in living down – the conclusion they came to was that the twin brother must have been switched for a girl in hospital, the birth of a girl having always been regarded as a tremendous misfortune in China.

In all that time not a day went by without her parents secretly visiting the Foreign Ministry, or the Department of War, or any temple they could find to pray in. They began by invoking the Celestial Goddesses, believing them to be the most helpful, given their superior knowledge of the local geography, and who knows... they be mothers themselves – in some distant and ephemeral dimension, of course. But on further consideration they spotted a flaw in this logic: the two nations were, after all, locked in a ferocious war and no assistance could be expected from Chinese gods. That put an end to all their hopes.

Three years on, they had resigned themselves to never seeing their daughter again and had given her up as dead. But no sooner was her name engraved on the traditional wooden funeral tablets for the family altar than the little girl

---

[14] A name given to Japanese people that were born abroad or are permanent residents of other countries.

reappeared – no one could say where from – carrying a canary in a cage. She was delivered to them by a Chinaman with a long wispy moustache, who introduced himself as 'Chin Li Foo Jr., Magician'. The girl arrived speaking fluent Mandarin and not a word of Japanese. But, despite a protracted conversation, neither party could understand a word the other was saying, so they agreed to communicate in ideograms, which they wrote on the black slate her brothers used for their homework. From what they could decipher – or rather, infer – the girl had taken a book from the Shin Doji Orai no Jiten Daizen[15] collection, which had been sitting in a half-packed box awaiting removal. She had then apparently hidden herself away in the little tea-house by the carp-pond and fallen asleep. No one knew for certain how much time had passed before the good man found her wandering the back streets of Peking barefoot and alone, clutching her book for she was worth. Nor did they ever manage to solve the mystery of how she came to be in such a place. Still, what mattered was that the magician had taken her with him, treating her like his own daughter. The girl must have had several years of excitement as they moved about the country in their small travelling circus, but she remained forever tight-lipped about that period of her life.

The fact that she had picked the first volume from the fukuro toji[16] collection was another stroke of luck. On the first page of that particular volume, on the ex-libris, was written the address of the house where the family had previously lived in Japan and where they would be bound to return one day. Her father's name appeared clearly: 'Chairman Ito Yoshimi', written in kuro sumi,[17] and in immaculate

---

[15] An encyclopædia for primary school children.

[16] A type of 'bound-pocket' book binding.

[17] India ink.

calligraphy. Indeed, it was the only page to have survived intact. The magician received a substantial sum for his generous actions before vanishing back into the world whence he came.

The girl and her family found it equally difficult to readjust to each other after such prolonged, involuntary exile. It was especially hard for her siblings, as she had learned a few tricks in their time apart, such as vanishing biscuits without a trace. Little did it matter if they used seven keys to locked her away; she would always escape her punishments; no one could do a thing about it.

This and other stories little Tanaka had heard about his grandmother convinced him that, wherever they might go together, their travels were sure to bring extraordinary adventures. As their journeys never took a straight line, but branched out to various old towns up in the mountains, Tanaka nursed the secret hope that one day they would reach places so far away that they would never make it back in time for school.

Oh, the summer nights in guesthouses! The old wooden inns with upright ladders, the little doors and secret cubbyholes in villages that had lain slumbering for over half a millennium!

Tanaka liked nothing in the world so much as to imagine that he and his obā-san were samurai marching along the historic Nakasendō Road[18] on a mission to Edo. In incessant monologues he would ask and answer questions, dishing out orders to his soldiers on make-believe steeds. Overhearing his whisperings, his grandmother would think his words were directed at her...

'Nothing, Obā-san, nothing. Just playing.'

---

[18] A mountain road in Japan, connecting Edo (modern-day Tokyo) with Kyoto.

Everyone seemed to be on familiar terms with his grand-mother. Greeting her like an old friend, often refusing to let her pay the bill, she would be forced to find other means of getting the money to them.

They would often sit in a circle with fellow travellers, roasting fish over the fire of the irori.[19] As night drew on, moved by nostalgia stirred by the rice wine, they would set to singing old peasant songs, which little Tanaka found utterly hypnotic. Then, when he was sound asleep, someone would hoist him over their shoulders and carry him to his futon. Half-awake but already slumbering in dreams, Tanaka would tamely let himself be tucked in, sliding into a universe of camphorated sheets and grain-stuffed pillows that gave under the weight of his head like a sighing field under the autumn sun.

They would wake up at dawn to the crowing of the cocks and linger long over breakfast. There was warm tofu[20] brought up in baskets, and dark salty seaweed from distant seas. Crunchy wild vegetables that grew in the mountains amidst rocks and by rivers where the sweet fish leapt.

Still swathed in the clean aroma of steaming rice, they resumed their journey to Hakone,[21] discovering the delight of locomotives rushing past at dizzying speeds, or of the soporific clackety-clack, as Tanaka rested his head on his grandmother's lap. After touring a few temples and lakes, it was time to embark on the last leg of their journey and board the little train. Night was almost upon them. They settled back into the wood and red-leather seats worn black at the edges. The perfume of the humid forest and

---

[19] A sunken hearth.

[20] Soy milk curd.

[21] A mountain tourist resort to the west of Tokyo, famous for its geo-thermal springs and the colours of its foliage in autumn.

the chirping of crickets intensified as they penetrated deeper into the mountains. By the time they reached their destination, the carriage was almost empty. His grandmother's cousins were waiting for them inside the small station, loud with cicadas. They exchanged greetings and bows before resuming the slow, laboured climb up a dirt track up a stairway of crisscrossing roots. There was nothing lovelier in this world than a path, Tanaka thought.

They paused frequently to chat. What they said to each other when they looked in the same direction could not be made out, for some reason, but had to be read in their eyes. After each brief interlude they would set off again in yet another apparently random direction. They would press on until they had almost crossed the small wooden bridge that hung over the channel of hot springs, where again they dawdled to chat, wreathed by sulphurous vapours, like wraiths encountering each other in the mists of the hereafter. They came at last to a path that descended a few yards to the garden of the old minshuku.[22] They exchanged greetings and bows with those who had stayed to prepare dinner, and everyone would start talking to Tanaka all at once: 'Look how you've grown, Tana-chan!' 'Have you already started school?' and 'Tell me, what grade are you in?' and 'Are you still in the kinder? 'Have you started school?' Then, as if Tanaka's answers weren't enough, they would proceed to grill his grandmother all over again: 'Is he still in the kinder? has he started school?' And they would press them further: 'Are you a good student? Is he a good student?'

But the best was yet to come. Tanaka was given his very own little table, a set of worn old pencils, meticulously manicured, some rice-paper to draw on, some brightly coloured squares for origami, or perhaps even a forgotten toy left

---

[22] A lodging house akin to a 'Bed and Breakfast' in Britain and the United States.

behind by another boy. But Tanaka and his favourite robots – Tetsujin-28 Go and Black Ox – were inseparable.

Tanaka and his obā-san shared a room with four others: the owner's cousin, her daughter and two sisters, whose mother he never managed to identify.

The doors of the minshuku were closed to tourists. They took advantage of that time of year to make any necessary repairs while enjoying a well-earned break, during which, needless to say, no one caught a moment's rest. One of the most important rituals was the cleaning, after the sami-dare.[23] The entire house would soon be plunged into chaos as everything was dragged outside and left in a jumbled heap to dry in the sun. These practices were part of the ceaseless strategic battle against the damp that accumulated over the year, mainly during the June rains. The garden would be transformed into a gypsy camp, where books, blankets and frying pans all shared the same unlikely space, and where, inevitably, everything would go missing. They would spend hours searching for everyday objects, as if in a flea market. 'Could anyone please tell me if they've seen the ladle?' 'Hold on a second, I'm trying to find the ruler.' 'Has anybody seen my glasses? I can't look for my glasses unless I'm wearing them!' 'I'd be glad to help out, but I'm looking for the book I was reading last night.' 'Oh! I may have put it out to wash with the sheets?' 'Oooooookā-san, what have you done with my doll?' 'Isn't that it, over there? The one Mr Dog's chewing on?'

Tanaka revelled in this disorder and was convinced that every house should devote at least one day to the creation of a wondrous chaos: a magnificent rebellion of objects.

Once their work was done, the women all plunged into the onsen,[24] their heads crowned with damp towels.

---

[23] Early Summer rain.

[24] Hot springs.

Incomprehensibly to Tanaka, they all seemed to enjoy this hellish treatment under the sweltering summer heat, after even the cicadas had evaporated. 'The December waters warm you up, see?' said one woman. 'And the August waters... well, the August waters cool you down!' rejoined another and, in possession of some shared secret understanding, they all burst out laughing. Such reasoning formed part of a collection of 'non-excluded thirds' that was beginning to open Tanaka's eyes to the relativity of the world.

Yet, in spite of such self-persuading arguments, peppered as they are with family myth, Tanaka refused to climb into the water. He would as soon have immersed himself in a cauldron of boiling soup, so he chose to just sit on the rocks and play with his robots, lulled by the laughter and the whispering world of 'women being all together'.

He was only allowed access to this exclusive women-only area[25] because he was still little. After all, 'no one wants a small child wandering about the place on his own,' 'What if he were to get lost or fall in the river!' And then, of course, he was quite irresistible, for as the saying goes... 'Nanatumade-wa kami no uchi.'[26]

He never ceased to marvel at the 'rejuvenating powers' his grandmother attributed to the springs, which could transform flat and wrinkled breasts into splendid buoyant ones. The effect was short-lived, though; no sooner did the women emerge, their bodies steaming, than their parts would resume their original droopy pocket shape. Not wanting to puncture his obā-san's illusion, Tanaka never said a word.

---

[25] Traditionally these baths were mixed, but were divided into separate areas for women and men when foreign tourism began, and have remained so to this day. In the mixed areas, bathers are required to wear a 'modesty towel'.

[26] 'Before seven [years], they (children) count themselves among the gods.' According to an interpretation by Arai (1992),

Night

It wasn't the dark that made him uneasy. He had always slept with the lights off, ever since the day he was born. No; it was what manifested in nature after nightfall. Tanaka had developed a theory – or rather an intuition – that the forest withdrew into itself during the daytime as if sleeping, as if oblivious to the world. But, as night fell, it began to awaken and, with it, the spirits of the mountains and the waters. The planets in their ephemerides and the stars looking on forever glinted in indifference at the changing scenery of day and night. But not the trees swaying in the wind, or the bushes, or the rocks, or the rivers, nor even perhaps... the peonies in the gardens.

'After all,' he thought, 'that would be the normal way of things: simply because in the timidity of birds, which take flight the moment we approach, lay the essence of all of nature.' Tanaka was overtaken by a profound sadness at the thought that he was doomed to be feared by birds.

Marked by centuries of stillness, the only thing left to the stones was to retreat into themselves. But at night, when folk retired to their homes, they could begin to breathe.

He remembered one time when, walking along the beach hand in hand with his father after dark; they had stopped for a moment by some black rocks jutting out of the sand like body-parts of some half-buried primitive animal. All of a sudden Tanaka distinctly felt a melancholy brackish exhalation over his legs. It was perfectly obvious to him: the stones were stirring from their reverie; there and then.

'No, son, they don't breathe,' his father had said. 'It's the kami[27] growing restless in the rock. It's only the kami, Tana-chan...'

The boy was surprised at his father's use of the words 'only' and 'kami' in the same breath, because, to him, a kami could never be 'only a kami'. It occurred to him that it was the other way round for people: they turned inwards at night and shrank from the revealed immensity before them, 'because darkness is always infinite, like the universe itself, even if you're sitting in a wardrobe.' Which was why people wrapped up warm – becoming like children in their mothers' laps – and prayed: 'Night, have pity on me, for I am but a man.'

Towards nightfall Hakone filled with unfamiliar sounds, hard to interpret. They had the property of being amplified by the woods, producing an echo that made even the lightest of droplets ring out. A light breeze in the bamboo was all it took to unleash a symphony of otherworldly hyōshigi[28] resonating out and across the mountains.

'Listen... there's something in the water! Something jumped, I tell you!'

Plop! There it was again.

'There's another!'

It could be 'this', but it might also be 'something else' – 'that' for which there is still no name. 'That' which singles us out, there in the dark – a 'thing' we cannot help sensing, even with our eyes closed.

'It's a frog!'

'A little frog diving into the pond!'

---

[27] A spirit in bodily form.

[28] Ancient musical instrument consisting of two pieces of wood fastened to each other with an ornamental cord.

'Like in the haiku!'[29] says his grandmother. 'The haiku... by Matsuo Basho.[30] Remember it, Tana-chan?'

'Yes, yes, you used to read it to me as a boy,' blurts Tanaka, eager for the conversation to be over with. Because his grandmother hasn't been paying enough attention, because they all talk too much, because out there is night, where everything that shines is a glance and far away howl the wolves out hunting rabbits in the moonlight. So you have to whisper or, better still, keep quiet! Quiet, so you can listen... But they won't. They've been prattling on all day and they still aren't done – they still have things to say. So many things that, if words were made of water, we'd all be drowned this instant!

And in the heat of the night a chill would run down his back as someone inevitably fell to telling obakebanashi,[31] ancient legends handed down night after summer night, prowling the huts like ghosts and raising the hair on the heads of generations for as long as story-telling and the nights themselves. Moments cherished yet feared, by the flickering little flame of the kerosene lamp and the crick-crack of the wood stretching awake in the rafters. Of all the obakebanashi, the one that frightened him most was the one about the Yamamba.[32]

Tanaka doesn't want to talk. He only wants to know one thing, something very serious:

'Obā-san,' he asks all a-quiver; 'is the Yamamba really real?'

---

[29] A form of poetry inspired by the perception of the instant.

[30] A famous seventeenth-century poet, alive in the Edo Period.

[31] Ghost stories.

[32] A demon taking the form of an ugly old hag with wild white hair, who lives at the foot of the mountain.

Young Ayako overhears him and answers with all her teenage impishness, her voice getting quieter and quieter:

'Tana-chan... Obā-san *is* the Yamamba,' she says in a whisper, then launches herself on him, tickling and shrieking at him, all the time laughing for all she's worth. Then all the others start laughing too and their laughter impels Tanaka's fright even further, so he runs out to nowhere, pushing all and sundry before him, stumbling, falling, and bursting into tears.

'Goodnessh gracioussh! Sshtop sshcaring him, Asshyako!' scolds Grandma, who's taken her dentures out, ready for bed. 'Come here, Tanasshan' she tells Tanaka, 'come to me... Ssho sshtop all thissh nonsshensshe, we have to go to sshleep.'

Sleep? Who said anything about sleep? Tanaka whimpers back to the futon and sits beside her.

'Come here, little one, come to me...,' she says, making room.

As night spreads its wings, Tanaka listens; his eyes as wide as windows... now the sluggish lollop of the prehistoric toad by the passageway door, now a low snore breaking rhythmically, like the rolling of waves on the beach... Then, out of nowhere, a dogless bark .

Tanaka shifts on the edge of the futon. What if grandma really is... the Yamamba?

Return

Obā-san and Tanaka will stay at the minshuku until the end of summer. Then, more than ever, he will wish to linger on, if only to find out how long the cicadas keep singing after the summer dies and the first kiri hito ha[33] falls to earth.

But before the September sun reached its zenith, the holidays were at an end and Tanaka was shunted back to school. Possessed by a supernatural sadness that prevented him understanding why they were doing this to him, he fell into a stupor, like a deer that, used to living in meadows of tall grass, would be dragged off to a train carriage. There, dazed by the lights and the milling throng, it could do nothing to block out the noise but shut its eyes tight.

It all felt a little different and sad when they got back home. His grandmother would usually stay with them for a few days to share stories of the trip, but eventually she would leave, and with her the last trace of summer. With her gone, Tanaka was bound to the round of shopping for school things. Holding his mother's hand, he would walk like an automaton, not knowing – or caring – where he was being taken. He was weighed down with packages, bags of shirts and white cotton ribbon to label his uniform, the itchy sweater and black flannel trousers he would be forced to wear even in hot weather because the school's 'Official

---

[33] *Paulownia*: famous in Japan for the sound its large leaves make when they fall, and accordingly has become a classic symbol of the arrival of autumn.

23

Calendar' pronounced the arrival of autumn. Once again he would visit the woman with the pin-studded mouth, whom his mother referred to as 'Misseamstress'. Once again she would launch into her haphazard lengthenings and short-enings and takings-in, insisting all the time on talking to him and asking him things through her pins, while she knew perfectly well Tanaka wouldn't understand a word of what she was saying. Tug him and prod him and prick him she would. 'Voo flease stov jiggling avout, child!' she would tell him, treating him like that black magic doll he'd once seen in a film on TV. And then there was that handicapped girl who lived with her... and spent every waking hour howling and whooping like a ghost train. He wondered what could have happened to the girl, whose shouts could be heard from down the street, balefully heralding their imminent arrival at Misseamstress's house. At least he was lucky enough not to live close by because he would probably never have got a wink of sleep, what with all that subhuman shrieking. The poor boy already had quite enough to handle with the stories of the Yamamba...

Then came the photographs, although thankfully he had already negotiated the ones on the first day of school by the 'official' cherry tree in the school playground, which marked the start of the first school term. He appeared in his school uniform, brow knitted, a stern glint in his eye. His mother laughed as she leafed through the family album and saw Tanaka always looking 'too serious'! Was he the only child who hated having his photograph taken? In fact, rather than loathing them, he found them a little 'troubled'. His mother said it was probably 'because they reminded him of days that were dead and gone.' The idea wasn't unreasonable: on the sophisticated side for a child, but true all the same, though he only came to realize with the passing of time.

Tanaka longed so badly for those moments of solitude when there was no one at home... He would go to the wardrobe, where the quilts and pillowcases were piled, in search of his little blue travel bag. In it, jealously stowed, lay his treasure: an old grey track suit suffused with the smells of holidays, safe from his mother's voraciousness for laundering. With eyes half-closed, Tanaka would plunge his face into its grimy folds and give himself up to smoky memories of bonfire after bonfire, opening a secret door to an ever vanishing summer.

Paper Graveyard

He contemplated jumping the train to go and see it. His workplace was only a couple of stations further. Yet he knew everything would have changed since its owner had died a few years back. He recalled his father's words: 'You can never revisit the places of your childhood; they simply don't exist anymore.' It was no use, there was nothing for him there; better just to enjoy the memory of it. And as the black and white landscape slid past the window, he was struck by a sudden insight into his reluctance to be photographed as a boy. He in fact felt intense curiosity about the hand-coloured photographs lining the family albums, though most of the people depicted in them had departed for the other world. They all now shared a common space between the sheets of tracing paper: Granduncle Kinjo-san, he of the shaven pate and abundant side-locks, one shoulder bare, sitting by a window fixing the body of a shamisen.[34] Next to him, on a bamboo bench, in front of a curtain decorated with autumn landscapes, squatted Koman, a onetime geisha in Tokyo. She wore her hair down. It reached almost to her feet. Below her was a double picture of the Miyagi-san sisters in striped bathing costumes – one in red stripes, the other in black – sleeves rolled up to their elbows, their hair done identically in classic Shimada chignons, immortalized on a 'handmade' beach strewn with seashells. They were holding an oar used to punt boats forward on the river-bed,

---

[34] A Japanese three stringed instrument.

not the sea as the background suggested. Beneath the photo, was a 'jokey' caption: 'Why aren't we wet?'... Yet another picture on the same beach, this time standing beside a gilded Greek column. One day he too would be there, and someone would write beneath his photograph: 'Why so serious?'

Wonder Boy

When he reached the station, Tanaka headed uphill, toward the Yamana residence. Along the kerbside ran an iron handrail so people wouldn't slip on the ice and crack their heads open. At the top of the hill he rounded a gentle bend to the left that ended in the high stone wall marking the boundary of the residence's grounds.

Tanaka-san used to enter through a little side door next to the front door. Both nestled in a wisteria-crowned arcade that sprang into bloom in mid-spring, doomed in winter to become a tangle of bare twigs worthy of the nest of some Royal Pterodactyl. A heavy zelkova gate divided the garden itself from the inner sanctum, which contained a cobblestone patio with a well from the Muromachi Period.[35] There were a few stories about that well that Tanaka would rather forget but they unfailingly sprang to mind whenever he passed it.

The gatekeeper sat there in his little cabin all day long, eyes glued to the monitor, intent on every movement beyond the walls. No sooner did Tanaka approach than the gate swung open automatically, giving him no time even to ring the bell.

'Ohayo, gozaimasu!'[36] he greeted him, waving him through like someone uncertain whether they're directing

---

[35] The Muromachi shogunate; 1336 to 1573.

[36] "Ohayō" is a greeting used in the morning. The addition of "Gozaimasu" is to make the expression polite.

traffic or performing a dance. Then he walked with him, as usual, as far as the edge of the garden.

A long way off Madame Yamana was waiting for him on a bench beneath the bare maples, with her little felt hat, her leather handbag on her lap and a small suit-case.

'Good day, Madame Yamana!' Tanaka greeted her, 'sorry to keep you waiting!'

She nodded curtly once in return.

'Tanaka-kun.[37] I just stepped outside because I knew you'd be arriving,' she said complicitly.

Then, looking at the sky, she asked:

'Do you think it will keep snowing?'

'By the looks of it, yes, Yamana-sama,'[38] replied Tanaka, approaching the car. 'It is quite cold, is it not. And the sky has that stillness about it...,' he said opening the rear door.

Madame climbed into the car and Tanaka stowed the suitcase swiftly in the boot.

'Tokyo this time?' he asked, anticipating her answer.

'Yes, as usual; to Tokyo, please. I shall be staying until the day after tomorrow. I shall call to tell you what time we will return.'

'Tokyo it is, then! We'll run into a fair amount of traffic on the road,' he said, rubbing his hands to drive away the cold. 'Looks like we'll have more snow in the evening. It's lucky you don't have to go back just today,' he added, turning the key in the ignition, 'goodness knows what the roads will be like. It's always as well to check before setting off... just in case,' he added.

She took a little mirror from her handbag, glanced at it and put it away again.

---

[37] The suffix '–kun' is used for employees or students, usually male, whom one has known for some time.

[38] The suffix '–sama' is a markedly more respectful version of '-san', used indifferently for any gender.

'Of course,' she replied. 'Are you good at weather forecasting?' she asked, adjusting her hat in the rear-view mirror.

Tanaka smiled.

'No, Madame, not really... I heard it this morning on the radio.'

He was being modest. Tanaka could predict changes in the weather with a sniff of the air. Indeed, as a boy, he had become famous in his village for just that. He would draw back the shoji[39] and provide an instant forecast. Often, in bright sunlight, he would take his mother by surprise, telling her it was going to rain, and his predictions were so unerring that he was, on more than one occasion, even suspected of summoning the storm. His explanations of the whys and wherefores of his conclusions were not without 'a certain scientific foundation'; the secret lay in his sense of smell. Air currents and atmospheric depressions, mists or dews, cirrus, stratus, cumulonimbus, even harvest time – every event in the year had its own particular scent, and Tanaka had learnt to unravel that interweave of damp, flora, fauna, tides, clouds, and village and country activity that went to make up any given meteorological situation. Because the weather isn't something that begins and ends in the heavens.

'The child can even smell the Wind-Rose!'

'Tana-chan!' his cousin would call from the terrace. 'What'll the weather be like tonight; I'm supposed to be going out with my boyfriend. Is it going to pour down?'

'I don't know, I haven't smelt anything yet.'

'Get smelling then and be quick about it!' Kaeda-chan would shout to him from the gallery, and Tanaka would start sniffing the air like a bloodhound. However, if the aroma of food reached his nostrils, blown on the air from

---

[39] Opaque vertical screens covered in waxed paper that slide sideways to redefine spaces in a room, or are used as doors or windows.

the extractor fan in the kitchen, he would run out to the stove to see what his okā-san was cooking up. 'I don't know, I'm hungry! Take your umbrella just in case!'

Nor was he only consulted by brides-to-be – reluctant as they were to spend their weddings getting drenched – but even by fishermen, afraid to set out to sea without checking first with him, the Meteorological Service being somewhat haphazard and the weather so mixed-up that it was difficult to make any hard and fast predictions.

'I baint be putting out this evening,' said one, unloading the previous night's catch, 'because The Lad said there'll be a storm... and a real blinder at that!' and '...if The Lad says so...' and no one blinked an eye at such phrases. They circulated around the sheds in the harbour in the wee small hours, even before the market opened – or even when no one had any doubts about putting out to sea because all the available semiology suggested otherwise. But what really disconcerted outsiders was to discover that 'The Lad' was not the nickname of an old sage, but merely of a five-year-old boy.

Long before almanacs, or even before the Chinese described the twenty-four jiéqì, [40] people oriented themselves by relating chains of events. Several centuries on,
this was how things still worked in his village and no one
needed to consult the calendar to know that the hydran-
gea blooms by the little tea-house announced the start of
June, heralding the arrival of the consignment of sincha [41]
from Uji. [42] The young women would sit by their aunts, sip-
ping tea and looking on with feigned indifference at the
procession of boys fresh and strong as new tuna, all the
time giggling nervously behind their fans. Not long after
that the rice would begin to sprout in the paddies. The bo-
nito [43] season was already upon them, and in just a few days
the westerly breeze would start to blow and the entire village would be swathed in the aroma of the smokehouses
where the honbushi [44] was being prepared. Then the sultry

---

[40] 'Solar terms': Developments of calendars over the course of three
consecutive dynasties (the Shang, the Zhou and the Western Han),
which divided the calendar into twenty-four microseasons of 15° each.

[41] New tea: the first month's harvest of a variety of green tea, character-
ized by its fresh aroma and sweet taste, available for only a short time.

[42] A tea-producing town.

[43] *Thunnus thynnus.*

[44] The process goes by various names, the smoking itself being called
'arabushi'. After the fish has been sun-dried it is known as 'hadakabu-
shi'. It is then covered with special mushrooms that completely remove
the moisture before it becomes 'honbushi'. It is approximately six

summer swelter broke loose, and there was no escaping its stifling embrace. As the nights grew shorter, the sudare[45] were no longer enough to keep the houses cool. People would spend the nights tossing and turning, cultivating a growing compassion for the lethargy of others, as everyone went about in a trance of exhaustion, sprinkling salt on their sweets and sugar on their savouries. Many slept outdoors under mosquito nets or just slumped on their engawa.[46] Shoji overlooking the street were flung open wide, all privacy temporarily suspended. Once abed, the sleepless neighbours were in the habit of talking to each other into the wee small hours, and protests from other houses were commonplace: 'You there! We're trying to get some sleep here!

Tanaka would put his futon under the netting on the verandah that overlooked the back garden. Before long his mother would join him. Then his father would arrive in vest and underpants, oppressed by the unrelenting heat, and all three would end up sleeping in the open air, one atop the other.

For all their efforts not to whistle at night[47] so as not to attract the snakes that frequented the gardens at that time of year in search of guinea pigs, they would inevitably end up sharing their futon with one at one stage or other. Worst of all, the only villager who knew the 'magic spell' to frighten them away had died a year earlier and nobody could remember it because no one had ever bothered to write it down.

---

months before it is ready to be sliced into what is called 'katsuobushi', the basis of an endless variety of dishes and broths.

[45] Green bamboo shutters.

[46] A narrow wooden deck along the edge of a house facing the garden.

[47] According to a Japanese superstition, whistling is thought to attract snakes.

In the summertime Tanaka's mother used to come home when it was still light, which created the illusion that she came home early. In this time warp, stretching from the end of the school term to his holidays with his grandmother, Tanaka's relationship with his mom seemed to 'depart from the script'. At times, overwhelmed by a strange sensation of seeing himself 'being a son' he wasn't quite sure how to go about it. He would watch the other children around him being with their mothers and try to do as they did. 'She's my mother,' he would tell himself in silence, but the more he repeated it, the stranger it sounded to him, until the concept lost all meaning. The anxiety – that of not being able to capture the essence of being 'a-son-for-a-mother-who-wanted-to-clown-and-caper' or who would simply sit beside him – was written in his body. A mother who didn't wear her apron or sit at the kitchen table doing sums on the abacus or checking his homework; no, she was a woman who attracted stares – discreet but real – from young men 'fresh and strong as new tuna'.

Sooner rather than later Tanaka discovered that one of the conditions of so-called 'childhood happiness' lies in not being darkened by the fear of losing it, as one day we are bound to...

So it was that, over the years, due in part to her burgeoning rheumatism, it became more and more difficult for his grandmother to get out and about. At first she sent him word that she 'may well' go, then that she 'may not', then that she 'wouldn't', which eventually became 'almost definitely... heaven knows.' Tanaka, meanwhile, emptied himself of all expectation, realizing that one thing was what was possible and quite another what was probable.

He wondered if his parents had considered the possibility of moving to Honshu[48] with her. He spoke to them then with unusual assertiveness, as if he had become an adult overnight. He explained that the future lay in the capital and that they couldn't fritter away their lives as if they hadn't left the Edo Period, which cast a shadow over their futures, and that there was a good reason why the young upped and left the village.

His parents looked at him with something between surprise and stupefaction.

'They teach you those things in school?' asked his mother.

---

[48] The largest island in the Japanese archipelago, on which stands the city of Tokyo.

Finally, his father, a dour and silent man whose mere presence was enough to shut the beaks of fighting cocks, lost his temper and spoke:

'No, we can't just go off to live in Tokyo, son. You'll have to wait until you're bigger, and then you'll decide all by yourself, and I don't want to discuss the subject again,' after which he got up from the table, without leaving the slightest room for appeal.

'But, Otō-san…!' sobbed Tanaka, a child once more.

His mother calmly laid down her knitting on the table and looked piercingly into his eyes. Putting her finger to her lips while watching his father slouch off grumbling, she said to him in a loud whisper:

'I don't know where you've been getting all those ideas from, Tana-chan, but don't be rude to your father!'

'But, Okā-san, I didn't mean…,' retorted Tanaka.

She interrupted him:

'…to tell him he's wrong, that he doesn't understand or doesn't know.'

'But, Okā-san…,' he insisted.

'Be quiet and listen!' snapped his mother. 'You haven't been on this planet long enough. You shouldn't behave as if you were on an equal footing, telling him his life has been one long mistake, that he should learn from the young ones who are leaving! What would become of our villages if all their inhabitants upped and left? We'd all be living in ghost towns!' she concluded.

Tanaka stood there looking at her with his deer's eyes but didn't understand a word of what she'd just said. Then, foundering once again on words, he stammered back:

'Okā-san, it's just that… it's just that I never… it's not what I…'

'Stop it, that's enough. Subject closed.'

Then, she inhaled deeply and started humming a tune. Tanaka sat up, bowed and asked permission to go to bed.

But once there, lying in his futon, sleep eluded him. He felt confused. His head was a tangle of words spinning round and round in an endless imaginary dialogue. His heart pounded beneath his pyjama top, his temples throbbed, the back of his knees and legs ached. He played over the events in his mind and realized he hadn't had a chance to explain himself: the syllables had tumbled out over one another. At no stage had he suggested his father's life had been 'a mistake'. Why would his mother have put those words into his mouth? Words he'd never uttered! Or had he? Could he have said them... perhaps without realizing? He didn't even understand their meaning. It had often occurred to him: as he didn't yet have the ability to express himself properly, people were wont to infer his meaning. Yes, they would interpret him and go off at a tangent. Grown-ups possessed a vocabulary he found fascinating: so different from his own, which was still somewhat clumsy and monosyllabic. He had always found words bewitching, their sounds even more than their meanings. So, more often than not he would allow himself to be 'said' by others. He preferred to fall prey to those incomprehensible musical complexities out of love for the way they sounded. He thought that such definitions of himself – not that he understood them, for it was like listening to another language – would sound far more intelligent to others' ears; yet, far from being positive, the result was painful. Tanaka seemed incapable of learning this lesson and would fall into the same trap over and over again. He wondered if ultimately it wasn't sheer vanity, but he always reached the same conclusion: no, vanity it wasn't; it was a profound respect for vocabulary.

It had also happened to him at school. The teacher had mentioned to the headmaster 'something that Tanaka had said', although, in fact, he hadn't – not *that way* at least. When the headmaster asked him about 'such contents', he went quiet and, through his silence, consented to let himself be 'said'. 'The teacher had no doubt put it better,' he thought. 'Why spoil it? It may have been in moments such as these that, inadvertently, he took the decision to devote his life to language; subjectivity was, in itself, too complex for someone else to decide what we mean, for someone else to come along and decipher us... when we cannot even decipher ourselves. If in any case he was fated to 'not be understood', he would at least rather it be his own choice to remain ambiguous.

Late at night he awoke to the sound of his parents arguing in the next room, with only the fusuma[49] between them. He couldn't tell what they were saying because they were speaking low. Would they carry on putting words into his mouth? Tanaka felt suddenly saddened. They would no doubt be talking about someone other than him – a ghost, some figment or other. If they could only see into his heart... Maybe then his mother would come to his bedside and apologize... But the light went out and the house sank into silence.

---

[49] A wooden framed door covered by thick paper used to divide the interior of houses.

❖

Deprived of his holidays in the mountains, the summers felt as if they would never end.

The rains would not come until the fourth lunar month, announced by the scent of damp earth on the southeaster. Then the people would sit in the engawa and sigh with relief as they sipped barley tea and listened to the incessant croak-croaking of the frogs. Every year they prayed the rainy season would be mild... as it was not uncommon for showers to summon tempests and typhoons that peeled the roofs off houses, tore up fence posts and chicken coops, and sent pigs flying through the air. His father used to tell the story of how, one day in '36, it rained sardines. The villagers took it as a miracle and no one could persuade them they had been gobbled up by the typhoon blowing in from the ocean and spat out right on top of them.

Meteorology in those parts wasn't a profession that could be trusted. As far back as anyone could remember, the person responsible for announcing any changes in the barometer was an elderly recluse who lived in the lighthouse on the hill that rose in the west, near the old abandoned port. Although surrounded by astrolabes, sextants and compasses navigational and mathematical, having been a sailor in his youth, it was his expert eye that made out the dawn or the veils of the moon. The problem arose when, because of the cheongju,[50] his sole companion, his

---

[50] Korean rice wine.

sight began to fail. So it was that old Nakamura-san – for that was his name – grew more confused with each passing day and wouldn't let the fishermen set sail, terrorizing them with his apocalyptic forecasts. The local Administrator, seeing the town on the verge of cataclysm – for, not only were fish not being caught, but the peasants had joined in the mass panic and refused to harvest in case they ran into a typhoon out in the fields – decided that from then on people should rely on their own judgment – whether based on experience or old folks' bones – until further notice.

So they went back to their daily lives, albeit with some apprehension, doing for the first time without Nakamura-san's predictions. By now the poor man was in the throes of full-blown delirium tremens, raving about mermaids' breasts and salmon striding through the hospice wing on stilts. He was adamant that his incipient blindness was due to ink squirted by tiny squid swimming through the ether of his room.

Later, when technology landed in the village in the shape of radio – and, later still, television – the people realized that weather forecasters weren't all that effective either, and so they began to trust in little Tanaka's sense of smell, nicknaming him 'The Wonder Boy', or simply, 'The Boy'. Though Tanaka could never have predicted a rain of fishes, he nonetheless knew when it was inadvisable to go out to sea because he could smell the winds even before they left the turquoise sands of Borneo.

The ceremony of Kawabiraki[51] was held by the Togetsu-kyo Bridge in Kansai, as it had been for hundreds of years. With these auspices the river was 'opened' to begin the

---

[51] *Kawabiraki* is held every summer to commemorate the year's catch and ensure safe fishing.

ukai,[52] a tradition passed on from China, via Korea. On that occasion many visitors arrived – including priests from Matsuyama[53] – causing chaos in the town, as it had not a single ryokan[54] or minshuku, only a small four-room hotel for the rare travelling salesman, where the most important guests were put up. In turn, the locals squeezed into the corners of their houses to accommodate the committee members, or slept on makeshift futons on the engawa. Being modest people who eked out a living from what little farming they could on their mountain terraces, from their paddy fields and the local fishing, they felt embarrassed about outsiders witnessing the simplicity in which they spent their days. Nevertheless, they were moved by the spirit of omotenashi[55] and freely gave what little they had. 'Well, then,' they would say, 'our little house may be humble, but please look on it as your home.' So where once five had slept, there now slept twelve, sometimes occasioning unexpected changes in the composition of families.

The streets became one big party, and people delighted in the food in the open air and the food carts selling sweet bean jam, candied sweet potatoes, jellies and colas. Some would even set up a yakitori[56] stall on the pavement outside their houses, taking turns to fan the hot coals with much enthusiasm. No one went to bed early and the general hullaballoo did not abate before dawn. They would stay up perching on the rooftops, watching fireworks brought in from China, even though the practice had been banned some years before because of the fires it caused in

---

[52] A way of fishing that uses cormorants.

[53] A town in Shikoku Province.

[54] A traditional inn.

[55] An ethic of hospitality and service.

[56] Savoury or semi-sweet grilled chicken brochettes.

the kaya,[57] and more than one had taken a fatal tumble in their drunken stupor.

The Kawabiraki would get under way with endless sutras recited in honour of the fishes whose lives had been sacrificed over the course of the year. Only then was the river declared 'open', and once the moon had sunk below the horizon the ayu fishing would commence. Lit by torches, the boats carried a crew of two oarsmen and the cormorant keepers, who would place a ring around each bird's neck. The ring was equipped with a hook, onto which a cypress bark cord was threaded. Once they were in the exact spot where the fishing was to take place, the cormorants were allowed to fly off in search of their prey. They would zigzag crazily through the air, and the keepers had to take care not to let their cords become entangled. When the birds caught the fish in their bills, naturally they couldn't swallow them for the rings around their necks. So the fishermen would then gently pull on the string, drawing the cormorants to them until they were safe on board again. They would then remove the fishes from their bills and toss them in a basket, cover it with the lid and repeat the process.

Although the cormorants often lived for fifteen to twenty years in captivity – almost four times longer than their wild relatives – and although they were virtually part of their owners' families – some kept them as pets and would even share their futons with them – this did not guarantee them a happy existence. Far from it. They were said to be affectionate birds, but this may have been because they were suffering from something similar to what many years later came to be known as 'Stockholm Syndrome'.

The hard truth was that, when they grew old and infirm, they were simply replaced with new birds that arrived – as once they had – from the coasts of Ibaraki. They would then

---

[57] Bunches of tall grasses known as 'susuki' and used for thatching roofs.

have to sleep outside, perched on some rotten, rickety plank on the verandah, freeing up for the newcomers the space they had once lovingly shared with their masters. There they remained, unceremoniously, the only change in their posture being to raise their heads once in a while. They no longer ate and, forgotten, their presence was only felt again when the stench from their inert bodies began to attract the flies.

From that first night until the end of the season, before summer's end, one of the most beautiful sights to be seen was the moment when the fishermen waited for nightfall, the fires flickering on their boats, as the moon slowly descended like a pink grapefruit over the sea on the far side of the island.

❖

He could remember the precise moment it happened. He had been sitting on the lawn, in the back garden at home. His father had managed to glue Tesujin-28 Go's head back on and his mother had graciously wrapped it up in a furoshiki[58] as if it were a gift.

'He's as good as new,' she said to him.

The paint on the right forearm, with the number 28 on it, had run a little, owing to the fraught life of this superhero, so regularly called on to save the world. Tanaka got ready to play as he always did, when suddenly something closed and locked him out. He stared at his toy, trying to work out what was going on. He rummaged in the bag for his tyrannosaurus and staged a battle between the two. But the dimension that made Tetsujin-28 Go's heroic feats possible was wiped out in an instant, transforming the robot into nothing but a bit of painted scrap metal, and there was no one who could revive him. It felt as though Tetsujin had been stripped of his soul. He left everything lying on the ground and ran to his room in search of a 'Black Ox' manga, thinking that perhaps something might occur to him. But it was futile; he didn't feel inspired. So he decided to try his luck with the fishing rod; perhaps he would run into one of the local boys. He went out into the street and bumped into

---

[58] A square shape cloth used in Japan to wrap items and carry them. There are quite a few designs which have different colours as well as meanings and traditions.

Masa-chan, who was going shopping with his mother and elder brother.

'Coming to play?' he signalled to him. Masahiro answered by pointing at his mother and crossing his eyes to convey his dissatisfaction.

Tanaka walked on, rounded the corner, and headed down towards the beach and the farthest rocks, hopping and jumping his way through. You could sometimes find crabs in the rock-pools left by the previous night's tide. They would sidle belligerently from one hiding place to another, then vanish beneath a stone. When he did manage to catch one, he added it to his booty of iridescent mussels, their blue mouths still biting on strings of seaweed.

At weekends many children used to swim in a natural pool that formed among the boulders. They called it 'The Pot' because it resembled an enormous saucepan. It had openings at the sides that let the fresh water in and out, making it an ideal refuge for small fish. Tanaka liked to lie on the smooth edge and would spend hours observing the marine life on the bottom. More than once he caught himself feeling an incomprehensible thrill welling up until it poured from his eyes. He didn't know what was happening to him. It wasn't sadness, no; it was more like a kind of marine nostalgia. He would feel a sudden irresistible urge to submerge himself in the blue, as if in a 'zone of impossibles'. Something inside him was grasping the fact that 'being human' meant inhabiting 'in-betweens', and he fought against having to accept such a sentence. He would think of the story his father had told him about some divers who drowned in the deep because of the pull of the abyss. Victims of this loving trance, their only desire was to go on diving until in the end 'Their blood began to fizz like soda water,' as his father put it. 'The fact is, us men can't run till we take flight the way we do in dreams, or build a nest in the branches of a tree or under the eaves; and we can't swim amongst ships like fishes do. Plying the skies, plying the oceans... from the day we're born it would appear we're denied the blue. Maybe that's why our souls will always thirst after it.'

Tanaka knew that, according to the theory of evolution, like all living things, we come from water, and have spent more time in the sea than on terra firma. From which it followed, he thought, that what was moving inside him was possibly something related to his origins... something clamouring to return? Tanaka realized then that life was 'round'. It would all one day end where it started. There was no way of knowing for sure; he just felt it. Later on, after mulling things over, he decided to ask his biology teacher if he believed a memory of the sea was part of our human genetic make-up. His teacher stared at Tanaka in amazement, tilting his head from side to side as if trying to reshuffle the knowledge within it, and answered that he 'believed' that genetics went far beyond the realms of biology. In any case, as this was a science class and not a lecture on faith, he could not give him a satisfactory answer.

Several years went by in Tanaka's life during which he came to think his future might lie in biology. He would go to the river with his friends to catch baby trout, which they kept in homemade aquariums adapted from industrial pickle jars. He used to observe the fishes at all times of day in the hope they would sooner or later reproduce. He tried creating a replica of their habitat, with stones and seaweed, but the trout died after spending a few days swimming upside down. Tanaka reached the conclusion that no one can learn about wildlife when it is taken out of context. 'If I want an aquarium to observe trout in, it'll have to be as big as the river itself,' he mused. That was when he gave up on aquariums.

A couple of miles from where he lived, there was a stone mound resembling a flattened pyramid. It rose above the surface of the water to a height of twelve or fifteen feet at high tide and could be reached on foot when the tide went out. It may have had something to do with the old military observation bases, but the general view in his village was that it was actually part of a series of constructions belonging to the ancient Mu civilization of Yonaguni Jima,[59] which had spread eastwards. Many people liked to climb up on it and would even take a picnic and perch on its top for lunch. One nevertheless had to watch one's step at the start of the ascent, as the algæ had thrived in the moisture from the constant contact with the water and the surface was very slippery. And then the steps that led up its walls were high and steep, and one had to haul oneself up with one's hands.

Tanaka preferred to visit it during the week, when there was no one about, and sit on the rock and read. One day – a day like so many others he spent there – the weather was so mild that he fell asleep. He often used to doze off for a few minutes, but this time, when he woke up, he saw that the water had covered much of the steps, making it impossible to get back down to the beach. It wasn't until midnight, when the tide went out, that Tanaka was able to make his descent. There was no moon, but the phosphorescence from the sea provided enough light to make out the silhouette of the land and he eventually made back it to the shore.

He found nothing romantic about the beach at that time of night, though taking your sweetheart moon-gazing there was part of his friends' 'academic romanticism'. No, it reminded him instead of shipwrecks. He imagined the

---

[59] The idea of 'Mu' as a continent and lost civilization first appeared in the writings of Augustus Le Plongeon (1825–1908) after his researches on the Yucatán Peninsula. The island of Yonaguni, which was occupied by American troops, came to form part of Okinawa Prefecture in 1972. It is the westernmost island of the Ryukyu island chain, and lies sixty-seven nautical miles off the coast of Taiwan.

Funayūrei[60] roaming the beach, not realizing where th
were, and remembered what it said in the Tibetan Book ⌣.
the Dead, the *Bardo Thodol*, that his father had found lying
beside the railway tracks in the port: 'When people die,
they have to go to the beach and walk on the sand. When
they look at their footprints, they see that they lead in the
opposite direction to the way they are walking.' The
thought filled him with apprehension.

'The dead don't know they're dead! What if I've
drowned and haven't realized yet? What if I'm at the bottom of the sea and my spirit's wandering around this place
and that's why my head is full of lost souls?'

Tanaka swivelled around unexpectedly to see if he had
left footprints in the sand. When he saw he had, he
breathed a sigh of relief and quickened his pace until he
reached the first of the cottages outlined against the murk,
in the vegetation covering the dunes.

The village lay in darkness. Not another power cut!

When he entered his house, he saw that a kerosene lamp
had been set on the table. He called out to his parents but
no one answered. He imagined they must be searching for
him in desperation. He couldn't decide if it would be better
to stay and wait, or to go out and look for them. Fearing
they would miss each other, he decided to wait. A few
minutes later his father arrived toting a lighted lantern.

'Son!' he cried when he saw him. 'Are you all right?
Where have you been? The whole village is out looking for
you!'

Tanaka felt bad that he hadn't taken the necessary pre-
cautions. He knew very well that the tide went in and out
twice a day, having been brought up among seafaring folk.
He felt properly ashamed at his blunder but... what could

---

[60] 'Sea spirits': the vengeful ghosts of people who have died at sea.

he do? He hadn't done it on purpose; sleep had got the better of him.

At that moment his okā-san came in and threw herself on him, her voice breaking as she said:

'Child! Where have you been?'

'He fell asleep,' his father answered for him, and repeated the story he had just been told.

'I fell asleep, mother,' said Tanaka. 'It was only... an hour, I think, but when I woke up I couldn't get back down.'

His mother burst into tears and Tanaka realized how gravely this episode had affected his parents.

After endless lectures, he was eventually banned from returning to the beach. Tanaka thought the punishment utterly absurd. He didn't think they could teach him something he'd in fact already learnt: to wit, not to go back up that rock without checking the tide table for that day. As well as being announced on the radio every day, these tables were posted on the door of the Port Authority building, not far from his home. He would also have to remember to take a watch, but clearly they also wanted to help fix this knowledge in his mind. So, as well as having to stay at home, he would have to show them that he felt ashamed and repentant – which was true; he didn't have to prove that to anyone.

Tanaka had to put up with reproachful glances and mean-minded gibes about the incident from people at the store every time he went there on an errand. From all this he was able to draw a couple of rules, which he angrily scribbled down in his notebook. The first was: 'I must avoid danger at all costs;' the second, 'I mustn't make mistakes.' He tried stubbornly to go back to being who he was before: a child who brings his parents peace of mind by acting in a way they can predict. From this he drew his third rule: 'Go on being a child forever!' This rule was extremely important: disobeying it had got him into trouble before...

Thinking differently was not something to celebrate; on the contrary, it was grounds for concern. His parents seemed to be uncomfortable with his questions and their explanations were almost always designed to fend them off rather than answer them. Deep down, something had touched bottom and was drawing to an end. For a few days, he accepted anything his parents insisted on, if nothing else to alleviate a seemingly unrelenting tension; yet no sooner did it ease than they would remind him of it again. So, having no choice, he stayed at home, helping out with the chores, feeling uselessly childish and striving to return to that place in the past. He tried to remember how he had done it, what things he had said or thought, but it was futile: he couldn't find the way back. He wondered privately whether 'that' might be what his parents sensed and what was really troubling them. Was staying cross with him an attempt to keep him as if he were still a child?

Trapped in a time warp, what happened that night on the pyramid, however, helped him to understand the process he was going through. He felt cast further and further away, towards some indefinite part of existence, but clinging lovingly to his solitude.

❖

Sometime later, one summer morning, his friend Oshima Osamu came to see him, carrying a basket that his mother had prepared for him to deliver to the old man who lived on the mountain a few miles away.

'Hardly ever leaves his house,' said Oshima. 'I'm taking him some food; rice, fresh eggs...'

Tanaka looked at his friend reluctantly.

Oshima insisted Tanaka keep him company, saying that the old man was a most interesting character who had travelled the world, and that they would take the path through the bamboo woods, as it was cooler that way. They could also have a dip in the stream on the way if the heat proved too much.

'Come on!' he begged, almost out of arguments. 'It'll be fun!'

'All right,' said Tanaka grudgingly. 'But you owe me.'

'All right,' said Oshima, trying to disguise his satisfaction at this victory.

The two boys crossed the village until they came to the main road, then entered the forest along an undulating track with steps leading to the stream. Along the way, on a bend in the path, hung a bridge of woven vines, which they had to cross to begin the ascent to the other side of the mountain.

Tanaka sniffed the air.

'Hmm... it's going to rain,' he said.

'How can you tell?' asked Oshima.

'I can smell it in the air,' Tanaka answered.

'That's weird,' said his friend. 'I'd like to learn to do that.'

'It's easy; all you need is a keen sense of smell.'

Suddenly Oshima stopped in his tracks.

'Hey... You're not that "Wonder Lad" they used to talk about in the village, are you? There was a boy who could forecast stormy weather. Remember him?'

'Of course I remember him!' Tanaka laughed. 'It was me!'

Oshima laughed too.

'I don't believe it,' he said, his eyes widening. 'So... was it true? I was only kidding when I asked you!'

Tanaka raised his eyebrows at him in surprise.

'Wow... that's incredible! "The Wonder Lad of the Storms," here, walking right here beside me,' added Oshima. 'I heard my mother talk about that "Lad" when I was very young, but I remember it perfectly. So how old would you have been?' he asked. "Five? Six?"'

'To tell the truth, I don't know for sure. It's something I've done all my life...'

'I have to tell my mother!' Oshima exclaimed, mopping up the sweat with the sleeve of his t-shirt. 'I don't believe it! "The Wonder Lad"!' he repeated.

'Your mother must already know!' said Tanaka. 'Seeing as she's a friend of my mother's...'

'In that case... why did she never mention it to me?'

Tanaka laughed out loud.

'I'm hardly a rock superstar living incognito!'

'You're way more than that, Tana-chan!'

'Oh, don't exaggerate,' chuckled Tanaka in embarrassment.

'"The Wonder Lad of the Storms"... I have to tell my mother,' repeated Oshima in a low voice.

They could make out the silhouette of a bamboo grove in the distance. Oshima pointed to a house that was only just visible, so obscured was it by the forest.

'There! There it is!' he said. 'It's that one, can you see it?'

Tanaka laughed and answered:

'Now I understand why you have to take food to the poor man. He'd have to be an athlete to be able to reach his own house!'

'You'd be surprised!' answered Oshima. 'He's not just *any* old man. He was a trainee at a shaolin temple for something like what... fifteen years? He's fitter than you and me put together.'

'A real shaolin temple? In China?'

'I'm not sure, actually. I think so. I think the one he was in is in China, but I'm not sure where exactly. He showed me a photo of himself once, sporting this long plait. You know, "shaolin style",' he laughed. 'So it isn't because he hasn't the energy to get up and down the hill that we're bringing him the basket. It's a gesture from my parents. The old man lives off his allotment and depends on no one, I can assure you. He is very frugal too... and you know what? Maybe because he never goes out, folk think the house is abandoned. I've met a few people along this path who hadn't the slightest idea anyone lived there,' he went on, almost out of breath. 'Only the other day an old man carrying a cane came down, stopped and asked me gruffly: "You boy, what are you doing here?"'

Oshima gave a carefree laugh.

'Growled at me like the mountain's guard dog he did! I almost asked him: "Well, excuse me, is this *your* mountain?"'

'What the heck did he care?' said Tanaka.

'Exactly! I thought the same thing myself. I would like to have told him "I've come to relieve my bowels",' he laughed.

Tanaka laughed again.

'And?' he asked. 'What did you say?'

'I told him I was going to see old Ito-sama, who lives up there,' said Oshima, pointing to the grove in the distance, 'and he replied: "Up there? No one lives up there."'

'So?'

'So I didn't like to say any more because I thought "This one's a bit barmy. He'd wallop me with that cane of his and that's for sure." But then I ran into this young man coming down the hill and, just to confirm, I asked him as well: "Happen to know where old Ito-sama lives?" And do you know what he said?'

'No... what did he say?'

'He said: "No one lives in these parts." That convinced me everyone must have been eating the same mushrooms!' laughed Oshima.

❖

Submerged in a tangle of ferns and creepers, Ito-sama's house seemed to be one with the forest. Courgettes and cucumbers hung from the beams of the verandah like Chinese lanterns, as Oshima walked up the engawa and, standing outside the door, called out:

'Ito-sama?' But no one answered.

After taking off their sandals, they entered the shaded walls. All was silence, the only thing to be heard were the cicadas heralding a storm.

'Hello?' he insisted.

'He's dead, Oshi-chan,' muttered Tanaka. 'Come on, let's go back!'

'Shhh!' his friend scolded him. 'Don't start. Let's go in.'

The room was cool and had a mossy smell. Tanaka's pupils, now dilated by the half-light, took in the vegetation that had overrun everything. Roots clamped to the furniture formed a web resembling a circulatory system embedded the length and breadth of the wood. Breaking in through the back window, a magnolia branch had taken shelter inside the house, enabling its flowers to bloom out of season. A creeper grew there, apparently supported by the pillars at the back of the house. In fact, its trunk had managed to dislodge them, tearing them from the ground in its loving embrace so that the roof balanced directly on top of it. Another window was practically covered. The sun filtered through a lacework of leaves, tracing a stained-glass window of light green and projecting its spectrum on the wall. A tiny gecko watched them, cross-eyed and motionless. No sooner did it realize it had been spotted than it scurried to its hiding place behind some cups on the sideboard, from which dangled strings of orchids.

Tanaka had the impression that the house had been built inside the trunk of some giant tree. Surprised, he looked at Oshima-san, who understood his expression and said quietly:

'I told you: he's an odd un this man is. Ito-sama?' he called again.

'Oshima-san?' asked a shaky voice from afar. 'Is that you? Oooh! Please, come in, come in! Come on in! I am sorry to have kept you waiting!' he said, ushering them inside. 'Come. Come, my boy. I'm tidying the allotment.'

'Excuse me!' said Oshima. 'I've brought a friend with me.'

Against the light emerged the figure of an old man, dressed in a hakama[61] with an apron over it. Next came the gushing of a water pump. Then he walked up to them and, drying his hands on the apron, bowed and greeted them:

'Come in, come this way and make yourselves comfortable. Do forgive the mess, it is just that I live alone...'

'Allow me to introduce you to my friend Tanaka-san,' said Oshima.

'Pleased to meet you.'

'Likewise,' answered Tanaka.

'This,' added Oshima, handing him the basket, 'is for you. Please, accept it. It's a worthless trifle.'

'Thank you, my son. Why did you go to all this trouble?' he said, taking the basket. 'How come you are always bringing me things? You really shouldn't. Goodness me! I am sorry to cause you so much inconvenience... Thank your parents for me. They are such good people... They always remember me. Over here, over here,' he said, opening a path for them through the cushions.

---

[61] A type of traditional skirt, worn by both sexes.

'Please, Ito-sama, don't worry,' begged Oshima. 'We've came to give these. We'll only stay a few minutes. We don't want to bother you, we know you're very busy,' replied Oshima.

'No, not at all,' answered the old man. 'It's no trouble, boys! No trouble at all! On the contrary! Two young men honour me with their presence when no one remembers this poor old man,' he laughed, 'and you've come all that way to get here…'

'You never go out, do you?' asked Oshima-san.

'Never,' he replied. 'I haven't left my house in seventeen years,' he said, chuckling and putting his hand to his mouth as if letting them in on a secret. 'Shall we say I'm a kind of… hermit.'

'You really like your house, don't you, Ito-sama?' Oshima insisted. 'You have everything you need here,' he said, looking around.

'It is true, I do like my house,' he confirmed. 'Nature and I live in perfect harmony here. We have grown accustomed to each other's company so to speak,' he laughed again and pointed to a space on the tatami.[62]

'Shall I make some tea?'

'No, please. Don't go to any trouble, I beg you,' pleaded Oshima.

'Let me see,' he said. 'There's enough wood to heat the water. No, no trouble at all. Let me see,' he repeated as he shuffled unhurriedly from room to room. 'Hmm, looks like rain,' they heard him say from the adjoining room. 'I can smell it on the air.'

Tanaka looked at Oshima and raised his eyebrows.

'That's just what Tanaka-san said,' remarked Oshima casually, '"The Wonder Lad!"' Tanaka kicked his friend to shut him up.

---

[62] A straw floor mat.

'As I am sure your grandparents will know,' Ito-sama continued, bearing down on Tanaka clutching an iron tea-kettle, 'in June one must always expect rain... unless it is already raining!' Laughing, he sat down next to them while placing the tea things on the small table at the side.

'Well, I've never heard that saying!' said Tanaka.

'You live and learn,' answered the old man as he poured the tea. 'Every day you live and learn.'

'Oh!' exclaimed Oshima, turning the cup in his hand, 'what a pretty chawan![63] This tea is truly special,' he added. 'You're very kind to share it with us. Where's it from?'

'Most kind, most kind,' he said, nodding several times. 'This tea... this tea... let me see... why, it comes from a small plantation in Shizuoka,' he answered.

'Shizuoka! That's a long way from here, isn't it?' asked Tanaka.

'It is a long way, yes, but don't think I go and fetch it in person?' the old man replied, and everyone laughed. 'I never leave my house, remember!' he added, joining in the laughter.

'The Chinese,' said Oshima-san, 'say that pouring tea like this – like a little waterfall, look – brings you luck.'

'Luck? You'll be lucky not to burn yourself!' replied Tanaka.

Everyone laughed again.

'Well,' said Ito-sama, picking up the thread of the conversation, 'let's just say that... they say it is a good plantation, and I for one believe them, it being famous and all. However, I don't know if this particular tea is that good; it is a late harvest. The leaves that are picked late,' he went on, waving his fingers in the air, 'are a little on the bitter side. The tannin, you know.'

---

[63] A bowl for drinking tea.

'But it's famous the world over. There must be a reason for them to say it's that good, mustn't there?' replied Oshima-san.

'Of course, it is what is called "vox popuri",'[64] said the old man. 'Do you know what "vox popuri" means?'

The boys looked at each other.

'"Vox popuri",' he went on, 'means "voice of the people" in a language called Latin.'

'Fascinating!' said Tanaka. 'I'd never heard of that language.'

'The voice of the people,' Ito-sama continued, 'speaks through stories.'

'Stories make the world go round!' said Tanaka.

'That's what wise old Kuzugen said,' replied the old man. 'In our family we have grown up with stories – but "true stories". Quite a number of them!'

'How so?' asked Oshima-san.

'Well, ours being such a big house, you see, each of us was a planet, with our own orbits. We even had an uncle who very nearly reinvented our language. Did you know?' he asked. 'I am sure I have told you before. Stop me if I have. I don't want to bore you with the same old stories all the time.'

'All right,' Oshima-san nodded as Tanaka asked:

'He reinvented our language? But how? Different from Japanese or a new dialect?'

'As you may know,' said the old man, 'during the Meiji Restoration the government ordered all commoners to add surnames to their given names, because until then, as you will have learnt at school, the "common folk" were the

---

[64] Vox populi: 'l' and 'r' are represented by a single distinct consonant sound in Japanese, making it sometimes difficult for Japanese speakers to distinguish the pronunciation of the two sounds in English.

property of the Shogun[65] and were not therefore allowed surnames. They were literally "alienated", as they say.'

The boys laugh chuckled at the double meaning of the word Ito-sama used to describe their condition.

'But, of course, to be one's "own master" was the exclusive right of the loftiest classes. Isn't it "alienating" to live like that?'

'I should say so!' laughed Tanaka. 'It's something you suffer throughout childhood.'

'And adolescence,' Oshima-san added.

They all laughed.

'Then what?' asked Tanaka.

'Then,' the old man went on, 'a lot of folk took historic surnames, for example. Others just made them up themselves or asked a local sage to do so for them. Our uncle wasn't strictly speaking a sage, but he had a most fertile imagination and a particular skill for reading what was written in people's souls. When someone asked him to do them the favour of making up a surname so that they could register in the census, he would first study the person, long and hard. After a good while he would decide what it was they needed exactly, and pronounce their new name. But that name was more than just the sum of its letters; it was "the word" that person had been searching for all their life, without even knowing it. It was what they urgently needed to know in order to find happiness. So they not only gained a surname, but an identity.'

'That sounds logical,' said Tanaka.

'Wait, for there is a twist to the tale,' said Ito-sama mischievously, and continued his explanation: 'The fact of the matter is that this renaming seemed to revitalize them, to give them the strength to go on or to start again, perhaps by going back to a wrong turning in their lives and giving them

---

[65] A General or military commander.

another chance to take the right one. It acted on their lives like an awakening! According to him, this happened simply because people – rightly or wrongly – find it hard to say "no". Imagine,' he continued. 'If you are sullen and bad-tempered, and everyone starts calling you "Mr Goodenough", how long could you last without taking up the call?' he asked.

The boys smiled and nodded and promptly set about giving each other silly names: 'Goodtemper Hikaru!' 'Clearmind Osamu!', and they roared with laughter at their bizarre names. Fearing he had been misunderstood, Ito-sama explained:

'Well now!' he laughed. 'I'm giving you a crude example, because obviously the matter wasn't all that simple. Being called "Goodenough" or something of that ilk isn't the sort of thing that would change someone's life completely. It was more like something "other"... something "hidden" that only he could see – what is called a kotodama.[66] Many people, on learning of these apparently miraculous events, came from far and wide and were willing to pay astronomical sums for his services, but he always flatly refused to take any money. Unfortunately, this meant that many charlatans started doing the same job, imagining it would be the fastest way of amassing a fortune. Obviously they did not obtain the same results, as they had no talent to see into the heart and therefore could not find the missing piece for those who consulted them. The fact of the matter is, in a manner of speaking, that this uncle I am telling you about thought that, if he could change people's lives by revitalizing their identities, he could also provide the service... on a universal scale!'

'Come again?' asked Tanaka.

'Ah!' Ito-sama exclaimed. 'Here's the most interesting part. Could he, perhaps, reinvent the language? A kind of

---

[66] A 'spirit of the word': the belief that a mystical power resides in words or names, the sound of which can magically affect people and objects.

re-editing of the Japanese language in such a way as to bring about positive changes on the metaphysical planes by pronouncing each of these words?'

The boys, who were listening carefully, raised their eyebrows.

He answered with a question:

'Why not? And so with that in mind,' he pressed on, 'he used ancient Shintoist knowledge which, obviously, he first had to acquire. And, after analysing all the existing Buddhist literature, together with some Confucian and other Chinese texts, he reached the conclusion that the original language was definitely contaminated, which was clearly the reason why it had lost its magic powers,' he said emphatically.

'And what did he do then?' asked Oshima.

'Yes, yes! What did he do?' repeated Tanaka.

'In that moment,' the old man went on, 'as you can imagine, the goal of "re-editing" the language became one of "Redemption". From then on he spent the rest of his days writing a feverish canon, almost twelve feet high, full of neologisms and cryptic signs which he intended to replace our language with.'

'Oh no!' they exclaimed in open-mouthed unison.

'Oh yes,' said Ito-sama. 'But the most curious thing was that a few years later, experts in linguistics and philology began to study it carefully – who can say why? – and concluded that it hadn't been written in a fit of derangement, but with impeccable logic; abstract, but impeccable. But what he never came to know was that, during all that time, he had stubbornly been doing alone what the Kokugaku School of Philosophy had already done throughout the Tokugawa Shogunate.'[67]

The three went on talking for a long time, telling different anecdotes about their respective families.

---

[67] 1603–1868.

'Where have your people gone, Ito-sama?' asked Oshima-san.

The old man couldn't say.

'Who knows, my son?' he sighed. 'Our family appears to be marked by encounters made and encounters missed. It is a peculiar karma that we suffer from. We have scattered ourselves across the world – all of us. It would seem, however, that the life-force that parts people brings them together again under the strangest of circumstances... We shall meet again!' he added optimistically. 'Though we probably shan't recognize each other, something in our souls will lead us home.'

Then the old man turned solemnly to Tanaka and asked him:

'Tell me, do you believe in reincarnation?'

Tanaka hesitated.

'To tell the truth...,' he said, staring into his empty tea-bowl, 'I don't know. Often, I see faces that look familiar to me, even though I haven't seen them before. Like yours!' he added with a smile. 'You remind me a lot of my grand-mother!' they all laughed.

'We old people all end up looking alike,' the man joked. 'At least in our aches and pains!' he exclaimed, grabbing his hip. 'Ouch, ouch!' he moaned in self-mockery.

Then, leaning in to Oshima-san, he pointed his hand at Tanaka and said:

'I like your friend, he is a clever boy.'

'He's still half asleep,' answered Oshima-san, and the laughter rang out again. 'Just wait till he wakes up,' he said, winking at Tanaka.

Night was falling. In the distance flashes of lightning lit up the hills. It had begun to rain.

Tanaka and Oshima would visit Ito-sama in the afternoons and stay until after five or six in the evening. Sometimes he would pluck a book from the bookcase and read out a passage to illustrate whatever it was they happened to be talking about. They never failed to be amazed at his remarkable memory. How did he manage to remember the exact place of every comment? They couldn't work it out, but their surprise was even greater when, as autumn drew in, the days grew shorter. On one occasion the room was slowly cast into shadow until it became completely dark. Out of politeness, they didn't dare say anything, and so they sat there in the dark until it was time to return home. Ito-sama got up several times, heated water, looked for a book and read out long paragraphs to them. If it hadn't been for that one episode, they never would have realized that Ito-sama was in fact quite blind.

Ware Tada Taru wo Shiru[68]

For the next three years Tanaka kept up his regular visits to Mr. Ito.

The old man would recommend books for Tanaka to read at home, and later they would discuss them. He assured him repeatedly that he could take whatever he liked from his bookcase, as he was now on 'the homeward leg' and had not come into this world to 'remain a seed'. All that was truly important to him he now carried within himself. Tanaka remembered his readings in the dark and wondered briefly why he would hold on to books whose passages he knew by heart. As if reading his mind, Ito-sama had said:

'I hold on to my books so that they remind me my journey is not yet done. Do you know something, my boy? In this world of darkness I live in, what I am afraid of is that one day I will die and not realize.' Tanaka imagined his friend walking along the beach, stopping and looking at the direction of his footprints in the sand. Could he then see them? He no doubt knew the Tibetan texts by heart.

They spoke often of school and why, after so many years and hours of classes, not to mention the extra hours devoted to Juku,[69] there were still fundamentals that they had not been taught. Tanaka felt he had learnt nothing that

---

[68] A saying meaning 'I only know what's enough' or 'I know the limits, and that's enough'.

[69] Private tutoring school.

would allow him to enter either university or the school of life.

'What do you mean you haven't learnt anything at school?' asked Ito in surprise.

'Well, not much…' Answered Tanaka sceptically.

'What do you mean "not much"? You've learnt to be Japanese, haven't you!'

Sometimes Ito-sama would jokingly call him 'my friend the philosopher'. It was no doubt due to his unerring vocation for living all coiled up in his own labyrinths. Yet, more than philosophy, more than anything, Tanaka loved literature and poetry. He knew his fate did not lie in the village among the squid and the octopi. And he wanted to share this truth that had started to burn him inside.

'My son,' said Ito-sama in a trembling voice, 'you have my blessing.'

They remained in silence for the rest of the night. It was the end of summer. The sunflowers in the back garden had started to wilt.

Ito Jun-san

It was early winter when Ito-sama left this world. The steps leading up to his front door were covered with straw, awaiting the snowfall. Inside, the bedroom was warm. He lay on the futon, his hand reaching out from under the quilt, clutching some bulbs no doubt ready for planting. But death, uninvited, had given them no time to reach the ground and two narcissi flowered there, tiny yellow suns between his fingers – small and twisted, open beside his se-hin no shisō[70] heart.

It was not unexpected. He had imagined it many times when he knocked at the door; the delay in answering made him wonder if his friend was still alive. He knew that if it wasn't today, it would be tomorrow, but that a day like this would surely come – a day when, touching the old man's hands, a cold stone would plunge the silent certainty of death deep into his chest.

Oshima and Tanaka washed and shaved his face and head, then dressed him in his pilgrim's kesa.[71] They cut the few chrysanthemums eking out a living in the back garden and laid them on his chest, now still and silent. Then they arranged some cushions so that people who went to pay their respects could make themselves comfortable. No one

---

[70] 'The Concept of Honest Poverty', a philosophy based on the purity of poverty as an expression of simplicity and virtue.

[71] A Buddhist priest stole made of linen fabric used by pilgrims on their tours of temples.

came. Only Oshima's parents, bearing a few simple flowers uprooted from the allotment. Perhaps it was better that way. They remained by the old man's side, alone. Later, some men came to lay Ito-sama out in his coffin and bear him away to the crematorium. After they cremated him, looking on indifferently, a clay urn was handed for them to lay the fragments of bone that were picked up with chopsticks one by one, starting with the toes. They kept the urn at home for some time, setting it to rest on the family altar. Later they moved it to the old local cemetery, where a small remembrance ceremony was held. Although Ito-sama had put down in writing his wish that Oshima and Tanaka should take over his house, it was something neither wanted to do. They did take the odd object to remind them of their conversations in his last years: his little chawan, his Buddhist lotus-seed rosary and a ragged old book of sutras. The rest they put up for sale. They didn't want to be present when the people turned up to ransack his house and haggle over his belongings now sleeping on the shelves. They were unwilling to watch outsiders carelessly touching them and dropping and breaking them, or examining them curiously from every angle to find a 'use' for them. But it all went off with no major hitches thanks to a clement aunt of Oshima-san's, who loved her nephew like her own son. It was she who took care of everything and finally handed over Ito-sama's last papers and faded passport to the boys. When it was all over, they returned to an empty house that had ceased entirely to be the one they knew so well.

Winter was well under way when it occurred to Tanaka to open their old friend's passport. A young man stared out at him from the photo, his eyes fixed on the infinite, like a lookout in the crow's nest. He read the date and place of birth. To his surprise, it wasn't Japan but China, in 1891, just three years before war broke out. Although his family, like many others, may have been forced to leave, just as his own grandmother's family had, it seemed too great a coincidence. That day, he asked his mother if she remembered at all the surname of his great-grandfather, who had been stationed in China all those years. She looked at him pensively and, after much chin rubbing, told him she couldn't.

'Do you think you could find out?' asked Tanaka as if gripped by a premonition.

'When your father comes, we'll ask him,' she said. 'I think he'll remember.'

Shortly after, when the long winter had still not come to an end, the unexpected news came of his grandmother's passing. So it was now too late to tell her that her twin brother Ito Jun-san – Ito-sama – had been living just a few miles away for almost half a century, quite unbeknown to anyone in her family.

"It would seem, however, that the life-force that parts people brings them together again under the strangest of circumstances... We shall meet again!"
Ito-sama

Still affected by the death of his old friend and the late discovery of their blood tie, Tanaka still could not come to terms with never seeing his grandmother again. For years he had harboured dreams of the moment he would pay her a surprise visit or go away on holiday with her, the way they did when he was a lad... He would dream of recreating situations and reliving them in every detail. He didn't register the fact that time was passing. It is what happened in his thoughts; there were islands that had broken away from the flow of life. His grandmother was one of those islands.

He walked his mother to the port, said goodbye and stood there on the wharf, watching the ship recede, smaller and smaller, over the horizon. He had to stay with his father to help him while she was away. He too all of a sudden had grown old.

Thirty-two days later, she returned from whence she came, her skin suffused with the scents of the city. She looked different to him: salon hair-style, dressed to the nines.

His grandmother had left Tanaka some money, enough for him to realize his dream of going to the capital to study. Some family friends, whom he couldn't remember but who did remember him, offered to put him up when he arrived. As he was leaving, his mother gave him a piece of paper, which she kept folded in an old handbag, with a short list of contacts on it. Tanaka and Oshima departed shortly afterwards, leaving behind their walks along the beach and the tranquil afternoons beneath the willow trees. They found temporary digs in a district of Hakone, at the home of some second cousins of Tanaka's grandmother, which doubled as an inn when the woods began to set the autumn alight. Somewhat later Oshima managed to get a job as an assistant in a small theatre company, which he had been in contact with for some time, and moved to Tokyo, leaving Tanaka at the inn, where he was about to start work. Tanaka began by helping out the owners with everyday repairs – learning more than he already knew – and restoring the little tea-house, which had been damaged in the last storm.

With the economic crisis fewer tourists visited Hakone than usual that summer. Out of concern for his patrons, who covered his overheads, Tanaka couldn't really see the point of having to sit around doing nothing. So he simply wandered about the house, dusting the rails of the screens and polishing the locks. One morning, like so many others, when he was washing the van just for the sake of it, the landlady of the hostel, Madame Miamaka, suggested that, in view of how little work there was, perhaps it would be best if he went to see someone of her acquaintance who needed a reliable chauffeur to drive her to Tokyo on a regular basis.

'Yamana Hinata[72]-sama,' she explained, 'is an industrialist who lives in the area. Perhaps, if you wish, you could work here again next autumn, when the season starts again. You know that people come here mostly to contemplate the maple trees.'

Tanaka took her up on the idea, and a meeting was arranged with this Yamana-sama.

---

[72] 陽向

Madame Miamaka drew a map on a page of her notebook, which Tanaka studied closely: 'When I get to the station, I have to walk uphill, then down the side-street with the pharmacy. I'll recognize it straight away: it's the only one with an iron handrail running the length of the street. Once I'm up there, I have to turn left, round a slight bend, after which I come to a stone wall that surrounds the garden of the Yamana residence. OK. Got it!'

Tanaka read the map carefully as he walked. When he looked up, he found he was at the big entrance gate. It was closed. He went to ring the bell, but an old man suddenly opened a panel in the door. Tanaka introduced himself with a brisk bow. The doorman beckoned to him to follow him inside. They entered an atrium that led to the garden, where a distinguished-looking gentlemen was waiting for them, whom Tanaka took for his future employer and who accompanied him to a room shrouded in shadows.

'One moment, please,' he said. 'Wait here.'

The young Tanaka stood there, by a collection of antique samurai armour and shields whose silhouettes gradually revealed themselves as his eyes grew accustomed to the dark. Voices could be heard somewhere deep within the house. Then a girl in a simple kimono appeared from behind the shoji and asked him to go with her.

A stocky man came up to them and introduced himself:

'Yamana Hinata,' he said, bowing his head slightly. 'Pleased to meet you.'

They exchanged a few words, after which he asked him to follow the young lady in the kimono, who led him to an office, where he was made to fill in some papers while she made a photocopy of his identity card and driving license.

'We'll call you,' she said.

Tanaka waited on tenterhooks all week, but there was no news. He thought he may not have met the job requirements... until eventually they contacted him: he'd been accepted. The job was simple and it would give him the chance to choose where he lived, in both Hakone or Tokyo. Essentially, it involved going once or twice a week to pick up the wife of Chairman Yamana-sama and taking her to the capital. He would stay there for one, maybe two days, sometimes longer. It was also possible that she would simply go shopping or have lunch, and would want to come back the same day. He had to be ready for different possibilities. He couldn't understand why she didn't take the train like everyone else instead of making things difficult for herself with traffic, but it wasn't his concern. As for board and lodging, the owners of the hostel had insisted he stay to live with them until he found somewhere more convenient to move to. So it was that Tanaka-san started working for the Yamana family.

After arriving in Tokyo and dropping off Madame, he would park the car, buy some lunch, and sit and read as he ate.

❖

People in the little village of Hakone Fuji were no strangers to gossip, so one would inevitably overhear all the latest news while queuing at the supermarket check-out or waiting to be served at the pharmacy. Tanaka gradually found out all about the locals' comings and goings. By all accounts, Madame Yamana, his employer, was half crazy. Shrieks had sometimes been heard coming from the house. They were said to be hers. 'Yes, yes, yes!' they would say, 'like a woman possessed.' It was rumoured that her husband, apart from being an industrialist or some kind of a minister – no one knew exactly what he did – was to all intents and purposes a Yakuza[73] leader, or some such figure, and that he was able to 'cover up' everything because he worked from a position within the government. It was also rumoured that the Chairman's mother had been murdered because "she knew too much" and that the murder had been committed by a woman who worked on the domestic staff.

'The Chairman's mother murdered? By the maid?' asked the lady stacking biscuits on the shelf. 'What is this? A novel by that English lady... the famous one... What was here name? Christo...? Or something like that,' she added, befuddled. 'The one who's all the rage...,' she mumbled, stacking the packets of noodles.

'Tabatha,' said the check-out girl.

---

[73] Members of transnational organized crime syndicate.

'Tanabata?'[74]

'No, Grandma, not Tanabata! She's a famous writer. Her books have been made into films and everything!' the check-out girl laughed.

'That's right, you go ahead and laugh!' snapped one woman, carrying a floral purse, 'but the maid's still free. Not only that, she has a job, as if nothing ever happened. And in the house!' she added in outrage.

'Ah! It's Agatha Clisti! Now I remember.'

'That's the one.'

'No, she isn't in the house because the old lady wasn't living there back then. She lived in the other house, the one by the river,' said the check-out girl assertively.

'How do you know?'

'Hmm,' hummed the check-out girl mysteriously. 'The things you pick up on the grapevine...'

'She'll never go to prison, because he's a very influential man,' came the reedy voice of a man weighed down with packages, leaning against the counter.

'What are you talking about? Didn't she murder The Chairman's mother?' asked a young girl with a squint.

'I'm telling you, she knew too much!' the lady with the flowery purse answered in a whisper.

'But she was his okā-san, for the sake of...!' insisted the cross-eyed girl.

'You just don't get it, young lady. Okā-san, my foot! To the Yakuza no okā-san's worth all that!' said the lady, opening her blossoming purse and carrying on regardless: 'How much is it? I'll take a tin of azuki too. I almost forgot! What a memory!'

'Naaaaaaaaka-chan!' shouted the check-out girl. 'Get us a tin of azuki from the sheeeeelf, will you!'

---

[74] A Japanese festival.

'Look, for a start, Yamana-sama is from a Kobetsu[75] family,' remarked a man with a little blue hat and big yellow teeth, who was standing in the queue. 'All this you're saying…,' he added, waving his hand as if swatting away a fly, 'there's no respect any more. Yakuza, my eye!' he cried contemptuously. 'Have none of you met his honourable father? Does no one remember him anymore?'

'No. I was very young when the Honourable Gentleman passed away,' came the thin voice of a woman in a hairnet, who looked as if she were suffering from some ghostly condition.

'Me neither. I never met him, but my grandmother did.'

'I don't remember him…,' said the old woman. 'I don't remember anything at all, not even what I don't remember.

'You're better off that way, Grandma; keep yourself sheltered from the storms of memory. What I'd give to forget it all!'

'No one in my family met him because we aren't from this prefecture; we're from Chiba.'

'Ah! Very nice! Chiba!' said the check-out girl.

'Thank you,' came the reply.

'Best peanuts!'

'That can't be right. You must have the story backwards,' said the woman accompanying her, whilst rummaging through the snacks shelf.

'What about a sense of loyalty?' asked an old woman in slippers, frowning.

'Something else: her mother – the lady of the house's mother, that is – was reputed to be a witch,' said a woman in little rubber boots.

---

[75] A branch of the Imperial Clan, supposed to descend from the Sun Goddess.

'Come off it!' interrupted a lady who had been rummaging through the snacks, while waving her hands to tell her husband to move up the queue.

'She had strange powers, I tell you. She was seen! Flying through the night on these bright red wings!' said the woman in the little rubber boots with a look of fright.

'Whose mother?' asked the lady, snapping her florid purse and picking up a shopping bag.

'The young lady's!' the girl in the thick glasses and the lady in the little rubber boots answered in unison.

'Shame on you!' the old lady bristled as she made her way down the aisle. 'Shame!' she repeated, her chin wobbling. 'Have none of you met The Chairman's honourable father! What has become of loyalty?'

The check-out girl whispered to the man with the packages, who was waving a bank note to pay:

'They're just things people say; I mean... no one can be sure they're completely true.'

Tanaka-san's hackles began to rise, but he pretended not to be listening. People in this part of the world were so superstitious they reminded him a little of his own village. He sometimes felt as if he had never left. When he returned to Tokyo, he could breathe again, lose himself in the hustle and bustle of the streets, become anonymous again and escape from an inevitable fate in which one day he would hear his own name slip from a pair of venomous lips. Yet stories troubled him: on the one hand, because they construct realities that, never having existed before, now come very much to life; and, on the other, because 'Kemuri wa tatanu',[76] as they said in his village. He feared all those things he had heard about The Chairman and his relationship with

---

[76] A proverb roughly meaning 'When the river roars, water it bears', or more loosely 'There is no smoke without fire'.

characters from the Gokudo.[77] In fact, now that he thought about it in that light... he himself had had the occasional mysterious character in his car. The Chairman's relationships ran the entire gamut, from judges and high-ranking public figures to distinctly shady types who looked like they had just crawled out of the sewer. Some of them were covered from head to toe in irezumi.[78] Yes, he had seen them in spite of the long sleeves and turtlenecks they wore to hide the red-eyed dragons on their skin. Sometimes, a simple twitch of the arm gave them away, a claw or fiery tongue flicking out from underneath. People feared them. Tattoos, in general, had even been banned in the onsen to avoid any misunderstandings. But, like many other inexplicable things in life, the Yakuza were 'all the rage'. They exerted such a fascination on people that there were comics depicting them as heroes. They aroused a curious sympathy. And the fact was that the kind of matters the Yakuza 'took care of' weren't dealt with by the police.

He recalled one in particular. He could sense something different in his wild eyes, something cold, something inhuman. He used to scan everything around him, one eye looking this way, the other that, as if he had been turned overnight into a chameleon by the power of a magic spell. He had overheard in these conversations that many of them belonged to the Inagawa-kai family.[79] If this were the case, then everything made sense! There was quite a leap, mind you, between that and involving The Chairman in these societies. Every tradition followed its own path and, like lanes on the motorway, they never crossed. A shoemaker

---

[77] Another name for the Yakuza.

[78] Tattoos.

[79] The third largest Yakuza group, based in the Tokyo-Yokohama region.

whose grandfather had also been a shoemaker was unlikely to decide to become a carpenter.

Whatever it was, and in all honesty, no one knew exactly what The Chairman did do for a living, and no one – absolutely no one – could conclusively claim that he had ties, even coincidental ones, with any Yakuza... Who knew whether the meetings that Yamana-sama took part in were really about the 'peace process', rather than one of collaboration? It is well-known that people love to fantasize, especially living in a village where nothing happens. The simple fact of living would not appear to be enough; people also wanted to be 'entertained', and 'news' spreads more by eagerness than by certainty. It was probably a load of old nonsense. As for himself, clearly the less he knew, the better. He did his job as usual, and that was that. 'He saw no evil, heard no evil, spoke no evil.' This last thought gave him butterflies in the belly.

Many people who had lived a simple, honest life were one day corrupted by power. How was it possible? He knew it couldn't happen overnight; that kind of a change had to be as gradual as the one wrought in the mirror by the passing of the years. Tanaka also knew that certain limits were fragile. It wasn't that he was drawn to the idea of getting mixed up with the Yakuza – of course not! His fear was that one day, sooner or later, something unusual would happen, something apparently innocent, that would end up reeling him in. What Tanaka desired most at the end of the day was to study, and he sincerely hoped he wouldn't run into the 'killer maid' in the garden at The Chairman's house.

Two crows on the wing of the roof

'It's 6:30 a.m. across the nation,' the radio blared as Tanaka stepped out of his house as usual. From the train he could see the motorway hovering above the urban landscape: a brutal slash cleaving through the buildings. The tracks ran alongside it, so close to the apartments that it was possible to see in close detail the laundry hanging on the balconies. Windows opened onto vistas of power poles amid a forest of bristling TV aerials. A thin man in a vest was smoking a cigarette and drinking something out of a mug. He was perhaps wondering whether he had been right to migrate from his seaside village only to end up living like a sardine in a tin. From the midst of all that concrete there rose a neighbourhood of little wooden houses. Small gardens and allotments. Scraps of paddy-fields and the short-lived solitude of the countryside, as the urban landscape never stops insisting...

As Tanaka crossed the bridge, he looked at the river and, towards one bank, at a heron poised on one leg, stalking its lunch. Stealthily it brought its head close to the surface of the water and waited until... splash!

'Oh, silly! You missed it!'

When he reached his destination, Madame Yamana was expecting him as always, sitting on the stone bench, her purse nestling on her knees. When she saw him, she stood up and they greeted each other.

'Oh, Tanaka-kun!' she said. 'Before I forget! My husband needs you to do him a favour... but he wants to speak to you personally because he has to give you precise instructions. That's what he told me. He's busy this week, but he'll call you. All right?' asked Madame, without waiting for an answer.

Tanaka paused, then nodded politely:

'Certainly, Yamana-sama. Anything to be of help.'

'Remember the car needs its annual service. For one thing you can tell them they have to change the upholstery on the back seat. It is stained, and someone tried to clean it and ended up completely ruining it,' she said briskly. 'So today, after you leave me at the house, you can drive it back to Tokyo and take it into the garage tomorrow. All right?'

'Yes... yes, of course, Madame,' answered Tanaka hurriedly, as an image of blood on the upholstery and someone trying to scrub it clean resolved itself into a whole series of horrible endings. He also wondered what this 'favour' he was supposed to do for The Chairman could be.

Tanaka and Madame Yamana put Hakone behind them.

As he drove, he kept wondering about that 'favour' and why he would have to talk to him in person about it.

'Have you seen the blooms on the azaleas?' asked Madame, interrupting his train of thought.

'Yes, I've seen them,' he replied. 'They're everywhere. Aren't they beautiful?'

'It's the season,' she said.

How could someone of The Chairman's status, so involved with high political office, need anything from this lowly, incidental chauffeur, a student of letters and the son of humble fish merchants?

'And the wisteria?' asked Madame Yamana. 'Have you seen the wisteria?'

'The wisteria?' repeated Tanaka, absent-mindedly.

'Yes, the wisteria... the one above the front gate. You've seen it hundreds of times,' she said, taking off her hat and adjusting her hair.

'Ah, the wisteria!' answered Tanaka.

'It's in full bloom!' said Madame enthusiastically.

'Yes, yes, very pretty,' he said, picking up the thread of his thoughts again: *they* never sort anything out *themselves*; *they* always rely on others to do it for *them*.

Not long ago he had watched a documentary about the Yakuza and how an ordinary citizen had suddenly quite inadvertently become embroiled with illegal activities. But he couldn't be sure it was true what they said about The Chairman's relationship with the Yakuza – although, according to the film, unlike the Italian Mafia, such things were not kept dark. Yet he just couldn't shake off the idea. He'd always felt a certain resentment and discomfort towards people in high political office. But was the Chairman's position a political one?

Tanaka was interrupted once again.

'It's the only time of year it looks pretty,' said Yamana-san.

'Of course, Madame,' answered Tanaka without the slightest idea what she was talking about.

Because of his position of power…? He had quite lost his thread.

He didn't even know for sure who The Chairman really was, but he couldn't refuse any favour he might ask of him. Either way he was trapped, not so much by loyalty to The Chairman as by fear of him. At that moment he saw the request as a kind of tacit sentence, the outcome of which could not be guessed at. But the fact was that, by the time Tanaka reached his destination, his apprehension had grown to the point that he would have chosen to disappear rather than have to meet The Chairman and agree to even the most innocent of favours. Even if it was just a matter of delivering a package, he told himself, suddenly remembering the severed digits posted in little boxes as proof of loyalty. 'Anything but a package!'

Madame Yamana asked to be dropped off in Ginza. She had to go to a famous shop that specialized in handcrafted hashi and hashioki.[80] They agreed he would pick her up at the Four Seasons Hotel at half past three sharp. She would be waiting in the lobby. Tanaka got out of the car and opened the door. Madame sprang out and immediately she was greeted by an entourage of saleswomen who appeared to have been expecting her. Tanaka immediately set off for Shinjuku. There were a number of manga stalls, where he could get hold of old editions of his childhood hero, but then he thought better of it and decided to seek out Oshima-kun and tell him what had happened, but on second thoughts... why trouble Oshima with things that might merely be a figment of his imagination?

His hands were frozen stiff and he felt unwell. His stomach churned but he couldn't tell if it was from hunger or something else. Something shook inside him. Perhaps it was the unsettled weather. Maybe he had caught cold in the morning.

He had to drive for a long time before he found anywhere to park. Still inside the car, he went over that morning's events, trying to find a clue as to The Chairman's mysterious request. Everything he had imagined paled in the light of a real meeting. He got out and started to wander. He passed a shop that sold cards and decided to buy one to send to his mother, as it would be her birthday in a few days.

'Dearest mother: How I wish I could be with you right now! I'm so looking forward to the holidays so I can come and visit you. Please send Papa my love.'

Then he headed for the city's main artery in search of somewhere to sit down for a while. When the lights changed, the people waiting across the street started crossing as well. He had barely taken three steps when a human tide drove him back to where he had started. But he stood his ground against the jostling throng and, summoning all his strength,

---

[80] A support to rest chopsticks on, placed under the thin end.

he breaststroked through the crowd until he caught up with those heading in his direction. Finally he plunged into this other throng, which dragged him along with it and deposited him on the other side of the street.

A small side-street with neon signs led off to the left. He walked into a snack bar: 'Tonkatsu Ramen' he read, 'a speciality of Kyushu.' Yes, that looked tasty and cheap! He slurped his soup and managed for a little while to keep his mind busy with the horseracing on the TV on the wall. He felt suddenly absent. He was tired and listless.

The girl at the counter had filled his tea-cup for a second time without him noticing. He finished off his lunch, paid and left, dragging his feet in the direction of the car. But when he got back to where he'd parked, it had gone. He could see the drinks machine and the electricity pole, and the railing separating the street from the railway... but not his car. He could have sworn that this was the exact spot he'd left it; he remembered clearly because he was in the habit of glancing around after a few steps to check where he had parked. But the streets all looked the same to him: they all had drinks machines and electricity poles all in the same positions.

He patted his pocket. The keys! He didn't have the keys! Could he have left them in the car? He walked up and down the block. His heart swapped places with the soup. What would he tell Madame Yamana? That it had been stolen? That he'd lost it? 'Madame Yamana, I'm afraid I'll have to escort you home in a cab.' But... how could he have been so absent-minded? The car was nowhere to be seen. How would he ever work now? He decided to go back to the cafeteria, but just then he saw a girl running towards him with something in her hand. The keys! He'd left them on the counter. Tanaka thanked her and breathed in relief. At least he hadn't locked them inside. But then... what about the car? Could it have been towed away? Had it been robbed and if so should he report it to the police? How long should he search for it first? Nothing like this had happened to him since his arrival in Tokyo. Had he left it unlocked in his distraction at The Chairman's mysterious request? Just then he felt like he did when he was a child: the same queer sensation... he felt like someone who had done something unforgivable and sensed that one day his dark secret would be revealed.

As he walked feverishly, he was no longer even sure where he was anymore. His legs hurt and he couldn't think. The very idea of having to take Madame back to Gora and then drive all the way back to Tokyo sapped him of all his energy. He didn't understand why she couldn't take the train like everyone else, although if she did...

He looked at his watch. It was already ten minutes to three! Running late now and with this traffic, he'd never make it in forty minutes. Suddenly he remembered he'd turned left when he'd come out of the cafeteria, having entered from the right of the building. With every drop of energy he could muster he ran to the door and, looking to his right, finally recognized the layout of the streets. He strode briskly, wading once again through the tide of people heading back from their lunch breaks. No wonder the street had looked so empty. It was an entirely different one! On reaching the other side, he spotted the car. It resembled a tame animal waiting to gobble him up and bring him back home. All Tanaka wanted was to sleep. Perhaps he could tell Madame he wasn't feeling well. As he walked over to the car, he saw on the back seat a rice-paper envelope tied with mauve silk thread. Madame Yamana must have left it behind. He picked it up and placed it on the front passenger seat where he wouldn't forget it.

As he waited for the lights to change, Tanaka saw out of the corner of his eye that there was something written on the envelope: '... Hikaru-sama,' a first name. Had she left it there on purpose for him to see it? It was odd… She never called him by his first name, but by his surname, like all the other staff: Tanaka. No, he decided to leave it where he'd found it and wait for Madame to give it to him. But then that might lead her to think he didn't pay enough attention. What to do? He could hand it to her and say: 'Excuse me, Madame, you left this…' No, he couldn't give her an envelope that had his own name on it because she'd think he was anxious to receive it, and that would not be good manners. So he decided to tuck it into the net in the front of Madame Yamana's seat so that she would realize he had seen it and left it to her discretion. Yes, that's what he'd do. How many conflicting decisions can one make in a day?

As Tanaka rounded the roundabout just a few seconds away from the hotel but several minutes late, he saw Madame Yamana leaving hurriedly in a taxi. She had clearly tired of waiting. She was being escorted by a young man. Would he have to take them both to Gora? He took the decision to follow them until they stopped at the first traffic lights. But, a turn up for the books, for once all the lights seemed to conspire to turn green.

Tanaka kept his eyes on the cab and Madame Yamana. She was smiling and nodding as she looked at the young man sitting beside her.

At last a red light. He was just about to jump out of the car to hail her when he saw the young man lean towards Madame and… kiss her! Perplexed at what he had seen, he clearly couldn't knock on the taxi window or he'd get a knock in the nose in turn for his boldness.

He waited. What else could he do? The taxi drove on for a few yards and pulled up at a corner. The young man got out – as luck would have it! – and Madame Yamana waved her young lover goodbye and went on her way.

Was it possible he had been driving her to trysts with this young man all year?

He stayed behind the taxi until it pulled up again. He shot out of his own car and tapped on the window. Madame started and looked at him in fear. Then, recognizing him, she smiled and put her hand to her chest in relief, signing to him to wait. She took some money from her bag, paid the driver and got out hurriedly. The lights had now changed to green and a line of cars was waiting behind them.

'Madame Yamana! Oh, Madame Yamana! Please forgive me!' Tanaka begged.

A thousand things crossed Tanaka's mind as he apologized: what to say, what not to say... 'The traffic!... Terrible!' 'The road was closed for repairs.' 'I saw you get in the taxi.' 'I didn't see you.' 'What a coincidence.' He monitored Madame's smallest gesture at full speed, stumbling over his words, while she floated, somewhere else, somewhere far away, not even appearing to hear him. Eventually she told him she had forgotten all about him!

'Take me to Mitsukoshi,[81] please.'

During the journey he tried to curb the urge to watch Madame in the rear-view mirror, but twice she caught his glance. She instructed him to drive around the block until he saw her come out of the store, as it would not be easy for him to find a parking space at that time of day. Was there a tone of reproach in her voice? It wouldn't surprise him if he had made her feel ill-at-ease. Worse still, would Madame suspect he'd seem them kiss? She must be trying to read the answer in Tanaka's face. 'Of course! That's why she won't take her eyes off me,' he thought. Should he tell The Chairman what he'd seen? At that moment, when things were going from bad to worse, he not only feared the 'favour' he had to do for The Chairman, but found himself caught up by chance in a web of complicity with Madame. And telling The Chairman would be a shocking act of

---

[81] Famous department store.

94

disloyalty after she had treated him so well. Who did he owe his loyalty to? What would Confucius say about this? Was Ito-sama right when he said he'd been taught to be Japanese at school? Who but a Japanese could be trapped in a dilemma of opposing loyalties? A dilemma for which there was usually only one solution...

He wanted to get home, throw himself on the futon and disappear for a long time. All day he'd been feeling like an orphan. His thoughts had turned out to be prophetic: people can become implicated in the most complex situations just by living and breathing.

He reproached himself forever having left his village. No doubt his fate would be more desirable working by his father's side, enjoying every summer and every winter, no longer picturing a future devoted to some insubstantial dream.

The journey back to Gora was tense and silent, though mercifully devoid of rear-view glances. As they neared their destination, Tanaka felt his stomach rumble.

The staffs were waiting outside the house and bowed reverently as the car drove through the gate and into the garden. They remained like that for a time, as if studying mushrooms in the gravel, then ran to help them with the boxes and packages, leaving these in the room by the kitchen for inspection. A bodyguard appeared from the back door muttering into a walkie-talkie: The Chairman was in a meeting, with who knew whom... Tanaka scrutinized all those faces, trying to work out who had been 'the murderer of Honourable Yamana's mother', but none of them looked 'outwardly criminal' to him.

A strong gust of wind blew around the garden and thunder rumbled in the distance. Tanaka shivered.

'There's no need for you to come back until next week, Tanaka-kun,' said Madame Yamana. 'We'll give the garage time to finish the upholstery. I'll call you!' she added, running into the house.

Suddenly everything went dark and the garden sank into a ghostly murk.

As he walked to the car, he noticed that the envelope was still in the net pocket. Perhaps a little higher, clearly showing his name? His heart leapt. There was no longer any doubt: it had to be meant for him.

Everyone had gone into the house except old Kobayashi-san.

'Son, can you see anything?' he asked. 'Wait, I have a lantern here. What with the power cuts…,' he said, getting drenched in the rain.

He waited for the boy to go through before closing the gate behind him.

'Thank you, Kobayashi-san!' he answered, at the top of his voice.

The old man waved goodbye and vanished into the shadows.

The darkness was spreading everywhere. He drove carefully towards Hakone Yumoto as the rain lashed the windscreen. He wanted to find a place to stop and open the envelope. Eventually he found a bend in the road where he could pull over. He turned on the sidelights, reached behind him and picked it out. Perhaps it would be better to leave it as it is, he told himself. When he arrived, in a couple of hours, he would call Madame and tell her she had left it on the back seat. The contents of that envelope with his name on it were clearly something that couldn't be spoken openly, he mused. It seemed almost like a 'game without words', an interplay of ambiguous gestures. He had reached a dead end and was seized by sheer terror. If he opened it, he would be implicated in its contents; if he didn't, he might appear 'uncooperative'.

'I'll leave it where it was and that's an end to it,' he thought. He decided to leave it on the back seat. He wouldn't do anything about it. It was for the best. Why should he? But... what about the garage? He couldn't leave it lying there, it would get lost. And what if it were lost? What if it should fall into the wrong hands? After all, he didn't know what it might contain.

He set off again and drove for several miles, breathing heavily and trying to think about something else. His chest felt tighter and tighter. He remembered the look Madame had given him in the rear-view mirror and wondered if all this might have something to do with The Chairman's request. Or perhaps Madame, forewarned of 'the request', was trying to pass him a 'counter-request'. Could it be related to what he had seen in the taxi? No, it couldn't. How could she be sure he had seen her?

❖

'That's some appetite for noir novels you have!' laughed Oshima-san when he heard the story. 'Leave it where it is. You call her tomorrow and tell her you've found an envelope but have chosen not to open it and that you're taking the car to the garage. She'll tell you exactly what to do with it,' he said, brimming with natural optimism. 'Now get under the kotatsu, I'll bring you some food.'

This, thought Tanaka, was an entirely logical solution. He could not understand why he had made such a fuss about it.

'Exactly, Tanaka. A scene out of a detective novel! You wind yourself up all on your own. You've rolled yourself a real snowball and sat on top of it! Call her before you take the car to the garage. I'm supposed to be the budding thespian, not you, and don't you forget it!' he concluded, prompting a nervous giggle from Tanaka.

'You're right,' said Tanaka, as if just awakening from some incomprehensible nightmare.

They both retired to their futon to sleep.

Tanaka spent the first part of the night quietly, repeating to himself what Oshima-san had been saying. He lay there exhausted and eventually drifted off to sleep. But at three o'clock he awoke with a powerful foreboding and a headful of worry. He couldn't stop thinking about it, turning it over and over in his mind. The envelope... could it be something to do with her lover, that young man she kissed? Maybe it contained some kind of a bribe? He had to find out what was inside, so he got out of bed and started downstairs on tiptoe in the dark. He was burning with fever. A step creaked under the weight of his foot. Oshima-san heard him and shouted:

'Don't even think about it!'

Tanaka jumped.

'You frightened me!' he exclaimed. 'What did you say?'

'Don't even think about it. Now go back to sleep. I know you're after the envelope. Don't even think about opening it,' he repeated.

'It's just there's something I haven't told you,' said Tanaka.

'Oh, Tana-chan, please! It's nearly four in the morning!' his friend protested.

Tanaka turned a deaf ear and, sitting at the foot of Oshima's futon, launched once again into his explanation of how nervous what Madame Yamana had said about The Chairman asking a favour of him was making him and having to do so 'in person', because he couldn't imagine what it might be and didn't care for either the tone or the idea of having to 'do favours' for someone with such an ambiguous reputation. Then there was the matter of the upholstery... He had seen the stain and it was too big to have been something that had spilled... And another thing: what had happened that afternoon with that business about the taxi? Maybe it would be best to tell them a problem had cropped up and he would no longer be able to work for them. He asked Oshima his opinion but didn't wait for an answer. They still had to pay the rent... He could last a year without a job thanks to the money his grandmother had set aside for him. But he was in a tight spot, that much was certain. What if he couldn't find another position?

Tanaka's monologue went on and, by the time he was done, Oshima-san was sound asleep. Who knows how long he'd been at it! Tanaka made an effort to put the whole story out of his mind and lay down again. But his head was abuzz. He couldn't take any more, so he got out of bed. Once again he tiptoed downstairs, this time avoiding the creaking stair. He went into the street and walked to his car. It wasn't as cold now but it was still raining, and the thunder echoed all around. He opened the car door. There lay the envelope, where he had put it. He picked it up and tried to open it, probing it with uncertain fingers, but his nerves got the better of him, and he tore both it and the note inside it in two.

'Oh!' he groaned. 'Why didn't I think of steaming it open? Damn it!'

In the bottom corner was a cheque that Tanaka managed to extract. It was a small cheque... a small cheque with a very big number on it! The light was dim. He managed to wipe the sweat and rain from his eyes, and to hold both pieces of the note up to the car light. Hands shaking, he read: 'Dear Hiyoshi-san, please accept from my hand this gesture of good faith and with it my sincerest apologies for the misunderstanding. Aiko'.

Hiyoshi-san? Hiyoshi-san? But... So? Who was this for?

Tanaka stood there, turned to stone, wishing the moment had never happened. The rain hammered down on him. Distant lightning lit the buildings. Seconds later came the thunder. It was too late now. Even if he did get hold of an identical envelope, he could never stick the note back together. He had violated his employer's private correspondence.

In the deep of the night
throbbed the silence like a human heart.

❖

Watanabe Aiko-san[82] had been born on the outskirts of Tokyo the same day and year as Her Majesty the Empress Consort Michiko Shōda. But, unlike the Empress, Aiko was interested neither in sport[83] nor in feeding silk worms. No. Her heart's desire was to become a great actress and perform Chinese opera.

Aged eleven she embarked on a long passage, starting out at the National Conservatory of Kabuki[84] Arts and Nogaku[85] theatre, which set her on the road to her dreams. She religiously took singing lessons with a private teacher who was said to have studied the Mei School technique with no less than Dan Mei Lanfang[86] himself. Her tutor had assured her she had a promising career ahead of her, confirmed that same day by the blind fortune teller who sold amulets at the local temple.

She could never have imagined the turn her life would take shortly after her father died. Nor could her mother,

---

[82] The family name comes before the given name in Japan.

[83] Emperor Akihito and young Michiko met in a game of tennis in Karuizawa.

[84] A drama performance with a history of over two hundred years, which includes dancing and singing.

[85] The oldest theatrical art in Japan.

[86] One of the four most famous Chinese artists in the golden age of the Beijing Opera.

Watanabe Emiko-san, who was present at that tragic moment, make out the sense of the last words her husband breathed: 'May you find it in you to forgive...' Having uttered them, his eyes fixed on some point in the ultimate void, and Watanabe Emiko-san was left alone with the echo of her own breathing, crouched in a room expanding endlessly into infinity.

The shadows of the first cherry blossoms were cast indifferently on the paper of the shoji overlooking the garden.

'It's cold,' she said to herself. 'The heaters will have to be turned back on. Just when we thought winter was over.'

'May you find it in you to forgive...'

Watanabe Emiko-san could not live out her mourning the way other academic widows did. Nor could she break down and cry over every object she found in the place where her husband was no more. There was no undoing the fact that he had waited until the last seconds of his life to ask for forgiveness. What hurt most was his lack of trust: that he hadn't dared tell her what was going on – whatever that might have been. But to leave her like that to face this labyrinth of possible outcomes stretching before her every night, felt to her unforgiveable. 'A blank cheque for a refund of conscience,' as she finally managed to put it into words- 'you don't do that to someone you've loved.' She felt saddened, her heart aching but also, humiliated, confused, wronged... and the worst of it was she couldn't yet work out why. She would writhe and thresh with a concealed anger that kept her awake until the early-morning witches sabbath of crows. They would attack the netting covering the rubbish bags, and she would have to go out into the street to keep them at bay with a broom until the refuse lorry came.

One day, in the middle of a storm that flooded the streets so badly people had to roll up their trousers, through the window Madame Watanabe saw a little man in bottle-bottom glasses, dithering outside her front door. He seemed to be trying to make out the numbers through the curtain of water pouring over his spectacles. Watanabe-san stuck her head out to see who it was. The man's suit was so creased it looked as if he'd been sleeping in it, and rain gushed from the brim of his hat.

'Watanabe Emiko-sama?' he asked, exuding clouds of mothball fumes.

'Yes, that's me,' she answered, raising her voice to make herself heard above the thunder.

The little man introduced himself formally and his sodden hands passed her a thick manila envelope.

'If you'd be so kind as to sign here,' he said, tugging a receipt from an inside coat pocket. 'Just to prove I've given you the envelope.'

That modest hand gesture from someone so utterly insubstantial, however, unleashed a tsunami that would shake the family's foundations to the core and leave them quite literally at the mercy of the elements. For several years her husband had apparently been indulging a secret gambling addiction. This became so all-consuming that it led him to pawn every one of his belongings, which – though not rich by any stretch of the imagination – were not in short supply.

She recalled the time, when her husband was still young and all he wanted was to show her parents that, although a late teenager at the time and a little insecure and carefree, he would soon be in a position to look after their daughter. The girl herself was a hard nut to crack and no suitors ever measured up. Her parents had already set up twenty-three o-miai,[87] always with the same outcome: she would find some flaw in them and the first date would be the last. They realized their daughter must be a case of kurisumasu keki[88] and decided not to waste any more time on her. Yet she

---

[87] Formal Marriage meetings organized by a go-between.

[88] Compares with "Christmas cake' that, if not sold by the twenty-fourth or twenty-fifth, will never be sold, hence widely spoken that young men who reach that age will find it harder to marry.

seemed to have developed a liking for this gawky boy, whom she had at first ruled out. Her parents clearly felt this was their last chance but, truth be told, they didn't take it that seriously. Then, after the second or third date, the boy vanished.

'You'll see, father,' said Emiko-san in a prophetic tone, 'he'll be back. Just when we least expect him.'

'Like death itself!' her father replied, receiving a kick from his wife under the kotatsu.

The young man did indeed show up again just when they no longer expected him, and gallantly offered their daughter the pinkest natural pearl they had ever seen. It wasn't a diamond ring as tradition dictated, but a Philippine pearl of dubious provenance was good enough for them by that stage of the proceedings. Her parents agreed that he could take her off their hands at the earliest opportunity, in case either party should change their mind. Though she was never in love – as she just wasn't that interested in married life with this or any other man and what she really liked was the open air – they nevertheless lived quite happily. Truth be told, she would rather have been trekking bareback across the Mongolian steppe than having to devote herself to raising children and preparing umeshu[89] every year at the end of June: It simply bored her.

For a long time, driven by his desire to marry her, her husband had devoted himself to work, and although the company hierarchy was set in stone and he would only be in line for promotion at certain ages, a series of lucky breaks helped him climb the ladder. One day, quite out of the blue, he had hatched the idea to take up gambling and, what was worse, to play for big stakes, something that was most unlike him.

His secret could not be kept dark for long, although his early death spared him the pain of having to witness the

---

[89] Plum liqueur.

cataclysm it wrought in his family, not to mention their reproaches.

Watanabe-san and her daughters found themselves living in a tiny minimalist house whose mortgage had been momentarily suspended by her creditors – partly out of sympathy and partly out of 'loyalty' to the deceased – but which in any event the widow would be forced to pay later on. In addition to this there were other debts floating in the ether, but no assets left with which to settle them. So it was that their lives came to be ruled by the binbōgami,[90] though it took them some time to understand this reality, especially her daughters. They felt as if they were living a bad dream and that, when 'the next day' arrived any time now, they would wake up and everything would be like it was before.

Mrs Nakamura, who had been in the family's service since Aiko was born, offered to stay and help without being paid her salary. It was with a heavy heart that Watanabe declined her generous offer, as she no longer had anywhere to even put her up.

'We should do like the Kuge,'[91] said Aiko sarcastically, 'and go from door to door, talking to the neighbours.'

'My dear, I am in no mood for joking,' her mother answered, trying to solve the puzzle of how to fit her daughters' clothes into the small wardrobe alongside eiderdowns, towels and blankets.

---

[90] A spirit, that incarnates in a person or a house and brings misery or poverty.

[91] Descendants of the Fujiwara family, which ruled over all aspects of court life during the Heian Period (794–1185). When power changed hands in the era of the Samurai, they fell into poverty. Every New Year, faced with the obligation to pay their debts, they asked forgiveness for not being able to do so, saying that 'perhaps they should burn their houses and escape in the night'. Terrified of the possibility of a fire in the neighbourhood, people would collect money for them to stop them burning their houses.

One possible solution to their cramped conditions, she thought, would be to have the three of them sleep together on the futon. Two with their heads facing east, and one in the middle, pointing west, or maybe... one facing south. Whatever she did, she would need a compass to make sure none of their heads were pointing north.[92]

'A penny for your thoughts, Okā-san,' said Aiko languidly, filing a nail that had just broken.

'I was thinking about the points of the compass,' her mother answered. 'I need to buy a compass.'

Aiko thought her mother was speaking figuratively about how disoriented she felt, what with all that was going on, and in an attempt to console her she said:

'Okā-san, I will have to give up my singing lessons too.'

Failing to pick up on her gesture, her mother answered with a reproach:

'Yes, dear. I know. Do you realize, all you think of is your singing classes, when your sister Keiko hasn't even finished school yet?'

Aiko took a deep breath.

'We shall have to learn to give up many things,' her mother added. 'We shall start a new life, different to the one we have always lived. But don't worry, dear. We will overcome. You'll see. We will overcome,' she repeated.

The two of them stood there in silence, utterly devoid of any belief in the likelihood of her statement. It was growing dark.

---

[92] The dead are placed with their heads pointing north.

❖

Aiko-san started helping her mother prepare Chinese dumplings which they served in a small makeshift 'dining room' on the ground floor. The curtain had come down on her aspirations for ever: her dream of being a diva lay on the other side, she had to give up rice powder[93] for wheat flour and cabbages. At times she would seek consolation in her sense of humour, telling herself she would never have made it to prima donna anyway, as she couldn't play the Onnagata.[94]

Suddenly, as if struck by lightning, she remembered that her Aunt Mika-san – her father's elder sister – had once told her that modern women must learn to type because, together with the sexual arts, it was a vital tool for women to 'get on in life'. So Aiko decided to take her advice retrospectively and register for a free state-subsidized typing course as part of a program for women of limited means. She preferred for now to leave the sex aside – which besides, as a 'means to an end', had nothing modern about it. Sometime later, while she was taking the metro to secretarial school, she wondered whether her aunt really had said such a thing or she had simply dreamed it. In an attempt to confirm the truth of her memory, she asked her, and her aunt responded with a belly laugh. It had definitely been a dream, and amid the laughter she added:

---

[93] Used for stage make-up, but also by geisha and maiko.

[94] The leading female character, always played by a man.

'But I think it's a stupendous idea!'

As her Aunt Mika-san was on the 'wayward' side, Aiko didn't dare ask her which of the two she was referring to, so she assumed she meant both.

Despite her fingers aching from pressing the keys of the rickety old typewriter, despite the icy temperature of the water in winter, Aiko didn't grumble any more. She went on slicing onions, making the most of the stinging in her eyes to cry away the cascade of tears it prompted and so avoid another scolding from her mother for being 'selfish'. Yet not a single day of her life went by without thinking she would sooner or later return to the theatrical arts. She would practice in front of the full-length mirror on the bathroom door, but the space was too cramped for her to truly express herself. Often, looking deep into her own eyes, she would hold dramatic dialogues with herself: 'Poor Aiko, how sad what's happened to her!' she would say. 'But what *has* happened to her?' 'What? Hasn't anyone told you? She's been found dead by the River Kamo,' she answered, devastated. 'The moon leant over her pale face!' she continued, drumming on her cheeks with her fingers. 'They found her frozen to death, and those darling eyebrows of hers... all frosted with snow! She's dead!' 'How dreadful!' 'Yes, such a great talent as hers... and now she's dead! Dead! Dead!' Then the mirror rippled and shattered, blurring the outline of her face. So she would shut her eyes tight and let the warm liquid run between her lashes, restoring her image in the bleak bathroom light.

❖

Her workplace was in the same neighbourhood where she had studied, and whenever she passed through, she would run into her old theatre friends. Once, she had seen a group of them in the distance, chatting outside the doors to the tea-house, their hands occupied with packages of costumes, masks and feathers. Two years had gone by and she wondered when there would be no turning back for her.

It was through her work that Aiko met the man who would become her husband, the young Yamana Hinata. He had gone to the office one afternoon for a meeting with her boss, who had been held up at one of the ministries, so they had had to reschedule. To make his wait more pleasant, Aiko busied herself with serving him tea and company brochures. They fell to talking and, as it was late, he decided to ask her to dinner at a restaurant in the same building, famous for its sukiyaki[95] – Aiko's favourite. At the end of the evening, he invited her the following Saturday to the Peking Opera, which was touring Tokyo at the time. It was an invitation she couldn't turn down, and she saw it as a gateway to the world she had left behind and so badly yearned for. They began to see more and more of each other, until one day he proposed.

Aiko had imagined that her life would become a constant round of theatre dates, on the move from stage to

---

[95] Sliced beef cooked with various vegetables in a table-top cast iron pan.

stage. She even speculated that she might teach her new husband everything she herself had learnt about the dramatic arts. This fact, which she seemed to be predestined for, changed the meaning of the family tragedy from conclusive to relative, making the famous words of Master Chuang Tzu[96] truer than ever: 'Bad luck? Good luck? Who can tell?'

---

[96] A fourth century BCE Chinese philosopher.

❖

Outwardly Hinata Yamana-san was an 'important' man, yet no one had the slightest idea what exactly it was he did for a living. His profession might, on balance, have been said to involve 'tying up loose ends' or 'acting as an intermediary': something akin to a 'broker' of political and trade relations among keiretsu[97] – a 'facilitator' of the impossible, as a client of his had once called him. Whenever something needed fixing and there was no one else to turn to, people turned to Yamana-sama. They had taken to calling him 'The Chairman'.

Madame Watanabe was happy with her daughter's choice of suitor. She realized at once that he was a man who knew what he wanted. He had 'a particular aura' about him, 'a certain charisma', and he appeared to belong to that caste of people who have the ability to conjure a 'yes' before the question has even been asked. Watanabe-san could finally take a break from frowning so much at the dumplings and once again smelt something she hadn't experienced for so long: the scent of 'Three Pagodas' soap on her skin, instead of onions.

Yamana-sama used to take Aiko, her mother and her sister for walks in the country. They would spend Saturday in the open air and have lunch somewhere special. He

---

[97] Fundamental, family-type units of banks and companies, that work together towards common goals and form the basis of Japan's industrial economy.

would sometimes have dinners of anything up to thirteen courses prepared in restaurants with private booths, just for the three of them. That summer he invited them to the seaside and set them up in a pretty ryokan, south-west of Honshu. He would visit them at weekends and then return to Tokyo to attend to business.

The resort was in some turmoil due to the presence of American troops, but people seemed to have grown accustomed to living alongside them.

Young Keiko would gaze in captivation at the Marines and the sweethearts strolling along the promenade. She had a romantic spirit which, until then, she had never been able to display openly anywhere but in her fantasies. If there was one thing she truly desired, it was to marry, just as her sister was about to do. When she caught that day-dreamy look on her face, her mother warned her not to go and 'get involved with those people' and that she 'had no idea what went on there.'

'But... so it isn't true,' asked Keiko, 'what they say about the young women who come here to find American husbands?'

Her mother rounded on her sternly and replied:

'You don't want to know what they find, Keiko. Just don't get mixed up with them.' And she went on: 'We will stay at the ryokan until the end of the holidays – out of politeness – but then we shall go home, back from where we came.'

Madame Watanabe was taken aback that The Chairman hadn't taken such things into consideration. She didn't understand whether this was due to his capacity for dialectical synthesis, whether he simply hadn't paid enough attention, or whether he believed she could manage two restless teenage girls on her own and keep them within the walls of the ryokan. It was inevitable: "kowai mono mitasa".[98] Predictably enough, the two sisters' curiosity about this brand new world led them to sneak out foolishly one night while their mother was asleep.

'Just to take a peek,' said one. 'Just to get an idea,' said the other. And with all the blasé callowness of youth they walked into the night through the brambles and across the meadows until they reached the town.

The streets were filled with people and music, hustle and bustle. Young men and women came and went from the bars, beer cans in hand. Boys wolf-whistled at the casually dressed girls walking along the pavement, their cat-calls meeting with winks or giggles; sometimes they would even join them.

'The people here seem very open!' said Aiko in delight.

'Must be the summer…,' her sister replied.

Seeing other girls like themselves entering the bars, they plucked up their courage and did likewise. They swore to each other that they would go back to the ryokan after one little drink as if nothing at all had happened.

In Tokyo they had been to tea-houses with their friends, or for sushi with their parents, but never alone, and never at night. To them it was all just a childish lark. Caught up in the energy of the place, they went inside, sat at the bar and ordered tea.

'What? Tea?' asked the waiter. 'The tea-house closed at six,' he added sarcastically, pointing through the door at the place across the street. 'We don't serve tea here, young ladies.'

'Well,' asked Aiko, 'what do you recommend?'

'We have rice wine… and beer,' he answered.

---

[98] 'There is the temptation to see what is feared,' or more familiarly, 'forbidden fruit is the sweetest'.

'OK... we'll have one of each,' said Keiko.

A young Japanese man sitting in a corner with some other young men kept staring at them. In the end he went up to them and offered Aiko a cigarette:

'Two honourable young ladies from a respectable family? At this hour? Alone? In a place like this?'

The question puzzled them, as they weren't the only women there. Many other girls were sitting there on their own or in groups of two or three. Aiko smiled, inhaling a mouthful of smoke, which, never having tried a cigarette before, made her cough and splutter. Then he took her gently by the arm.

'Come,' he said, 'you'll have a good time. Tell your friend to come too.'

He led her over to the table from where he had been watching them. Aiko looked for her sister over her shoulder and saw that she was following them. So she let him lead her, as if the decision weren't her own but had been taken by some inescapable fate bound to run its inescapable course. Her sister sat down beside her, squeezing in between her and a young man drinking beer from a can.

'Japanese and Americans,' whispered Keiko, 'drinking together? Just like that? As if the war had never happened?'

Aiko felt like a woman possessed and could no longer tell if this was bad or whether she should simply 'surrender' to what was written in the stars. So she answered her sister, who gripped her arm tight:

'If you don't want to stay, go back to the ryokan. But don't go to sleep! Then you can open the door for me.'

'Have you completely lost your mind?' asked a frightened Keiko. 'You'll be sorry, Aiko-chan! Oh this is crazy! You'll regret it!' she repeated.

'Oh, I might, little sister, I might,' she replied, 'but the crazy things you regret most in this life are the ones you didn't do when you had the chance to.'

Being the younger of the two and given the sisterly tone of this pronouncement, Keiko knew not to insist, so she set off back to the ryokan, worried and angry with herself, and fretting about Aiko, all the time thinking she should have stayed. As she tottered over the cobbles, she broke the hanao[99] on one of her geta.[100]

'Oh, damn!' she cursed.

She knew this was a terrible omen and felt an overwhelming urge to rush back for her sister. But she thought better of it when she pictured Aiko's fury, so she trudged all the way back to the ryokan barefoot.

She slipped through reception, past the landlady, who had fallen asleep in a chair in front of the television. She went up to her rooms, slid back the screen with all the stealth of a snake and lay down on her futon, half undressed, trembling from head to toe. Her mother, who had been on sleeping pills since her father died, was snoring peacefully, but Keiko didn't get to sleep until dawn, when Aiko came back drunk, her hair tousled, her clothes a mess. She helped her to undress in the dark, took the clothes and placed them in a bag at the bottom of the suitcase.

Keiko had to wait until well into the afternoon the following day before she could talk to her sister. She hadn't wanted breakfast and they hadn't been able to put away the futon to lay the table, so they had to improvise one on the engawa and keep stepping over her. Her mother noticed nothing untoward, nor was she surprised at how long Aiko slept in, putting it down to the sea air and to general exhaustion.

The young man who had courted Aiko on that infamous night with his beautiful, strange, Abyssinian cat's eyes had

---

[99] Thongs.

[100] Traditional high wooden clogs with two supports on the bottom and V shape thongs between the big toe and the other toes. Breaking Hanao (thong) is considered bad omen.

also succeeded in stealing her only dowry, which she had been at such pains to keep intact. She couldn't even remember how or where it had happened; she remembered practically nothing. She didn't know whether someone had drugged her or whether, unused to drinking, she had simply had one too many. Nor could she remember how she had made it back to the ryokan. All that came to mind were flashes of a struggle: octopuses wrestling in a tangle of desire, pain and repulsion; a young woman – not Japanese – watching her, telling her to kiss her and laughing when she did.

When she went into the bathroom that night, Keiko noticed several bruises on her sister's arms, neck and ribs, and began to cry inconsolably. She couldn't make out Aiko's attitude. She wondered how her sister could have been so self-destructive: how come she hadn't sensed the danger when it was staring her in the face? All of a sudden she felt she didn't know her, despite having spent every day with her for all these years, that she wasn't the sister she had grown up with, but a total stranger bent on making her suffer. A stranger she adored, for whom she would have given her life and yet who acted indifferently toward her. Aiko, for her part, was in a kind of trance. She seemed not to hear Keiko, answering without thinking, as if miles away.

'You don't remember anything?' Keiko asked angrily. She must be doubly stupid, she thought to herself.

Aiko had nothing to say in her own defence; her mind was quite empty and she needed to rest.

Keiko spent the rest of the holidays crying, which her mother took to be one of her 'tantrums' with her sister.

'Instead of being happy for her wedding… just look at you!'

Then, realizing the best thing would be to give her hope rather than fanning the embers of her resentment, she added flatly:

'It'll be your turn soon, Keiko, don't despair. You're still young. You'll soon find your Prince Charming.' This only succeeding in making Keiko burst into a fresh flood of tears.

But Aiko's story didn't end there. One morning, two months later, when the young man's face had been wiped completely from her memory, she discovered a strange whitish liquid leaking from her nipple. The pain was so intense she had to hold her breasts in order to get out of the futon without screaming. She grew thin, as everything made her nauseous. Her sense of smell became so acute that most of the time she went around with her nose covered to stop herself being sick.

Aiko would never forget the afternoon she broke the news of her conspicuous pregnancy to her okā-san. They were sitting on the tatami, surrounded by mountains of bills from her creditors. Her mother was handing her a copy of an IOU signed by her father for her to read, as the light was too dim for her tired eyes.

'I'm pregnant,' she said, 'and it's not Hinata's.'

Her mother froze in mid-gesture, holding the piece of paper in her outstretched hand, staring into the void in the century of an instant. Then her eyes foundered on the shores of Aiko's gaze.

That was the moment that sealed her fate: the wedding would not be called off.

With a sang-froid that restored Aiko's confidence, Madame Watanabe immediately made the necessary preparations to send her away on an emergency visit to look after her 'sick' aunt for the term of the pregnancy. There she would give birth and return, fresh as a daisy, ready for her wedding to Yamana Hinata, The Chairman. With barely any time to bid her fiancé goodbye, Aiko was duly shipped off to the island of Sato one windy autumn morning, and her mother placed a pair of the girl's geta on the front step; one looking out and the other looking into the house, to ensure her safe return.

❖

Most people have never heard of Sato. According to her mother, this is due to the fact that, 'Sato lay just beneath the Dragon's left fang.' Dragons, apparently, and all manner of fearful and ferocious-looking animals were painted on the edges of maps. The message was that beyond, stretched perilous unexplored territory, which induced in sailors a kind of 'edge-of-the-map' syndrome. As if that weren't enough, amidst the kanji,[101] an inscription would read: "HC SVNT DRACONES".[102]

This tradition, it would seem, had been taken up by cartographers from the Low Countries,[103] the only western territory with which the Empire of the Rising Sun had maintained any kind of contact. It wasn't known, however, if the custom of dragon painting dated back to the days of Marco Polo.

The Dutch had settled on the island of Dejima in Nagasaki Bay. From there, with the Japanese watching their

---

[101] Chinese ideographic character used in Japanese writing.

[102] 'Here be dragons'.

[103] The Dutch navy assisted Japan in its struggle against Portuguese missions, which had started to attack Buddhist temples and establish its Inquisition in Japan, just as it had been imposed on the Iberian Peninsula and in all the countries that conquered by the Portuguese. Due to the conversion of the occasional Daimo (local ruler) to Catholicism, people started being burned alive. This, plus the fact that the West was dividing up the world like cake, made Japan decide to permanently close its borders.

every move, they acted as middlemen for the rest of the world. They also traded and obtained, among other things, illustrated books on human anatomy and surgical instruments for the Japanese, who were prohibited for religious reasons from performing dissections. In exchange they received copper, camphor leaves, porcelain, lacquerware, rice. Japan's borders remained closed to the rest of the world for more than two hundred and fifty years.[104] No one could enter or leave. In those days, if anyone dared to abandon the territory for whatever reason, they were considered a traitor to their country. Moreover, anyone who was part of the traitor's family would never live to tell the tale.

The stories sailors told must certainly have been terrifying. Sailing through a storm with fifty-foot waves crashing down on the deck must have filled many a seaman with the fear they were about to be devoured by a pack of wild beasts living just over the horizon.

Clearly, if the island of Sato was to appear on maps of the Orient, 'the dragons' would have to be the first to go. And they wouldn't go until the buccaneers working for the Crown could be certain there was nothing worth exploiting there. So, in spite of the natural fears such dark seas might arouse, there more to this game of hide-and-seek than met the eye, something that only they were privy to.

Aiko, who was lucky enough to have seen some of those original navigation charts at the Naval Museum of Edo, observed that the dragons generally wore childlike expressions that inspired laughter rather than fear. She could almost hear them saying: 'I can't move from here because I'm painted on, and as it's my job to make sure no one ventures across these seas, I'll just have to stay put!'

Though she found it hard to admit, Aiko discovered that in a way the sailors were right: the experience of sea travel

---

[104] The Edo Period: 1603–1868.

was remarkably similar to being tossed about in the bowels of the Yamanata-no-Orochi.[105] Just as she had lost all hope of finding calm waters, the sea changed colour and the ferry soon put in at the bay. In the distance, surrounded by mountains, she could make out a little port and some people on the quayside fluttering white handkerchiefs at the incoming ship. Amongst them she picked out her aunt and uncle, waving their arms and calling to her: 'Aiko-san, Aiko-san! Welcome! She was wearing a little pink hat for identification.

Aiko was filled with emotion on sensing the goodness radiating from these two humbly-clad figures as they stood on the jetty. They were all got up in their Sunday best to welcome her. She later noticed their shoes were rather worn. She had heard a lot about them and seen photographs of her aunt as a child sitting on a rock somewhere near Okinawa. She remembered it because she looked ever so funny in her little blue, hand-coloured sailor's cap, with her two front teeth poking over her bottom lip like a rabbit. She hadn't changed much, either in terms of her expression or her teeth.

Her aunt and uncle shared a curious first name – Michi[106] – so everyone found it more amusing to call them 'The Michi'. It may not have been very formal, but it came to be a family custom and the name stuck.

As she was debarking, Aiko collapsed as if drunk, the journey having left her unable to stand on terra firma.

'That's landsickness,' said her Uncle Michi-san. 'It'll soon pass. I have just the thing for it.'

So her uncle rigged up a hemp hammock on the verandah overlooking the back garden and fastened it to the crossbeams. There Aiko remained, rocking beneath a broad,

---

[105] The 'eight-branched serpent': a dragon with eight heads and eight tails.

[106] Used interchangeably for men or women.

light-green mosquito net with crimson trim, isolated from the force of gravity. When it was time for bed, her aunt had to climb into the hammock to undress her, gently sliding her leg into the pyjama bottoms as she rocked alongside her.

Every morning her uncle would be up with the lark and off to work. He would have a brisk breakfast of fish and soup, which his wife had prepared the night before. Her aunt spent the whole morning rushing about hither and thither with a cloth in her hand, wiping away dust that only she could see. Sometimes Aiko would go to market with her. There she would listen in transports of delight to the local dialect, unscathed by the passing of the centuries. She wandered through that whispering world of woolly gestures in a state of lucid torpor, without feeling obliged to understand or enter into conversation – which, anyway, she preferred to avoid. She enjoyed the unexpected relief that came with letting go of language and responded to everything with a 'Yes!', or would simply thank people with a smile that they would sometimes find perplexing. She believed that this way she would live up to everyone's expectations, so she let them think whatever they wanted. This strategy led her to observe that the ambiguity of the reply revealed whatever folk hoped to confirm. In fact, it was something that happened in any case after long explanations, so it made no difference.

The mile-long folds of correspondence sent her by her future husband arrived in dribs and drabs. Sometimes she would receive two or three letters at once but then go for more than a month without hearing from him. When this happened Aiko's mood would swing from feeling overwhelmed by the reading to fretting about the delay. She always wondered whether Hinata-san suspected anything about her sudden departure. She was conscious of how paradoxical her replies were. Years later, when she came across her letters in a drawer of her husband's desk, she wondered again how he could ever have believed the whole story. 'You'll see, dear Hinata. My aunt will be better in no more than five months and then I'll be able to come back.' At the time she felt her missives should have been cleverer, though she felt no guilt at spinning him such a barefaced lie. Why should she? She knew that telling the truth would mean her family would be cast away on the rocks of shame and destitution. Her mother had been right when she'd said that meeting Hinata-san had been a rare stroke of luck in life. They couldn't face going back to living in the conditions thrust upon them after her father's death. She also felt a great deal of affection for this man who had been so understanding and thanks to whom her prospects were now looking up.

The days passed, the peach trees blossomed and the light refracted through their shimmering flowers brought a ghostly, angelical atmosphere that descended on the whole village.

Hikaru-chan was born on the same day as the Buddha, April 8th, in a spell of torrential rains. He weighed almost nine pounds and did actually rather resemble a Buddha, ready to be popped on a shelf. No one understood how he could have come out of those hips of Aiko's, which were as narrow as a twelve-year old's.

When the rains finally let up, the whole village came back to life. The little allotment on which the sun now beamed was left to grow to seed. The rains had spoiled it, but no one had any time to tend it for now. The cherry tree, though bent by the years, remained true to the spring and burst into flower.

Sitting on the little stone bench in the garden, by the freshly-washed clothes hanging on the line, Aiko would feed her son while the wind shook a flurry of pale petals off the cherry tree. Her Aunt Michi-san would settle down beside her with obedient devotion and massage her feet with red tea, or cook cold green tea soba[107] nests or thick gelatinous soups of junsai[108] and somen.[109] She also cared for the boy as if he were her own and could even distinguish between his different cries. Meanwhile Aiko rested and dreamed of staying forever, floating on the wind like a cherry petal. It was a dream secretly shared by her aunt, who had told her that it was entirely up to her whether she stayed or left: 'Our little house is humble but please look on it as your home.'

Eyes welling with tears, Aiko thanked her and said her aunt would surely know how to care for her son better than she did.

'You deserve him far more than I do,' she said. 'Don't worry about a thing, I'll cover all your costs. It'll be our little secret forever,' she added, solemnly.

The pact between the two was sealed.

When the time came to leave, young Aiko said goodbye to her son with mixed feelings. She laid him in the cradle as if he were a doll waiting to be played with next holidays, kissed him, then headed for the jetty with her aunt and uncle. Just as her mother had, after Aiko left for Sato, her aunt observed the custom of placing a pair of geta at the front door – one pair facing out, the other facing in – in the hope that one day Aiko would have a change of heart and come back to them.

They saw her off just as they had welcomed her months before, got up in their Sunday best and fluttering their white handkerchiefs.

---

[107] The Japanese for 'buckwheat', synonymous with a fine noodle made from buckwheat flour.

[108] *Brasenia schreberi*: a perennial aquatic plant belonging to the same family as lilies. Its shoots are wrapped in a gelatinous substance and are highly appreciated in Japanese food.

[109] A fine noodle, similar to angel hair.

During the crossing Aiko could not shake off the feeling that she had forgotten something. The weather had started to warm up and the enforced lethargy of the cabin was becoming unbearable, so she decided to sleep outside. Several times she awakened in confusion, not knowing where she was.

The pitch-dark night stole in, and all that could be heard was the hum of the engine and the splash of water against the metal hull. Her hands were cold and her stomach churned. Her child would be asleep by now, she thought. She would never have been able to love him, anyway. Who could tell what kind of person he might become? Through the night she wept in slow, heavy sobs that merged with her dreams and gradually evaporated towards dawn. When they pulled into the station, she spotted her mother and her sister through her swollen eyes, waiting on the platform with a bunch of flowers. The three women embraced and burst into tears. In a moment of clarity Aiko realized she was making the biggest mistake of her entire life, yet still she abandoned herself to her fate without a backward glance.

Her mother took her immediately to see the same doctor as had confirmed her pregnancy to stem the ceaseless river of milk flowing from her breasts. And as they dried up so too did her memories. After a few weeks she was horrified to find one morning that it all felt like a dream and she had begun to forget.

Her mother had had to perform miracles to stop her fiancé travelling to Sato to see her. Whenever he suggested doing so, she would wipe the idea from his mind, saying she was almost home and it would only be a few more days. Then, when she still didn't come back, she told him her sister-in-law's condition had worsened, but that things would surely work themselves out soon – for better or for worse. All that time Yamana Hinata-san went on visiting the family, taking gifts and money dignified with discretion in a little envelope. He had decided that the best way to secure Aiko's affections was to take care of her family as soon as possible.

Sekihan[110]

Aiko and Hinata were joined in wedlock in the solar month of November, eleven being considered a lucky number.

While Hinata-san's mother felt his choice of wife to be unsuitable, he was her only son and she spared no expense, shouldering the cost of the hotel where the ceremony was to be held, as well as the reception after the ceremony.

For all that times had changed, it now being the done thing to serve specialities of French cuisine, Madame Yamana wished to do things the way they had been done her whole life long: in strictest accordance with tradition. So she ordered lacquered trays decked with arrangements of autumn leaves and fresh crab, chawanmushi[111], pink rice flecked with fine flakes of pure gold leaf, kombu[112] broth and clams, kazunoko,[113] adzuki bean sweets and other delights to promote a full and fertile life. She had the menu printed in kanji and translated into French, which the groom's guests found very chic, and the bride's utterly snobbish and futile. Although tradition dictated the two groups be kept separate, they were easily distinguished: anyone entering the function room could work out who

---

[110] White rice with adzuki beans, known as 'happiness rice' and eaten on special occasions, such as births, marriages or recovery from illness.

[111] Egg custard.

[112] Seaweed.

[113] Fresh herring roe: *kazu* means 'number' and *ko* means 'child', symbolizing the desire to be blessed with numerous offspring.

was from Hinata's family and who was from Aiko's, even though all the married women were in black kimonos and the single women in coloured ones.

Aiko wore the traditional dress with herons embroidered in silk and gold. She took the precaution of ensuring that it was her time of the month so that a few drops of blood on the nuptial bed would bear false witness to her lost virginity. She had to wrestle with the astrologers, who were stubbornly opposed to the wedding being held on that date. But on the night, after retiring to their rooms, The Chairman was so drunk that he fell fast asleep, while Aiko prepared her nuptial nightdress in her dressing room with the aid of two young seamstresses. The giggling girls wished her luck and withdrew. Aiko walked triumphantly from her dressing room, proud of her new status, only to end up sitting on her wedding bed listening to her new husband snoring, so loud it rattled the Coromandel screens. It took no great insight to realize she wouldn't get a wink of sleep that night.

They left the following morning for Rome, "the most romantic city in all of Western Europe", according to Hinata. It was the first time Aiko had made such a long journey by plane and again she got no sleep. As soon as they landed, she realized that Rome possessed none of the romantic qualities her husband had spoken of. Even less so in the month of November, when it was cold and wet and wasn't encircled by the flame-red geraniums she had seen in postcards of the Spanish Steps. Her husband turned out to be a history buff, plain and simple, just like his father, so Aiko ended up spending her honeymoon being dragged from museum to palazzo, forced to learn the history of characters that were of not the slightest interest to her. The Romans certainly had nothing to do with Japan, nor with her, nor even with themselves, if the differences between the people of centuries ago and these others parading before her was anything to go by.

As she came and went, hobbling through the ruins, twisting her ankles on the cobblestones, then hopping about to fix her shoe, she told herself that these streets could only have been designed by men who didn't understand high heels, and that all she was going to get out of this was a return trip to Tokyo with her leg in plaster.

During their sightseeing Aiko would lag behind while her husband marvelled at the porticos, the domes, the arches, and marched ahead, perfectly heedless of her. He would often disappear into the crowd, and Aiko would have to stay put and wait until Hinata noticed she was missing and came back to look for her. As if that weren't enough, she also had serious issues with the acidity of the food and the rice being generally undercooked for her liking. And what about those apparently harmless little coffees her husband insisted on drinking in the mornings, the ones strong enough to wake the dead? She had tried one once and it left her heart pounding till long after bedtime. Then, to cap it all, there wasn't a single place in the whole city where she could take refuge in a nice, quiet cup of green tea.

Her husband patiently taught her to recognize the word 'pesce',[114] for that was what, relatively speaking, most pacified her gastronomic discontent and confusion. From that moment on he decided to compile a dictionary of 'tentative similarities' including such specialities as *cotolletta alla milanese* – a rough equivalent of tonkatsu[115] – or *fritto misto* – which bore more than a passing resemblance to agemono.[116] Aiko was even known, on occasion, to venture as far afield as *ravioli, raviolini, tortelloni, tortellini, agnolini, agnolotti, capelletti, sorrentini...*

---

[114] Italian for 'fish'.

[115] Fried pork in breadcrumbs.

[116] Deep-fried vegetables or fish.

'They're variations on gyoza, like the ones your mother used to make,' he said in a valiant bid to convince her. 'Then you have *riso in bianco*, which is a lot like gohan,[117] and then there's *fettuccini*, which is something like ramen, and *vermicelli*, which are almost first cousins with somen because... as you surely know, Marco Polo...,'[118]

No, she wasn't the slightest bit interested in Marco Polo, who, according to his log, had discovered pasta on his voyages to the Orient long before Italians made it their own.

Looking back, it *had* been a fascinating trip, but there was something inside her that put up a passive resistance to anything the encounter with this culture could give her, because she felt betrayed. It was not the honeymoon she had hoped for by any stretch of the imagination. If at least they had been in a group... But Hinata preferred they went alone. And for what? For nothing.

'The Goodwill Dictionary' – Aiko's name for it – that her husband had put together was extremely generous in its ideas, but fell well short of her gastronomic expectations. Had her mother been there, she would have explained to him that her attitude was no more than her 'princess airs and graces' rising to the surface and that he'd better start getting used to them.

Aiko eventually ended up eating in a grubby Japanese restaurant on a side-street off the Piazza della Repubblica. Anything was better than having to subject herself to the whims of that foreign food, whose acid intensity she deeply distrusted and whose meteoric effects disrupted her sleep.

'Do you think it's normal,' her husband reproved her with a hint of frustration as he popped a piece of raw fish into his mouth, 'to end up eating in a place like this when

---

[117] In this case used for steamed rice.

[118] There is a theory that it was Marco Polo who introduced pasta into Europe after visiting China.

we're in Rome? Considering how famous Italy is for its cuisine, I mean?'

But in time Aiko's palate acclimatized and scaled the peaks of delight when she discovered *pizza Margherita*.

'That's what I want,' she said, standing before a succulent photograph of bright red tomato sauce, creamy white mozzarella and deep green basil leaves.

Her husband looked behind the poster to find out what she was referring to.

'Pizza-o; that's what I want.'

After this epiphany Aiko declared she would eat *pizza Margherita* and only *pizza Margherita* for the rest of the trip and possibly for the rest of her life. Hinata had to negotiate this faux-pas, being reluctant to spend the rest of their honeymoon luncheoning and dining in pizzerias or, failing that, grimy 'Japanese' dives staffed by gaijin.[119]

'What do you say to some *calamaretti fritti?*' he asked on the third day, sitting in a pizzeria on the Campo de' Fiori.

'What's that?' asked Aiko.

'Ika tenpura,'[120] he said. 'Just wait, you'll love it!'

On more than one occasion poor Aiko found herself walking barefoot into the lobby of a hotel, being in the perfectly logical habit of automatically removing her shoes with a sharp tap of her heel on the edge of the step before entering.

'*Signora. Mi spiace... le scarpe,*'[121] the concierge whispered to her on one occasion, glancing discreetly at her shoes.

Aiko stood there staring at him, unable to work out what he was referring to.

---

[119] Not Japanese.

[120] Very light frying.

[121] 'Madam! I am sorry... the shoes'

'*De shooseh…,*' he repeated, his gaze flitting from Aiko to her shoes and back again.

'Ku tsuo!' her husband translated, pointing with his eyes at the offending articles, neatly set on one side.

The concierge, who was a Neapolitan, understood this to be an expression from his own language[122] rather than Japanese and thought her husband to be a man of rather strong temperament. Anyone can make a mistake, after all. But he was amazed at the man's astonishing fluency in the Italian language.

'*Bravo!*' said the concierge. '*Ma nun se proccupà…,*'[123] he added, noticing Yamana Hinata-san's embarrassment and trying to keep him sweet.

'Dis a something dat a happen all a de timeh,' he repeated, with much gesticulation -in case his words weren't enough and something was lost in translation-.

Of all the places they visited she found Venice the most disconcerting. The outward appearance of this city from the 'Arabian Nights' was deeply intriguing, but she couldn't understand why they'd built it at water-level, without any apparent concern for the tides, when to the west there was such a vast expanse, the occupation of which could have been settled with a battle between republics.

'Besides,' she complained, 'who came up with the bright idea of building an entire city on wooden stilts?' Her conclusion was unimpeachable: they were on a raft. Besides, the Roman engineers and architects who had dominated much of the western world with their plans for cities and giant aqueducts were of a different race – surely extinct – from these so-called 'Italians'.

---

[122] 'cazzo' is an Italian swearword, sometimes emphasized by the 'aoh'. It has many meanings, among which is 'penis', and is considered vulgar.

[123] 'Don't worry' in Napolitan.

Water was a constant bugbear in Aiko's mental trigonometry. So much so that one night, having spent the whole day paddling in the *aqcua alta*[124] lapping at the shores of Saint Mark's Square, she dreamt that, when she awoke in the morning, they would have arrived safely in Tokyo aboard *La Serenissima*[125] no less. The huge 'ship' was outside the Basilica of Santa María della Salute. They docked on the jetty, as if it had been the *traghetto*.[126] Standing on the shore, her mother and sister were waving white handkerchiefs, just as her aunt and uncle had when she had put in at Sato.

'You have too vivid an imagination,' laughed Hinata.

'Are dreams supposed to be logical?' laughed Aiko.

Yet, secretly, in the deepest coves of her mind, the dream wasn't so absurd. It didn't require much imagination to realize that Venice and all its magnificent palazzi might one day drift off and away across the Adriatic. Of that she was quite certain.

---

[124] A high tide that sometimes covers part of the city.

[125] A name for the Venetian Republic.

[126] A Venetian ferry.

❖

Once the novelty of the trip had worn off and the anecdotes had been repeated to relatives ad infinitum, Hinata's family started to wonder why Aiko wasn't pregnant yet. The couple had had plenty of time to produce a child, so Hinata's mother and sisters agreed it was time for a visit to the doctor and the Sumiyoshi[127] to make enquiries. At home, the servants had even taken to planting lucky charms, which an indignant Aiko would discover hidden in her underwear or under the futon in the mornings.

She delayed the visit to the family doctor for obvious reasons: he was bound to realize her womb had previously harboured life. So she decided to secretly consult the specialist who had seen to drying up her breastmilk after she gave birth. His verdict was conclusive: there was nothing to suggest Yamana-san wasn't capable of reproducing like a rabbit. So she decided the matter was settled, but it turned out not to be as easy as she would have wished. The issue of her pregnancy came and went. It would, from time to time, erupt again, especially when her husband's cousin Masako-san became pregnant or gave birth (which appeared to be her favourite pastime, with no more than ten months elapsing between one child and the next). Nevertheless, recriminations were generally avoided in the interests of family harmony, although the subject was not

---

[127] A temple of fertility.

outside the realm of easily legible signs and everything seemed to conspire to bring it up. Even a perfectly innocent remark from the cook about a laying hen would prompt a great deal of blinking, evasive glances and mouth-twisting – the heavy artillery in the repertoire of daily warfare. To her in-laws it was obvious that there was only one person responsible: Aiko. 'Never in this house has any male been incapable of breeding, still less Hinata, who is descended from samurai stock.' Not Hinata, whom his mother used to put outdoors to sleep, exposed to the elements in the middle of winter, so that he would grow as tall and strong as a sughi.[128] Several times he had to be snatched from the brink of the death from pneumonia. Sterile? Hinata? Never! That would bring the greatest possible shame on his family: not being man enough as expected of a first-born son. No, not Hinata... Aiko! A skinny little slip of a thing who doesn't look a day over twelve! And all she eats is that funny Italian bread when she should be getting some washoku[129] down her, the way the rest of his family has always done. 'Proper food, Japanese food.' It all made the very air unbreathable. That constant tension could not last forever. But two years went by and nothing changed.

Life seemed not to offer many alternative dimensions to galvanize Aiko. The only change was wrought by the seasons: the bouts of winter flu, the dinner parties, the embassy receptions, the festivities and tea ceremonies carefully arranged by her mother-in-law. Aiko began to wonder whether she had inherited her mother's celibate genes and to question whether she really was cut out for marriage. She started seriously considering the possibility of going back to singing, dancing and acting. But in her heart of hearts she knew there was no turning back the clock. It

---

[128] Japanese cedar famous for its longevity, strength and height.

[129] Traditional Japanese food.

would only be a way of recovering the happiness that had been ripped up in this nuptial wilderness. She decided to speak to Hinata and ask his opinion. But she soon discovered this was a mistake when his sisters began to intervene, as if the decision were of public concern rather than a private matter.

She couldn't stay here like this, doing nothing. She had even stopped preparing umeshu every year at the end of June because she was in the way in the kitchen, which had become foreign to her. So she began to explore the grounds in search of somewhere special to call 'her own', somewhere she could feel free of the ever-watchful eyes of her mother- and sisters-in-law, who tracked her every movement and corrected her manners from the moment she opened her eyes until she closed them again. Eventually she came across an abandoned hut behind a copse of giant Thai bamboo. She'd read in the local paper about restoration projects for buildings like this as part of a heritage protection scheme. She decided to mention it to Hinata. He might be able to pull some strings and get them into one of the programs to cover some of the costs. Eventually she persuaded him.

'It's Chinese opera or the old minka,'[130] she said.

To which he replied: 'The minka. Do what you like, it's yours.'

At the start of summer Aiko embarked upon the colossal task of refurbishing this elephant of a thing slumbering amidst the bamboo. Both her husband and his family considered it a 'pointless passing fancy'. But deep down Hinata knew that, in the long run, it was best for him.

'While Japan progresses and does away with those filthy old places,' said Hinata's mother, 'she goes and takes it into

---

[130] A house of adobe, wood and bamboo, with a thatched roof, used formerly by peasants, artisans or tradesmen.

her head to "restore" them. What does she think it is? The Imperial Palace? And just as I was going to call the council to have it pulled down and sow my peonies there!' she added in a fit of pique.

'I warned you, Hinata,' grumbled his sister. 'The girl has a screw loose, you'll see, sooner or later. Fancy restoring a minka…! Okā-san's right!'

'Have you ever heard of such a thing?' added his other sister. 'You don't want to know what this is going to cost you!'

Hinata decided to have a tête-à-tête with his mother and explain the procedure to her. Five experts would have to come from Kamakura to assess the project and start the restoration work.

'Experts,' she asked. 'Experts in what? In huts? How can one be an expert in huts?'

'Yes, mother. Five of them will be coming down from Kamakura, as I said,' he replied.

'Where's that?'

'About forty miles away.'

'Why do they have to come from so far away?' she asked. 'Can't she use local workmen? I bet they'd know how to put the kaya back on,' she pointed out in annoyance.

'It isn't just the kaya,' replied Hinata-san. 'There are other things. Besides, what do you mean by put it "back on"? The kaya's useless, I don't think it can be saved.'

'It will cost you a fortune!' said his mother.

'It's restoration work. They'll have to take it to bits like a jigsaw puzzle and piece it back together again – at least part of it, because it's falling to pieces as you well know… practically in ruins.'

His mother listened, head tipped back, hand cradling the tip of her chin. She scrutinized Hinata's every word, incapable of believing he was talking about an abandoned hovel at the end of the garden, of no interest to anyone.

'You're serious…'

'Of course!. And I'll tell you something else: they won't use a single nail,' he added. 'Do you know what that is? Real craftsmanship, that's what.'

'It is because nails weren't used in the past: they were deemed taboo,'[131] said his mother. 'I still have boxes of the natsume[132] we haven't used, and guess what: there isn't a nail in them. But one thing is a box, another is a minka. Besides, then is then and now is now.'

'Oh… well, Okā-san! I *am* surprised that you of all people should say that; as I always thought you felt that "now" should be exactly as it was "then".'

His mother pursed her lips, tilted her head back and looked towards the window.

'How long will we have those men in the garden?' she asked.

'A year? I haven't spoken to them yet. Wait until they come and I'll fill you in with all the details. Don't worry, they'll use the back entrance gate, you won't even notice…,' replied Hinata. 'But tell me… I bet you didn't even know there was a hut there…'

'Certainly I did!' his mother replied. 'Your honourable father used to play there as a boy. It was the only one left standing. Those places are so dark…!' she said, rubbing her arms as she shivered. 'A spider trap!' she said and pursed her lips again. 'There were two more, further down the hill, near the river,' she added. 'A hermit moved into one of them and… they wouldn't kick him out, imagine… In fact, they used to take him rice and tea, I think. But one fine day he upped and disappeared.'

'Disappeared?'

---

[131] The nail-head signified the Emperor and could not be hammered.

[132] Lacquerware used for the tea ceremony.

'Just like that. Vanished. Pooff! No one saw him ever again. Must have found another hut. Of course, my father-in-law had them pulled down to prevent any further mischief. They were small, much more so than the one at the back there,' she said, pointing over Hinata's shoulder, 'and they were already falling down on their own by then. They just needed a little push. I'm talking about before the Meiji Restoration, mind you. Perhaps she would like to live there?' she asked sarcastically. 'Like the hermit?' she said, barely stifling her laughter.

'Oh, what are you talking about, Okā-san?' Hinata scolded her, as he turned on the lights of the tokonoma.[133]

'She wants a doll's house to play in, then.'

'Right,' he replied, knowing the subject was now exhausted – as indeed was he. 'That's settled then,' he said.

'Well, if you agree to this...'

'Sheer folly, I know,' Hinata interrupted her. 'But I have my reasons, Okā-san. It would be complicated to explain, but trust me.'

'Trust you? Are you asking for a token my faith? You do so because you have no logical arguments,' she laughed.

Hinata laughed too. Sometimes the things his mother said...!

'Well I don't understand you, I don't and I don't,' she said, heading for the kitchen. 'What is there for dinner tonight,' she added with a sigh to no one in particular.

---

[133] A ledge raised slightly above floor-level on which any art objects are placed.

The minka

Blackened by kurobikari,[134] the massive bamboo beams had stood aloft for over three centuries. Their original golden chestnut colour was revealed on removing the ropes they were lashed with to support the roof. They piled up the canes at the back of the garden; there was a mountain of them, a game of Mikado[135] ready to be played by giants.

Over the following year Aiko worked with architects and craftsmen, carting about ropes and plans, tying off posts, serving tea and caring for her employees as if they were members of her own family. She even took to wearing a pair of nikkapokka[136] to allow her more freedom of movement. The project inched forward at watch-maker's speed and had to be put on hold throughout the month of June due to the constant rain.

One day, like any other when Aiko entered the kitchen balancing a tray of dirty tea-cups, she ran into her mother-in-law. She had been doing her best to avoid her, the tension between them having rekindled thanks to the recent arrival of yet another baby from Hinata-san's cousin – who did nothing else apparently but give birth. Madame Yamana could not help glowering at Aiko from head to toe

---

[134] Covered with tar to form a black lustre.

[135] Japanese jackstraws.

[136] Traditional trousers, usually black or navy blue, baggy at the thigh and narrow at the ankle, used by building workers. They are knickerbockers originated in the Netherlands.

and, disregarding the presence of the cook, who was scaling fish, she spluttered and choked:

'A married woman... does not go about... dressed as a man or...,' she coughed, '...fraternize with labourers! Now I see!' She raised her voice. 'You are a boy! Not a shadow of a doubt! No wonder you have refused,' she coughed again, 'to give your husband... a... son,' and, on the verge of apoplexy, burst out sobbing.

Aiko stood rooted to the spot. She looked at her mother-in-law, but couldn't tell if what she was seeing was real or a dream. She had known Madame's words had been just bursting to get out and was sure it wouldn't be long before they did. And she'd been right. Finally, she had spat them at her in an outpouring of anger and resentment, heaving with pent-up rage that couldn't wait another minute.

Standing in the middle of the kitchen, clutching a pair of poultry shears, her face reflecting the green of the branches of the sansho tree[137] against the glass of the window, eyes sunken, mouth pitch dark and puckered by the black furrows of her fury. She looked like... like... an apparition! Yes, that was it! A demon from the Tibetan Book of the Dead!

'Oh, thou of noble birth! Harken closely! [...]
Any thing fearful or strange that thou mayst see'[138]

Aiko felt a volcanic wave well up inside her and, as her breathing quickened, the animal stirring within began to roar. Staring straight into her mother-in-law's eyes – something she had, out of respect, never done for more than a few seconds – she managed finally to find the words:

---

[137] *Zanthoxylum piperitum*: Sichuan pepper.

[138] Recitation from the Tibetan Book of the Dead – 'Bardo Thodol' – warning the deceased of the horrific apparitions they may meet on their passage through the afterlife.

'Oh...!' She bit her lip hard to stop herself saying more. But from somewhere came a 'You!'

Aiko gave a deep bow

"I am so sorry...! Forgive me, please!" and stormed out of the kitchen, cheeks blazing, temples pounding, about to explode. Meanwhile, she heard Madame Yamana's outraged spluttering and wished with all her heart like she had ever wished before: 'I hope the old hag coughs herself to death!' The coughing faded as Aiko walked away. She felt something warm trickling down her chin. When she touched it, she realized she was bleeding from the mouth. She had bitten into her lip.

For better or worse, those two minimalist words would fly the kitchen that very day and spread across Hakone Fuji in all weathers. By night and day they wended their way, and barely a year had passed before they reached Tokyo high society. The meaning of the words gradually changed. They were even set to music and became a source of laughter for generations to come:

'Oh...! You!'

For the first time in her life Madame Yamana Hotaru felt defeated and decided –albeit grudgingly – to move from the house she had lived in for over forty years. She returned to visit only to keep up appearances. Aiko, as might be expected, was anything but sorry. In fact, everyone silently enjoyed the extra few cubic feet of air to breathe.

Mrs Kato

By the start of winter the restoration of the minka was complete. Night and day at the heart of the building the irori fumed away, the door shut to smoke the ceiling and waterproof it with tar.[139] Aiko was a regular visitor to the little village of Miyanoshita, where there were several shops of "objets d'art" and antiques. She was looking for something for her minka, more for the simple pleasure of browsing than with anything specific in mind.

As her husband's father had lived in the area all his life, Miyanoshita's older inhabitants remembered him well. His family had once owned far more land than they did now. Much of it had since been donated to the Council for a public park that ran on to what much later on was declared the Fuji-Hakone-Izu National Park. The property included a few buildings – servants' quarters, barns, granaries, stables – that passed into the hands of the Agency for the Protection of Cultural Properties of Japan at the end of the nineteenth century. It also boasted a large two-storey adobe-and-palm-fibre kura,[140] still intact despite the harshness of the climate and the passing of time. Its antique contents had been donated by her father-in-law to the National Museum.

---

[139] A method of gradually waterproofing roofs with a coat of shiny, black tar.

[140] A semi-enclosed storehouse constructed beside the main house, used to store screens, furniture, crockery and other movable valuables brought out seasonally or for special occasions.

Mrs Kato's little shop stood directly opposite the famous Hotel Fujiya, and she had a clear recollection of all the stories and events, as well as Aiko's father-in-law, the Honourable Yamana-sama.

'Certainly I remember him!' she said. 'He was always at the hotel, meeting with high-ranking government figures, intellectuals, men-of-letters... writers who had country houses in this neck of the woods. Sometimes after his meetings he would come into the shop to browse, or pick up the occasional item. He was quite a lot older than myself. He was a great art lover and had a keen eye for what was valuable and what wasn't. I specifically recall a Heian[141] painting he had taken a shine to – an extraordinary thing,' remarked Kato-san, pausing a moment to dust the dragon on a Ming vase. 'Who knows what ever became of it?'

According to Mrs Kato, Hinata's father was one of the most interesting men she had ever met: intelligent, funny, witty... He brimmed with brilliant ideas and was uncommonly cultured.

'Someone you could discuss any subject with,' said Mrs Kato. 'It happens when one has lived a great deal. One comes to the conclusion that all centres are ultimately peripheries. Which was why he always avoided being judgmental.'

'How wonderful!' said Aiko in amazement.

'Yes, he was someone very special indeed. His death left a big hole in many people's lives,' Kato-san went on. 'Including, I imagine, his wife's.'

She vividly remembered the funeral: it had even been attended by members of the Imperial Court, as many had summer houses around those parts.

'Not the Honourable Emperor in person, of course. Some of his relatives came, however. Government officials

---

[141] 794–1185.

stayed in that hotel. Oh!' she exclaimed, 'if you could only have seen it, Madame Yamana! Now that is what I call a funeral!'

'Did you attend the ceremony, Kato-san?' asked Aiko.

'No, I didn't go,' she replied. 'How could I have gone? No, I didn't go because it wasn't, shall we say a... public affair. We did, however, go to see the procession. And what a procession! So many people! There, can you see?' she said, rising from her chair and pointing through the window.

Kato-san took Aiko by the arm and led her to the door.

'That one. Do you see it? That one over there, across the street. The food is still splendid there,' she added. 'Do you know, people came from miles around to say their goodbyes. From far and wide! I remember the shops closing in the village and the flag flying at half-mast on the monument up the road. They are things that stick in your mind – things you never forget.

'Half-mast!' Aiko exclaimed. Why did my husband never tell me? she asked herself, then added aloud: 'He must have been a truly important man!'

'Important? He was the village patriarch! Someone much-loved,' Mrs Kato assured her and went on: 'I used to live... not far from here, with my mother. She woke me with the news, though it was already two days since his death, as we later found out. Anyway, she woke me and, in a broken voice, she said: "Daughter, the Honourable Yamana-sama has passed?. Break out the funeral kimonos, we are joining the procession." She knew I knew him from here, from the shop. I was quite overcome... just to see the effect his death had on everyone. You think people like that will never die, that they'll be immortal, like the Emperor. The Emperor denied being immortal because the Americans forced him to... What a nerve!' she said, indignantly. 'Still, I do believe he was immortal. Everyone was too scared to contradict them,' added Madame Kato, lowering her voice, 'but he is... he was. The Honourable Emperor Showa will never die. Oh no, indeed. This story resembles the astronomer Galileo's. Do you know the story of Galileo?'[142]

Aiko shook her head. Just then, someone rang the doorbell. Madame Kato got up from her stool, looked at Aiko and said:

'I'll tell you another day. Come back and we'll talk some more. Oh, if only you knew...! I have so many things to...,' she broke off. 'Oh, good morning, Madame Nakazato! Or rather, good afternoon! One loses all track of time in an antiques shop!' she chuckled.

Mrs Nakazato bowed and, removing her rain-soaked hood, handed her umbrella to Kato-san. Aiko bowed her head in turn and set off home, without having heard the Galileo story.

---

[142] 'Eppur si muove': Albeit it does move.

Madame no longer lives here;
she is gone to stay...

'Madame no longer lives here,' Aiko told the house-keeper, 'so please be kind enough to give me the keys.'

Lowering her eyes, the housekeeper responded fear-fully:

'With all due respect, Ma'am, only Madame has the keys.'

Hinata had just come into the kitchen looking for fresh water. Taken aback by their exchange, she asked:

'What keys? What's going on?'

'Hinata,' said Aiko, 'please tell her to hand me the keys to the kura.'

The housekeeper remained silent.

'Do you have the keys to the kura?' he asked, as if return-ing from an interplanetary voyage.

'No, Honourable Chairman,' she replied. 'I've already told your honourable wife that I don't have the keys. As you are well aware, your honourable mother took them with all the other keys to the upstairs wardrobes, the ones from the big closet in the anteroom next to the dining room and the little key to the attic, the ones to your hon-ourable father's dressing room and, of course, the ones to the kura – even the ones to the...

'All right, all right, Murayama-san!' Hinata broke in. 'I don't need an inventory of every door in the house,' he said, talking over Murayama as she finished explaining:

'... which were flooded last year.' She breathed in.

'What was flooded?'

'The cellars, Sir,' replied Murayama..

'Very well. I haven't the slightest idea what you're talking about, but very well. Has it been dealt with?'

'Yes, Honourable Sir, but it's good to keep that door open to dry the damp. When her Honourable ladyship lived here, she...'

The maid was cut short.

'The Honourable Yamana-sama's honourable mother no longer lives here. Please explain what we are to do about the keys,' said Aiko.

'Aiko, please...,' interrupted her husband.

'Yes, Ma'am. Please, forgive me,' said Murayama-san, bowing deeply.

'How is it that she doesn't have the keys?' asked Aiko, looking at her husband. 'What happens if we have guests tonight? What china are we supposed to dine off?' asked she through gritted teeth.

'I understand, Ma'am,' answered the maid, bowing again. 'Please forgive me.'

'Murayama-san, will you be so kind as to go back to work?' said Hinata. 'And you, Aiko, come with me one moment, please.'

Aiko didn't move a muscle.

'Excuse me, Honourable Chairman,' said the girl.

'Go, just go. And you, come with me,' he repeated, staring at his wife. 'Come, Aiko, come with me at once,' he insisted, taking her by the arm.

She resisted a moment, but then gave in and followed him to the domo.

'Don't you think the domestic staff have witnessed enough scenes in this house? Don't you see there's no reason for them to know my mother isn't living here?' he asked, turning to her with a dour look.

'But... Hinata!'

'And other thing!' he cut in. 'Murayama-san belongs to a family that has been in our service for five generations. Five generations!' He repeated. 'Do you understand me?'

'Yes, of course, why wouldn't I understand you? I understand perfectly.'

'You start arguing with her... She's already told you she doesn't have the keys. Don't you believe her? Why would she lie to you?'

'It's not that I think Murayama-san is lying to me.'

'Well then? Why do you insist?'

'Hinata, I have nothing against Murayama-san, but her attitude...'

'What attitude? Tell me, what attitude? Because I didn't notice any attitude at all. She simply told you she doesn't have the keys.'

'I don't know...,' said Aiko, incapable of describing what she sensed. 'I just want those keys. I have the feeling everyone's conspiring against me in this house. I can't get anything done.'

'It isn't a feeling. It's quite real. But it has nothing to do with a conspiracy! It so happens that in this house you have nothing to do. You have been fortunate enough not to have to look after the house – a predicament many would give their eye-teeth for. You can go out all day if you so please, to play cards, buy knick-knacks in Miyanoshita, or drink tea with your friends.

'But what about the china, Hinata?'

'They know everything there is to know about the china. Are you forgetting that they've worked here all their lives?'

'No, I'm not forgetting. But if the keys aren't in the house, how will they get into the kura to look for the things for the tokonoma? Or how will we change the china? I need those keys! Your mother used to go to the kura with Murayama-san. Now, she doesn't live here. Is the kura suddenly off limits? Will we never be allowed inside it again?

Have all the wardrobes been closed for ever? Must we sleep in the same sheets for the rest of our days? Where does Murayama-san get the towels? She must know what to do in these cases! Isn't that right?'

'Very well, but she doesn't have them. She doesn't have those keys. She told you again and again. Yet you insist!' said Hinata in annoyance.

'She said 'the Honourable Madame Yamana is the only one with access to the kura,' but I know that's not true because I've often seen her going in there to fetch china or a scroll for the tokonoma.'

'Because she went in there with mother! That's why you've seen her go in there! In any case, you must talk to *me* about that, Aiko, not to *her*.'

'You? Since when have you had anything to do with the kura? Or the house for that matter?' she asked.

'I'll ask mother for them,' he replied, 'and I hope that that's an end to it.'

'Call her, but please do it right away,' said Aiko, folding her arms.

'What's got into you? Why is this so urgent?' he asked.

'Now, Hinata... Please...!' she repeated. 'I know you. I know that if you can put off calling her, you will, and then we'll have to have this conversation all over again.'

Hinata hesitated for a few moments, rapidly casting around for an answer he didn't have. Then, looking at Aiko, with a deep sigh of resignation he said:

'Very well, I'll call her.'

'Now, please,' Aiko insisted.

'Now, now!' he replied. 'Such a hurry, woman!'

Hinata went into his office, closing the fusuma behind him.

Aiko could sense the tension in Hinata's tone of voice as he spoke to his mother but couldn't make out what he was saying. Considering he was simply asking for some keys, the phone call went on longer than Aiko had expected and she ended up falling asleep in the sun, which beamed down on the tatami.

'Why do you force me into these things?' said Hinata, flinging open the shoji and making her jump. 'You know how much you hurt my mother. It's quite unnecessary!' he stammered in irritation, tripping on the step. 'Shi…!' he exclaimed, kicking the offending feature.

'Calm down, Hinata, and listen,' she said, dusting the cobwebs off her cat-nap, the solution then is for her to put herself to the trouble of coming over every time we have guests to decide which china we're to use.'

'Perhaps that would have been for the best,' he replied ill-temperedly.

'The issue there is… what would you do if she were ill? Would you still make her come?' she added, as Hinata marched off. 'Where are you going?' asked Aiko.

'To fetch the damn keys!' he answered. 'Isn't that what you wanted?'

'But, what's wrong? What did she say?' she asked, eager for an answer. 'Hinata?' she shouted, jogging behind him to keep up. 'Hinata!'

But he didn't answer. He didn't even do her the courtesy of looking back.

Aiko heard the car door slam and the engine roar. He got back after dark, reeking of alcohol, and tossed the bunch of keys on the table by the door without even a 'hello'. Aiko left them there to 'cool off' until everyone had gone to bed. Then she tiptoed over to what she saw as 'her coronation'. She thought that, under other circumstances, a 'handover of power' like this should take place with great pomp and circumstance, but she settled for this simple act of mastery without glory in thrall to the austerity required by the situation.

'Let's hope they're all here,' she said to herself, picking up the keys, but unable to stifle a triumphant smile.

It was stronger than she was; from that day on she could never resist the temptation to jingle them in her pocket whenever she came across any of the domestic staff.

When her father-in-law had died, his rooms had been closed off. None of his children had had the courage to change the layout of the objects or go against his dying wishes. His things had remained exactly as he had left them and were never, ever touched again. No one went in to do the dusting. No one even crossed the courtyard where the plum tree of Kato-san's story stood, which must have been nearly a hundred years old. Only the man who cleaned the water tank ventured in from time to time.

'Apparently, that afternoon he ordered tea,' said Mrs Kato almost secretively, recounting those blighted moments, 'as he was in the habit of doing. It is possible,' she went on, 'that, soon after that, the Honourable Yamana-sama was taken ill. They say his personal valet, who was normally to be found in the adjoining room and spent his life following him around through the shadows, anticipating his every move, for some reason was not at his post that day at that precise moment. The Honourable Gentleman then apparently got to his feet and walked to the main domo on the other side of the courtyard, perhaps in search of help. He then supposedly called for his wife, who claimed not to have heard him. Anyway, it wouldn't have done the poor soul any good, as he never made it across the courtyard and dropped stone dead at the foot of the plum tree in full bloom.'

Thunder rumbled outside Kato-san's shop, making the windows rattle, and they both turned to look at the same time.

'But... how did they find out he called for his wife?' asked Aiko, her voice quavering.

'The gardener...,' she replied. 'He was the one who heard him,' she said, cupping her ear as if trying to hear a distant sound. 'He ran and ran to where the voice was coming from. Night was falling but it was still light, and there he saw him, eyes fixed on the crown of the plum tree. They say the blossom began to fall on the breeze.' Madame Kato threshed the air with her hand. 'They say it fell thick and fast, covering his face.'

Aiko hid her own with her hands.

'Oh!,' she sighed. 'As if I were seeing it!'

Madame Kato went on.

'Could it have been an act of compassion from the plum tree's kami?' she asked.

Aiko remained silent, then answered:

'Yes.' In her mind the image of her father-in-law lying there, on the flagstones, petals strewn over his face, was so immediate it made her shudder. 'That must surely have been it: an act of compassion from the plum tree's kami...'

Rain lashed the shop window. The funereal chimes of a wall-clock reminded them it was four o'clock. Aiko came to in the darkness of the antiques shop, as if she had just woken.

'Oh!' she said, looking for her handbag. 'It's so late! I'll have to call them to come and pick me up. There's no way I'll be able to get back in this storm!'

'Yes, my child. Here's the phone. Please feel free to make your call,' said Mrs Kato. 'Call them to come and pick you up. It's cold outside, do you want some tea?'

Now, in possession of the keys, Aiko finally had the chance to explore the forbidden world of her own abode. She now had access to the parts from which she had been tacitly exiled, despite living there, by her mother-in-law's territorial policy. But of all the rooms she could now enter, Aiko had only one in mind: that of the Honourable Yamana-sama, her father-in-law. The thought threw her heart into a flutter and the keys burned in her hand.

It was six in the evening. At that hour her husband would be accompanying a committee in Osaka and wouldn't be back for two days. The butler and the housekeeper would be in the kitchen chatting to the cook or polishing what was already clean just for the sake of cleaning, or to show they could improve on work already done by the other. The elderly gatekeeper was away, as his only great-niece was getting married, and he had left his even more elderly father to hold the fort. Aiko feared he might drop dead on her at any moment there in the little hut, at the slightest breeze making him sneeze and setting his ribs a-rattling.

'Good evening... Are you all right? Have they brought you anything to eat?'

When he saw her approach, the old man struggled to his feet. He bowed but couldn't straighten up and, bent double, had to grab something to keep himself from falling. After that Aiko resolved to keep an eye on him every now and then to make sure he was still breathing.

Clutching the keys in her pocket, Aiko headed for her father-in-law's quarters. She crossed the domo and climbed a couple of steps to the small rear enclosure that opened onto the engawa overlooking the patio. She crept across the wood chips, over the mossy cobblestones and past the plum tree, which still bore some leaves. A few steps further and she was standing right outside her father-in-law's study. A cobweb, pearled with dew, stretched between lintel and jamb, guarding the entrance. She mounted the step and, standing now before the tightly-locked shoji, she took a short breath. If at that moment anyone had come across her, she would have found it difficult to produce a convincing explanation or to conceal the frantic pounding in her chest. Aiko drew the keys close to the lock, trying to gauge which one would fit it, and tried them one by one all the while casting cautious glances left and right. A light wind blew her hair across her face, covering her eyes. Annoyed, she brushed it away with her arm. She was beginning to lose hope, for the lock would not give. Perhaps, she thought, the key had been deliberately removed from the bunch.

Suddenly, a noise. Something had fallen. It sounded metallic and went on clanging on the floor for a few moments – a pipe may be? She immediately put the keys in her pocket and crossed back the courtyard. Then she went and sat on the doorstep of the domo, facing her father-in-law's study, and waited until everything was quiet again. She remembered the story she'd heard about the girl who had drowned in the well, right there behind the study. Its waters had brought on premonitions ever since, or so they said. With the apprehension caused by this legend, and the Honourable Gentleman's death by the plum tree, that part of the house was considered 'blighted', and the staff tried their best to avoid it. In one of the trees growing between the well and the courtyard, some pieces of papers with writing on them had been tied to the branches, along with a few amulets. Aiko had seen this custom in some shrines. Such trees were said to be inhabited by a kodama[143] and were festooned with hundreds of strips of paper bearing petitions and prayers. She didn't know if that was the case here, or if it was, who might have registered such a presence in that place or started the tradition of making these offerings. She chose not to come any closer.

Aiko plucked up courage and crept back across the courtyard and up the engawa. She tried another key. It slid in effortlessly, but once inside it wouldn't budge. Then she found she couldn't remove it! She jiggled it back and forth until she heard a click. It must have jammed in the rusty lock through lack of use. Gingerly she turned it and the bolt of the lock slid back. She let out a sigh. Her shirt was stuck to her back and her hands were soaking wet. Possessed by a determination that made her shake, and feeling her heart beating in her throat, she drew back the shoji a crack and, still wearing her zori,[144] slipped through in profile like an Egyptian carving. Once inside she immediately slid the shoji shut behind her.

The room was in half-light, flooded with a pungent smell of rotting leaves. Was it already thirty years since the Honourable Gentleman's passing?

She tiptoed over to the window and slid open the shoji, letting in the golden beam of dust from the last of the December sun. She edged closer to the stage of the last scenes of the Honourable Gentleman's life. 'I'm surely committing some unforgiveable act here,' she said to herself.

Madame Kato's story echoed over and over in her mind. 'Apparently, that afternoon he ordered tea, as he was in the habit of doing...' There it was, intact! His chawan! She felt a blast of cold running up her back. Its contents had

---

[143] Spirits sometimes inhabiting trees.

[144] Traditional sandals.

evaporated to leave a darkish ring at the bottom. She leaned in to see better in the twilight and at that instant something creaked, making her jump back. She listened intently for a few seconds and concluded it must have been the wind... On the keyaki[145] wood table rested a fountain pen on a sheet of yellowing rice-paper coated in a layer of fine dust. She could make something out, written on the paper. It was in kanji and appeared to be an unfinished haiku: '"Wasurejimo...,"'[146] she read. 'Why do people have to die in spring? Why do they leave poems unfinished?' she wondered, overcome with sorrow. A veil fell over everything around her, an invisible haze of pain and sadness emanated from the torn and faded tatami; from the silent walls against which leant swords from days gone by... portraits and flags reduced to nothing, with no one left to tell their stories. All the past glories she had heard so much about were now reduced to these orphaned objects, destined for oblivion...

She had no right to be there. Suddenly aware of it, she walked gingerly over to the window and shut it, leaving everything as she'd found it; but every step she took had left a print in the dust that she could not now erase.

She swore to herself she would never return. Yet back she came in the afternoons, like someone visiting the infirm old man and, strangely, her sorrow began to turn into tenderness.

She would leave before nightfall, for fear of the dark, but came to prefer doing so after everyone was in bed to avoid being seen by the staff. The fascination this sealed room wielded over Aiko led her deeper and deeper into areas she never thought herself capable of penetrating. Until one day she boldly ventured to open wide the windows,

---

[145] The zelkova serrata or Japanese elm.

[146] A name for the last frost of spring.

shake out the cushions, light the incense sticks and arrange some flowers in the vases she had been smuggling in. She breathed life back into the room so successfully that even the deceased – had he been able to see it – would have been deceived that he was still in the land of the living. She brought a systematic order to each shelf and drawer, and the further she delved, the further she dared to delve. She opened the drawers and read the letters, fearing she would discover something she perhaps ought not to know. She found postcards from Edo – some written, others blank – and a portrait of His Majesty the Emperor Shōwa, autographed and dated 1937, before he renounced his divinity. 'Ah!' she thought, 'Mrs Kato would like that!' She came across a collection of antique kesa sewn with hemp-fibre and covered in seals that no doubt had belonged to his grandparents; as it was common at the time to go on pilgrimage with a group of friends and relatives, the way one might go on an excursion to the country. She found silks so delicate they disintegrated at the slightest touch into an opalescent dust that hung in the air before her eyes. In one of the chests there was a little box of aloe wood incense, which was hard to come by in nowadays, and she thought she might take some to burn at the family shrine beside the offerings. Bundles of sandalwood root still scented the places where they stood. Most remarkably, she came across a universe of writing, and she was sure that all one needed to know of the world could be found within that room full of neatly bound volumes. Some stacked on the floor, forming little staircases; others lined with leather and silk, and piled on tables. Books on arithmetic and astronomy, biology and geography, botany and philosophy. Inside one wardrobe, a volume of the classic, *Ise Monogatari*, by Ariwara no Narihira, wrapped in Madagascan spider silk exquisitely embroidered with peonies, and fascicles printed on rice-paper with ink drawings of tiny snails and crabs. There were also gracefully painted ants marching in single file up bamboo shoots. The sheaves were dated 1723, all bunched together and held fast with an indigo cotton ribbon. Among the pages were descriptions of the habits of many crustaceans and insects. One in particular caught her eye: the kamakiri.[147] Its name also appeared in kanji, expressing the Latin term in katakana:[148] 'Mantis rerigiosa'.[149] According to the description, the name came from the position adopted by the insect's front legs, as if at prayer, before it attacked its victims. They devoured them alive by sucking out their innards! She had always thought of cruelty as a capacity possessed only by humans. Then the image of her mother-in-law came to mind.

There was this restaurant... near the Tsukiji shijō[150], she used to go to with her father when she was young, that was. She couldn't quite remember its name. The place looked much like any other restaurant, but what distinguished it was the concept of the 'freshness' it offered its customers. Not only did they keep live fish and octopus in a tank, but when a customer chose one, the cook would take it, fillet it and serve it ikizukuri-style: with its heart still beating. Aiko would sit and stare at the fish slowly gulping its last atop a few strands of white radish. On other occasions a lobster's antennæ would go on twitching as it lay on the plate, or a slippery octopus tentacle would clamp its suckers to the table in a bid to flee its fate. Meanwhile, her father would

---

[147] 'The one that cuts with the sickle', known in the West as *Mantis religiosa*.

[148] A Japanese writing system used for foreign or scientific names, to express sounds or to emphasize a word.

[149] The 'praying mantis': following the phonology of Japanese, its writing system does not recognize the letter 'l', assimilating it instead to the 'r'.

[150] Fish Market in Tsukiji.

express his delight at the pearly flesh, calling it 'the purest act of commitment to freshness'. As a child, none of this appeared to have affected her. But it did much later in life. The horror it caused her was projected into her future to produce a retroactive traumatic effect. In a flash she understood the Buddhist conception of life. Octopi and sea bass then joined the chain of events that reduced her to a wash of tears.

One day, when she tried to broach the subject with her father, he replied with an appeal to reason:

'Aiko, everything we eat has been alive or has fed on something living. It's the way of things. It's natural.'

'That may be true, but there's a difference between eating salmon as sashimi and eating it while it's gasping for breath on the table. Say what you like, that's not need, it's sadism,' she argued.

Her father replied as he often did, with a question:

'How do you think tuna fish die? Gasping for breath on a fishing boat! Do you really think they kill them compassionately one at a time?'

He explained to her that the only difference lay in whether she 'saw it or not' and that, besides, eating them in fact made her an accomplice in that 'act against life', to use her own words.

'I'd accept your argument,' he added, 'if – and only if – you became a vegetarian or a Buddhist.'

Her father's point was that it took far more courage to accept the animal's sacrifice and that looking away while someone else did the 'dirty work' didn't redeem us from a 'certain complicity'. It was part of our animal essence.

Aiko, for her part, concluded that nature was indeed extremely cruel and that she was ashamed to be a part of it. She believed in showing compassion towards animals and from that day on was determined to be a vegetarian. But Aiko's sudden awareness of her unity with the cosmos soon vanished at the sight of the cod caramelizing in miso sauce over the coals.

The years passed and in her father-in-law's encyclopædic library Aiko found the answer she would have liked to give her father all those years ago: 'The fish used in sashimi have to be killed and iced instantaneously.' This was done to prevent the build-up of lactic acid, so they could never be killed by asphyxiation the way other fish were. It was always happening to her this: finding the perfect answer when she no longer needed it.

Aiko read everything she could lay her hands on, from the writings of Fukuzawa Yukichi[151] to the life of Silesian bees. She hadn't been aware until then of her insatiable thirst for knowledge. Her father-in-law's library became both a refuge and a gateway to a world of wonders. She even managed to smuggle in a step-ladder to reach the less accessible parts, with their hidden treasures.

So it was that one day, as she was arranging some volumes of the *Encyclopædia Britannica* on a shelf, a scroll tied with a black bamboo cord fell on her head. Aiko stooped to pick it up and unrolled it. Before her eyes lay an ancient map of Japan with a dragon drawn on the lower left side, just like the ones her mother used to tell her about, which she had later seen for herself at the Naval Museum. She couldn't find Sato in the drawing; it must be hidden just under a fang. Yes, indeed! Judging by the position, it should be the left one. The beast's head was twisted to one side, with one eye looking up and the other staring pop-eyed into space. 'A cross-eyed dragon!' she chuckled to herself.

Coiled around its outer surface was another map that, in one quadrant, specifically showed Okinawa Prefecture in

---

[151] A Japanese writer and political philosopher whose ideas on government and social institutions were of great influence in Japan during the Meiji Era.

the south-west and the entire series of islands, including Sato. Aiko took this rather odd fact as a message from beyond the grave, but couldn't work out exactly what that message was saying. Nevertheless, she took all the maps and the book on entomology, placed them carefully under the haori,[152] slid the shoji shut behind her and fastened the padlock. It was still light outside. As she passed the plum tree – still bare in the winter – she couldn't help looking at it and thanking it for the compassion it had once shown her beloved father-in-law, a man she had never met and was now getting to know. Hair swirling in the wind, Aiko ran into the house.

As she listened to Hinata's father's stories and traced the course of his life through his writing, photographs and personal effects, a feeling of love for him slowly began to dawn in her. A platonic love no doubt, but love nonetheless. A love inviting her to plunge into an 'imaginary relationship' that felt real, in which 'they shared' a world of interests. Dislocated as they were in time and bizarre as it might have seemed, she missed him. She knew for certain they were soul-mates; somehow she had made him hers.

In the month of January the famous Nayoroiwa Shizuo[153] – Oozeki[154] – passed away. Hinata said his father had told him that the young man, who was no great wrestler, enjoyed people's admiration and affection nevertheless. He was often preferred over others stronger and faster than he was, because what people appreciated most were his daily efforts to achieve his goals. When Hinata-san recalled him on this occasion, one of many, these words came to mind: 'Leave perfection to Greek marbles; they are dead,'

---

[152] A jacket covering the yukata (cotton kimono).

[153] A famous sumo wrestler (1914 –1971).

[154] A rank in sumo wrestling.

he said with his natural Taoist spirit, which seemed to raise him above routine miseries.

What Aiko could not understand was how this exquisite being, capable of appreciating poetry, with that immense cosmos of curiosity, humour and sensitivity, could have married such a woman. The contradiction seemed to her irreconcilable, until one day she heard someone who had known her mother-in-law long ago, in her youth, and then she understood: she hadn't always been that way. The sea change in her character had followed the premature death of her husband, whom she had idolized. It hadn't been an arranged marriage, but one built on love.

The day he died, she had shorn her flowing lock herself and left it plaited beside her husband's body. Then she had shaved her eyebrows[155] and finally every last hair on her head. This dull and searing anguish had plunged her so low she would have done better to incinerate herself at his side than go on living. She let herself be dragged toward a dense bitterness that made her hate anything 'happy' in life, a happiness they had lived together, and so it was that sunny spring mornings only deepened her grief. The cherry blossom… that flurry of petals, that reviled breeze bearing aloft their sweetness. What did they matter after that fateful day she had found him lying there, dead? What difference was there between a plum, a peach or a cherry tree when they all lodged in her soul with the same torment? How dare the music? How dare the laughter? What insolence blinds them to the knowledge that the world has lost him? Only the June rains, only the storms… Oh, shaking earth! Oh, spitting volcanoes! Oh, blood spilt! You will not console me!

And thus she spent the rest of her life, scratching at her cell of invisible stones. How could she have let go of every-

---

[155] An old custom among widows.

thing human? Yet understanding filled Aiko with compassion. Yet she knew she would never be able to get close. Her mother-in-law had become a truly venomous snake. 'A *Rhabdophis tigrinus*,' Aiko told herself, showing off her late knowledge of the natural sciences. 'Or perhaps an *Agkistrodon blomhoffii*. Or, better still, a *Mantis*. Yes! Exactly that: a *Mantis rerigiosa!*' Just like the one she had seen in her father-in-law's encyclopædia, ready to suck out her living innards.

Her mother-in-law could only be happy wherever suffering reigned, so she made sure she had a daily supply of little cruelties, 'bloodless' pleasures to appease her fury at not having died with her husband.

Aiko knew this woman's pulse would not skip a beat when it came to destroying her.

❖

As extremely respectful as the Honourable Yamanas were over the whims and fancies imposed by their ancestors, raising them to the hights of 'traditions', it was, hardly practical to go all the way to the Shimogamo Jinja[156] in Kyoto every year. Yet it was a custom rigorously observed, and no one had ever thought to question it. It ranked alongside family pilgrimages through mudholes, starting in the middle of the June rains and tolerated for the amusement of shared stoicism. After one of his daughters contracted the quartan fevers, the Chairman's father decided to put a stop to these peregrinations and imposed a new norm of celebrating the Hotarubi no chakai[157] in his own garden. He then prevailed upon the priests from a Nara temple to perform the ceremonies, and they could hardly refuse, having received financial support from the Yamanas for several generations. So, seated in a litter, the girl was able – through the veil of a mosquito net – to enjoy the spectacle, which brought her relief from the torture of the quinine rations, and a 'new tradition' was born.

---

[156] The Shimogamo Shrine, in Kyoto.

[157] *Hotaru* means 'fireflies'; bi means 'fire' or 'splendour', and chakai means 'tea meeting'.

Before nightfall there was a concert of koto,[158] shamisen and shakuhachi,[159] accompanied by singing. This was followed by a formal tea ceremony, at which the guests were served the first dishes of 'a mouthful and a half' in a strictly established sequence. As it grew dark, the garden was lit up by lanterns, which in those days were still fuelled by camellia oil. People held their breaths in anticipation of the moment, heralded by a long silence, when hundreds of fireflies were released into the garden and they would watch them fly about like tiny wandering comets.

Later in the season, when the nights were still warm, it was agreeable to sit out by the pond and contemplate the glow-worms, now acclimatized to their new habitat. The neighbourhood children would come out to hunt them and trap them in little woven bamboo cages, which they then hung on their verandahs. In one small bedroom of the house Aiko had seen watercolours portraying this hunting of lights.

In those days Aiko and her mother would often dine out in the garden under the moonlight, on a makeshift mat spread out in the midst of the irises. Of all their topics of conversation one – always the same – remained off limits: Aiko's son. It was a tacit arrangement that they had grown accustomed to until the night Watanabe-san asked her in a deliberately casual tone:

'Tell me, Aiko, have you given *that situation* any thought?'

'What do you mean "that situation"?' she asked.

'I mean your son. He must be a young man by now,' her mother replied.

'Okā-san, please...,' pleaded Aiko. 'I thought we had an agreement, you and I.'

---

[158] A traditional stringed instrument.

[159] An upright bamboo flute.

'I know, I know,' replied her mother, 'but… is it really "a pact for all eternity"?' she asked, raising her eyebrows.

'It's been so many years…'

'That's precisely why I'm asking.'

Puzzled, Aiko could not work out why her mother was talking to her as if she hadn't been her accomplice, as if she had played no part in the matter. She was asking her what she had intended to do about a situation she herself had orchestrated. At that moment she was holding her responsible, but she hadn't consulted her at the time. No. There was nothing to consult her about. She alone had decided what would be best for the family and had left no room for any appeal, embarking her unceremoniously on a journey to an inexorable fate. And now she was asking her whether she had 'given that situation "any thought"'. Aiko was astounded. Drawing on strength from where she hadn't any, she replied:

'Look, Okā-san, it was very hard for me, but we came to an arrangement, didn't we? So… well, that's it.'

'Oh, my dear… dear daughter!' replied her mother, 'arrangements can always be unarranged, can't they? Have you no desire to see him?'

'I don't know. Now, after all this time…,' she answered.

'Does that mean you've forgotten him?'

'Forgotten him? How do you think I could have forgotten him? Not only haven't I forgotten him, I dream about him all the time. Especially just recently… but it's too late,' Aiko replied. 'I shall have to live with it for the rest of my days as I have lived with it until now.'

Her mother gazed deep into Aiko's soul and realized she was on the brink of tears, though she was unsure which of the two of them would be the first to weep.

'Oh! Forgive me, daughter… Forgive me, please. How tactless of me…!' she said, handing her a handkerchief which she kept in the bow of her yukata. 'Have you really been dreaming about him?' she whispered.

'I have. I'm sorry, please don't ask me. I'd rather not talk about it,' answered Aiko, her eyes welling.

'Look, Aiko, I don't think it's too late. Too late is when you die, when you're cold. Then it's too late. There's nothing you can do about it then. But you're still young, Aiko, dearest!'

'I feel two hundred years old, Okā-san. If only you knew...'

'I... You have seemed so upset over this business...'

'Oh! What are you saying...? Me? Upset? I'm not upset, I'm just exhausted,' replied Aiko in a flash of annoyance. 'I've grown used to living like this, I tell you. Can't you see? Can't you see how life has carried on?'

'Don't be angry... It's just that a mother sees "things". "Things" that are hidden deep, deep within. "Things" invisible to other people's eyes.'

'Okā-san,' begged Aiko, 'I don't know what you're up to. But you won't think of... I don't understand you. You always... I... Why now?' she asked in confusion.

'There there, little one,' her mother consoled her. 'I was just wondering how long it will last. Where will it lead. You see, these things... It's only normal after all, don't you think? To want to know how you feel about all that's happened, seeing as we haven't spoken of it since.'

'No, not "all that's happened". You mean "all we made happen".'

'Well, be that as it may,' said her mother, 'but remember, I shan't be around forever, and after I've gone, no one will ever say anything again. If I can't raise that question, who will?'

Aiko looked at her sadly, waiting for her to go on.

'You know what torments me most? Seeing your sadness. The sadness I can see this very moment...'

Aiko lowered her gaze and turned her face aside.

'Look, dearest, after your father died, all I could think of was getting by. I wondered what would become of my daughters. Especially you, Aiko, because your sister Keiko, well, you know... she looked like a hopeless case. But I believed in good faith I'd done all I could. Imagine: me, Watanabe Emiko, a cook! Remember?'

'Yes, of course. You weren't so bad,' answered Aiko, smiling. 'But it was also a very special time, Okā-san. We were closer back then, and I know you acted in good faith and tried everything you could, and you did it very well.'

'But I pushed you, I know I did. And perhaps I pushed you into something you would never have chosen.'

'Okā-san...,' Aiko replied in an effort to relieve her mother of the burden.

'Let me speak, asked her mother. 'There are things I have to tell you.'

'All right, I'm sorry... Tell me.'

'I know I gave you no choice. By "trying everything I could", I never asked myself if that really was the way you'd be happy. My darling...,' she added, her voice trembling, 'I so badly need you to forgive me for that...!'

Aiko took her mother's hands in hers.

'Times were different then,' she said, 'and I think we both did what we had to.'

'I don't know, daughter, I don't know. That's why I say I'd do anything to bring the two of you together...'

'Yes, okā-san, the years have made you very sentimental, but I appreciate it.' She smiled. 'If forgiving is appropriate, then thank you for not waiting until the last minute the way Papa did.'

'The swine...,' her mother muttered, clenching her fists.

They both burst out laughing.

Soon the sunflowers in the fields were dipping their golden heads and the air was growing cooler and smoother at night.

Watanabe Emiko-san

Locked up in the early winter of the body, who does not begin to fear the time the living soul will beat its wings unable to escape, like a wild bird in a cage?

The young don't understand the process; they're too busy being young. Heedless of all, they ride roughshod over their time on earth. Youth swallows up their lives, whole. It consumes them in its fire, as it has also consumed me. The young do not understand the process. Nor did I when I was oblivious to these things. At that time I lived to defy the world, but the world has followed its course and has done so without me. Like horses on the Mongolian steppes the world runs free, crying 'Catch me if you can!' But I no longer have any wish to climb onto its crupper. Wishes? Yes, sure... I've had them. But my body has won the day. My body has said 'Leave me be! Can't you see I'm tired?' and has put the fear of stumbling and falling in my veins... of being knocked down or broken by the thronging masses that elbow their way through the streets. Fear of falling and never being seen again, of sinking into the blackness of the asphalt like I used to dream when I was a girl. My mother used to have to console me then, reassuring me again and again that my feet were free and separate from the tar.

The young don't understand the process. They wade on through, the water up to their knees, through the midst of the mire, and they aren't afraid of falling. They scale the mountains, reach up and touch the clouds. They cross the avenues at night, when the city lights fill their hair with glints and gleams, and make them shine. They zoom about on flying boards, drinking in the wind, heads down and defying gravity. And all the while my body tells me 'Leave me be. Take me closer to the ground, I want to rest. Take me home,' it tells me, 'with your cups and your spoons, and lull me in your slippers in front of the TV.' There's nowhere else it wants to be, but close by the serene simplicity of the rice and the bubbling of the water boiling in the iron kettle.

The young don't understand. They don't understand and they presume to tell us how we're supposed to live our time on earth. They think they know it all. Aiko's no exception, but she persists like the flies in the summer months. She never gives up. Ever. Sometimes, carried away by something she's read, she decides that what one needs is calcium. So she brings her cow's milk and yoghurt and other things she isn't used to. Why should she change her diet? And when did she organize games of Go for her at the local old folk's club…? Why should she, who had always hated board games, have to play Go with a gaggle of idle old women? She, who didn't even like clubs, never mind 'institutions', because they're so exasperatingly cold and impersonal, because they're so full of big old brightly-coloured posters stuck up all over the walls and 'happy' garlands the mere sight of which makes you realize they're destined inevitably for 'sad' places. 'Give it more colours! Make it brighter, more colourful! Let's see if you can brighten this perpetual gray! Let's see if you can gladden these old ladies till their dentures crumble and tumble out!' and then… then there were the indulgent smiles of the organizers, whom you weary with your deafness and who treat you like a child, pronouncing every syllable just in case you've suddenly gone deaf.

That was her daughter. She felt a need to 'organize' her. She belonged to that tacit institution of 'Daughters with old mothers whom they felt an obligation to entertain', and the best way to do so is to treat them like babies. Why *is* that?

It would seem that old age, whose territory has spread endlessly, is a place at the end of the road that no one is sure what to do with. In the past people worked themselves into the ground until they dropped from all the labouring, the seafaring, the sun, the salt, or there in the countryside, amidst the paddies, driving on the oxen. But nowadays old age is the expanding universe and, like a piece missing from the puzzle, it eventually happens, just like children waking at three in the morning. What can you do with a child that won't go back to sleep? It isn't mealtime or walk-time or potty-time... So the young resort to a kind of 'basic knowledge' for their dealings with old people. They develop it by crossing out options: strictly speaking, you aren't an adult any more: you wet yourself, you eat baby-food because your digestion's gone, you sometimes say silly things, you don't sleep much, you lose your teeth... you're a little girl. Or aren't you?

Aiko would sometimes say to her: 'Okā-san, you need a change of scenery. You can hardly breathe in Tokyo!' The next thing you knew, she'd get up one fine day saying that what she needed was a change of scenery. Was it a dream she'd had that had conjured such an emergency? No. Aiko's decisions were nothing if not arbitrary. One day this, another day that... dis-con-tin-u-ous. She never realized that no changes are welcome after a certain age because one never knows where they will lead... Painstakingly, one carves and stitches one's whole life, and there's a reason why it is its current shape. And goodness knows, it isn't easy to adapt! Any change, even the beating of a butterfly's wings, could unleash a typhoon! -So they say...- So one gradually learns to be happy with one's routine: a little rice, a little fish... and that's enough. It's fine. Always the same. That way you know where you've lived, where you've been

– that way you don't lose your glasses, your scissors, your keys.

She had now twice lost her dentures at Aiko's house, and a key ring. She used to tell her that what she was probably losing was her memory. No. They had just moved her to a different room a couple of times and that was what had confused her.

She needed her routine, to anchor everything in its place.

Sometimes, weary of the struggle for a 'change of scenery' on which she had embarked all alone, Aiko would end up traipsing reluctantly over to Watanabe-san's house. They were plainly visits to 'clear her conscience' and generally occurred after some row or other. Watanabe-san knew her daughter would spend the time lecturing her on how to live her life better as an old lady and, once convinced of success, she would be off, like someone leaving the house spick and span and absconding on holiday with a sigh of relief. But Aiko had never been there, to the land of old age. She did not understand. Not because she was stupid but because she was young, because the young always believe they know more, because the old aren't 'cool' and all that nonsense. Besides, they spoke a language that didn't sound like Japanese, a language no one could comprehend.

She was independent, but her daughter would never understand the kind of independence that kept her within those four walls all day. What's more, Aiko had already questioned her about it on a previous occasion, and she had replied: 'Well, it's the independence of doing whatever I feel like.' Unhappy with her answer, Aiko insisted with the same perseverance as a drip that eventually wears a hole through the cup. It clearly works for her: she nearly always gets her way. What she lacks as a strategist, she makes up for in perseverance, eventually wearing her opponent down. But two can play at that game. She must have taken after someone, after all, and who else if not her mother? The apple – as the saying goes – never falls far from the tree.

Often, in reply, Watanabe-san would give a wry laugh. She laughed because she saw it was futile and had no wish to provide explanations. The only advantage of having reached that age, which she thought was detestable, was being 'olly olly oxen free' from giving explanations. She didn't have to justify anything to anyone, but her daughter would always return to the attack.

'Why do you drag me all the way over here when you could be living like an empress over there, Okā-san?'

'You don't have to come if you don't want to.'

'You know perfectly well I worry about you. I can't relax knowing you're alone.'

'I understand.'

'Okā-san...'

'Tell me, what are you going to give your cousin Sayuri-chan for her wedding?' said her mother, changing the subject.

'Okā-san...,' Aiko replied, drumming her fingers on the table in impatience.

'Look, Aiko, I'm elderly. Living with someone else is a very tricky business: one day we love each other, the next we're getting under each other's feet. What you find convenient may not be for me. In life, what's convenient isn't always what's best. And what's best isn't necessarily what's useful,' she said in an apparent jumble of words. 'It's what makes you feel good in here,' Madame Watanabe concluded, touching Aiko on the heart, who let out a low moan from under her yukata.

'How odd...!' thought Aiko. They were the 'least Japanese' words she had ever heard from her mother's lips.

❖

Winter came, plunging the copper forests into a dark mire whipped up first by the strong winds, which flew away the leaves from maples and then, the rains. The weather turned so severe that the roads had to be closed in the interests of safety.

Once again Aiko's mother turned a deaf ear to her daughter's pleas. 'Don't worry, I won't go outside, I promise I won't go outside,' she reassured her. But they both knew it wasn't true and that she only said it to put a stop to her daughter's nagging.

So it was that, one afternoon, Madame Watanabe wanted some soy milk, because, as she put it, 'Cow's milk is for calves.' She looked in the refrigerator and realized they had run out.

'I could have sworn I'd put another bottle in there...,' she muttered to herself.

Glancing out of the kitchen window, which overlooked a small back-yard, she had the impression that the weather had improved. Only a light breeze stirred the neighbours' willow, the torrential rain having finally given way to a fine and gentle drizzle. So she plucked up her courage, wrapped herself in her coat, picked up the red golfing umbrella Aiko had given her – assuring her it was a tad peculiar to walk around Tokyo with a paper wagasa[160] – and stepped out

---

[160] An umbrella with bamboo ribs and a canopy of greaseproof paper.

into the street. The little Family Mart[161] was only down the road, and she had known for quite some time the woman who ran it. She would often send her own son to deliver the shopping, but it was too much to ask her to do this for something as trivial as a drop of soy milk. Besides, it was a bank holiday and her son would be out playing baseball. The street was deserted, which meant she would be able to walk without being trampled underfoot by the crowds in their permanent urban hurry. She did, however, notice that the pavement was rather treacherous, and the rubber soles of her zori skidded slightly, wetting the tips of her socks.

'Oh, only I would dream of coming out in my flip-flops!' she thought. She was worried in case she fell and broke her hip, so she set off at a slow pace, hugging the wall. She could hear the wind somewhere in the city but could not feel it; it howled through the skyscrapers in search of who knows what. Perhaps it would be better to turn back and do without the milk, but then… soy milk is so easy to drink! Especially when she hadn't eaten a thing since the day before. She forgets to eat sometimes…

Just as she turned the corner, an icy gust lifted her six feet into the air. Madame Watanabe flew towards the next block. The wind caught in the umbrella and eventually bent the ribs upwards, depositing her on the ground with a bump. Then another gust pushed the umbrella back into its original shape and into the air she rose again.

Two days later, worried when her mother didn't answer the telephone, Aiko called her neighbour, Yakimoto-san, to check up on her. 'Maybe her phone's out due to the storm,' she thought. 'It wouldn't be the first time.' Yakimoto-san went over at Aiko's request and rapped several times on the door. To no avail. Watanabe-san wasn't answering.

---

[161] A supermarket chain.

'No one answers, Yamana-san!' the old woman told Aiko. 'What shall we do?' she asked.

Aiko could hear the elderly neighbour shouting from the landing while she clutched the phone:

'Watanabe-san! Neighbour! Are you there?' she cried, and through the earpiece came the sound of renewed knocking.

'No. Nothing... nothing. Neighbour!' she insisted, now hammering on the door with her fists.

'Listen, Yamana-san, I'd come over if I were you. I can't send for a locksmith to open the door, you understand?' asked the old woman.

'Oh, goodness! Has she fallen and hit her head?' asked Aiko in concern. 'She could be seriously injured... or even dead?'

'Hmm... possibly,' answered the old woman. 'That's very common at our age...'

'I'm on my way over. My sister may arrive ahead of me. Listen, Yakimoto-san, my sister's name is Keiko. Did you get that?'

'Keiko-san, yes,' replied the neighbour.

'I'm telling you so that you can open the door to her if she gets there ahead of me,' Aiko repeated.

'Keiko-san. Of course, my dear! So which one of you is coming then? Are you coming or that other one... what was her name?' she asked in constant confusion.

'Yakimoto-san, I'm on my way, but if my sister *Keiko* gets there first,' said Aiko, 'please open the door to her. I'm not sure if she'll have the outside keys!' she added.

'Keiko-san. Of course! Keiko-san... how odd,' she hesitated, 'I had an aunt called Keiko, yes. Was it Keiko? My late father's sister. Such a pretty name, Keiko, Keiko...'

'Goodbye Yakimoto-san,' said Aiko and hung up.

The old woman remained on the landing talking to herself.

'Such a pretty name, Keiko... Mmm... what was I doing holding the phone? Oh, yes, the neighbour!' she remembered, and started hammering on the door again. 'Neighbour? It's useless. Ah well, she must have gone out,' she said eventually and went back into her own apartment.

The wind slammed the door shut behind her.

An hour later, Aiko's sister arrived with the key. She put her ear to the door. She could hear a sound she didn't recognize coming from within. She went inside. The television had been left on; the channel wasn't broadcasting. She called out to her mother as she made for the bathroom, expecting to find the worst. But there was nothing. She wasn't there. How long had she been missing? Where could she have gone? Perhaps she had got lost, she thought. That sometimes happens to old people: they go out and can't find their way back. But not her okā-san: her okā-san's mind was sounder than hers and her sister's put together.

Hearing noises, the neighbour came out of her apartment and entered Madame Watanabe's.

'Who are you?' the old lady asked Keiko.

'I'm Mrs Watanabe's daughter. Keiko, Yamana Aiko's sister.

'Ah...! I haven't met you before. And what are you doing here?' asked the old woman.

'Yakimoto-san, I came because my mother hasn't answered the telephone in days. Did you seen her go out at all?

'Perhaps it's broken,' said the neighbour, picking up the earpiece and tapping it on the cradle of the phone.

'Yakimoto-san, please put the phone down,' she begged the old lady. 'I'm calling the police.'

'What are you calling the police for? I only came because I heard noises and wanted to know what was going on...,' she replied, groping for an alibi.

'Please go home. I have to see about my mother. Please, Yakimoto-san, go now. I'll let you know if I find out anything,' said Keiko, going to the door and ushering her outside. 'Thank you most kindly, I'm very grateful.'

'Well I... How impertinent! Young people today...,' grumbled the old lady as she entered her apartment.

Again the wind slammed the door shut, making Keiko jump.

'Yakimoto-san, please!' she shouted.

Keiko rang Aiko and together they embarked on the long pilgrimage of telephone calls to the police, the hospitals... But no one had reported anything. No one had seen her. They knew nothing. Nothing but 'An old lady came in last night – It's her – It isn't her – She doesn't know – You'll have to come in and identify her yourself – She's hospitalized – She's in the morgue – We'll call you as soon as we hear anything – Please remain calm...' And then 'What do you mean remain calm, officer? My mother is nowhere to be found. How do you expect me to remain calm? People don't just vanish into thin air!'

'Let's see if the Chairman can help us, Aiko, why don't we?' Keiko entreated her sister, 'I can't see us finding our way out of this one by ourselves.'

'He already knows, Keiko. Obviously, I told him. We should have news any time now,' she added.

Indeed, The Chairman had launched a citywide search for Madame Watanabe. Even the fire brigade was involved. Two days later she was found a mile from home, on a piece of wasteground that had been used as a community allotment. Her body had been covered by wilted pumpkin leaves, and her hands still clutched the handle, all that was left of her red golfing umbrella.

Watanabe-san's tiny body was cremated along with the remains of her umbrella – which could not be prised from her grip for fear of breaking her fingers – in the Shinto tradition, to which the family belonged.

'Don't you think it's a mark of disrespect to cremate her with that umbrella handle, Aiko?' asked Keiko as the body was being taken away.

'No, leave it. Can't you see it accompanied her on her last journey?' she replied.

'Yes, maybe you're right. But... I don't know, it's so strange.'

'We've hidden it under the flowers, Keiko. I'm sure she would have wanted to take it with her,' Aiko replied. 'Would you rather they'd broken her fingers?'

'Well, I don't know...,' she answered. 'Anyway, you knew her better than I did.'

After the proper number of days her remains were taken – umbrella and all – to a small Buddhist cemetery in Tokyo, where she could find peace alongside her husband. A few months later, however, thinking it over... Maybe she would prefer to be with her daughter, so they moved her to the family cemetery in Gora.

The Prophecy

'You aren't telling me those were normal circumstances that her mother died in!' said Madame.

'Well no, they aren't. Of course, they aren't,' answered Hinata-san.

'A lady ought to die on her futon, surrounded by her family,' replied Madame bad-temperedly, and added, 'As is customary!'

Aiko realized the comment was aimed directly at her and retorted sarcastically:

'I wish it had been. I've hidden my thumbs[162] at every funeral procession in my life and I've never once clipped my nails at night.'[163]

'Oh!' exclaimed her mother-in-law. 'What is your wife saying?' she looked at Hinata.

'I'm saying that, unfortunately, one doesn't get to decide on these matters. She replied recovering her dignity.

'Okā-san,' interrupted Hinata, 'please avoid making those remarks in front of Aiko. And you, Aiko, what are these superstitions?'

---

[162] An ancient superstition that one's parents will die earlier or will not be present at the parents death bed if one does not hide one's thumbs when a funeral procession passes.

[163] Whoever cuts their nails at night will not be present at their parents' deathbed.

'*We* were referring,' she said, emphasizing the generalization, 'to the fact that *we* all expect you to take proper care of her now.'

'Of course, Madame Yamana. As I always have!'

Her mother-in-law tutted loudly and added ironically:

'Yes, yes, you always have. All that caring... and look how things have turned out!'

'With all due respect,' Aiko pressed on, fighting to contain her fury, 'but... if it's true that people die the way they've lived, as the saying goes, then such an exceptional being would also have to make an exceptional last journey.'

'Oh, Aiko! Please, do stop telling stories,' she riposted. 'How many times did I tell you she ought not to have been living alone? Last journey my foot...,' she repeated, dismissing Aiko's theory.

'Yamana-sama, with all due respect, Hinata-san is a witness to all the times I pleaded with her to come and live with us,' she said, looking at Hinata for confirmation that was not forthcoming.

'Enough now... This isn't the time to argue. Honourable Watanabe's ashes are still warm!' Hinata intervened.

'But surely you can see that this has given idle tongues something to wag about in Tokyo? And that after my son's influence managed to keep this calamitous news out of the papers. I am certain that, had she been living here, this would never have happened,' she asserted confidently.

Aiko fought to control herself, but it wasn't easy. Her mother-in-law was doing her very best to make her feel worse than she already did.

'None of us can be sure how we're to die. You, for example. We don't know. Or do we? Do we know? No, we don't,' asserted Aiko.

'Aiko, that's enough!' interrupted Hinata, raising his voice.

'We just do not know, Hinata!'

Madame Yamana pursed her lips and squinted at Aiko out of the corner of one eye.

'Maybe…,' she continued, 'poised to strike? Like a praying mantis hunting insects?' she said, without premonitory intention.

'That's enough!' exclaimed Hinata, getting to his feet.

Her mother-in-law put a hand to her chest and stared at her in puzzlement. No one could tell exactly what Aiko was talking about. On the one hand, the natural sciences were not that family's particular forte. On the other, obsessed with weevils and cobwebs, her mother-in-law was forever cleaning and spent her time scaling the furniture to reach all the nooks and crannies the maid had missed. So they didn't know whether to take it as a compliment or an insult, but none of them would ever have dreamed of taking it as the prophecy that in fact, was. Not two months later Aiko's words came true when Madame Yamana died falling from a ladder, hunting for insects. Well, at least one in particular: *Tineola bisselliella* – a moth.

They should have fixed that silly stepladder long ago. It had a wobbly leg and one of the steps was loose. But, for one reason or another, they'd always let it go. And so it was that as she tried to swat that moth off the ceiling with a kitchen cloth, carried away by the impetus of imminent victory, Madame Yamana miscalculated and clattered down the ladder, scrabbling at the air and hitting her head on the stone flags of the floor. She, who had always been an implacable woman, a woman of tempered steel, died in the most stupid way imaginable, losing the battle of her life to a common moth. The housemaid, returning with the insecticide pump, found her lying there, her eyes fixed on the spot where the cheeky moth was daintily shaking the dust from its wings.

It was lucky no one recalled Aiko's words, for they would not have worked in her favour.

While no one lamented the Chairman's late mother's passing, the funeral, with all due pomp and circumstance, lasted for thirty-five days. The urn with Madame Yamana's ashes subsequently lay in the family shrine, and parents and friends visited her residence, keeping the incense burning around the clock. Once again Aiko played her part, even shedding the occasional genuine tear destined for another recipient: her own mother.

Inside and Outside

Back in the days when the Honourable Madame Yamana was living with them, the Gregorian calendar, stipulating the first of January as the start of the year,[164] was not used in the house. Instead, the tradition – which lasted until 1873[165] – was kept up of celebrating the new year at the start of spring[166] in accordance with the lunar calendar. It is true that, along with all the positive changes wrought by the Restoration, came others that, taken as a whole, many people considered an 'ideological colonization'. Many families and generations with links to the arts and philosophy resisted – passively and actively – the new cultural icon of 'modernity'. In the name of modernity everything was transformed and devoured, slowly but inexorably. It was impossible to remain aloof from the game being played out across the world, and they could not escape the massive pressure being exerted by the United States and Europe.

It isn't known whether it was in a gesture of irony or goodwill that a carpenter from the little town of Tsumago in the mountains in central Japan built a high table in the

---

[164] The Gregorian calendar officially came into force on 1 January 1873.

[165] The date refers to five years after the Meiji Restoration, whereby Japan's borders were again opened to the world and the lunar calendar was swapped for the Gregorian or solar calendar. In the Judæo-Christian tradition January 1st marks the day of Christ's circumcision, eight days after his birth on December 25th.

[166] As was done in China, Vietnam, Korea, etc.

purest western style[167] on the occasion of Emperor Meiji's[168] visit to a noble house in the area. He was courteously invited to eat at this table, which was set, as expected, for a single diner. The owner of the house himself left proof that it had been made there, etching the date of the event on the underside of the table-top.

Had Hinata-san's mother been present at this highly symbolic scene, her indignation would have caused a state incident and no mistake. Madame had within her a spirit that married the deepest ideals of the kuge and the samurai. She resolved this dialectic without contradiction as she went about her daily task of survival, cloaking it in the splendour of a 'divine mission'.

In this version of Japan, which had flowed through her veins for generations, there would clearly be no space for what, echoing Confucius, she called *'the vulgar manner in which purple detracts from the lustre of vermillion.'*[169] She resisted in every way known and unknown the changes she felt were being wrought against her will, the everyday sacrifice at the altar of 'modernity' for the good of the 'future'; for her, the only possible future lay in the past. On more than one occasion she had said in public that she would rather die than have to see her Japan become just another country, because 'Being just another country was tantamount to being less of a country.' In this assessment every January 1st became a penance both for her and for anyone in her vicinity, albeit for diametrically opposite reasons. So much so that,

---

[167] In Japan trays with legs or low tables are used, and diners sit crosslegged to eat.

[168] Who would proclaim Japan's transformation to a western-style democratic government.

[169] A reference to the *Analects* of Confucius. Vermillion being the colour of the Japanese nobility, 'I detest purple for displacing vermillion. I detest the tunes of Cheng for corrupting classical music.' (*Analects*, vol. 17, 18).

when the fireworks started and the air was filled with the explosions of rockets, Aiko's mother-in-law was mortally offended if anyone dared so much as drop a hint that they wanted to go out into the garden to enjoy the spectacle.

'That is all we were short of!' she would protest, year in year out, always using the same words. 'First they foist a new way of eating on us, then needless to say they end up changing our ways of farming! Then they take away our New Year!' she said, covering the ears of her little shiba dog, who was whimpering in fear at the din outside. 'It's a disgrace!' Close the doors!' she would shout.

'They're closed'! someone would reply from somewhere in the house.

'The way things stand,' she went on, 'they are ripping up our calendar! The future generations... mark my words now, because this is very important!' she added, seeing that no one was paying her enough attention.

'Yes, Okā-san, I *am* listening to you!' Hinata fibbed.

'As I was saying, the future generations will find themselves performing empty ceremonies.'

Hinata, quite distracted by the racket outside, tried to humour his mother with the last words still echoing through the labyrinth of his ears:

'What do you mean "empty"?'

'You ask me what I mean by empty? Isn't it obvious?' she asked. 'They'll end up doing things like the Oosouji[170] and the Setsubun[171] in February in order to see in the New Year in January.

---

[170] A cleaning done twice a year, by Autumn and Spring. She is referring to the one before New Year.

[171] A reference to the ceremony of the last day of winter, when beans are thrown to drive out the 'demons of the house' and to usher in good fortune along with the spring.

'Oh! Now I see what you mean,' said Hinata, pretending to be concentrating.

'Is it not utterly foolish?' she enquired.

'It is,' Hinata corroborated, passing his mother a small glass of plum liqueur.

'Thank you, son. And what will be next? I ask you, son. Well? What will be next?'

'Don't ask me, Okā-san. I can't answer that. Kampai!'[172]

'Kanpai! Itadakimasu,'[173] everyone chorused.

'But, would *you* go out into the garden?' his mother insisted. 'Would *you* go out or wouldn't you, Hinata?'

'Well... it *is* rather eye-catching, Okā-san. That's all. Wanting to go out into the garden doesn't mean I agree or disagree with the change in the calendar, mother. It's true what you say, but one can hardly live in caves, cut off from the rest of the world. Don't you think?'

'Caves is where we'll all end up! Can't you see? Can nobody see? Have you all gone blind to what's happening?'

'Tell me, what *is* happening?'

'It's modernity, my son. That's what's happening. This monster will devour us all in the end if it hasn't done so already. You mark my words, if it hasn't done so already!' said Madame emphatically.

'What you call modernity is something that's been going on for more than a hundred years. And if you think about it, save for a few exceptions, tradition has stayed the same. But I don't see anything wrong in people now being able to vote, or not being a mass of isolated territories deliberately kept apart by dirt roads and broken bridges, or not living under the curfew. Don't you think?'

His mother didn't answer.

---

[172] A toast meaning 'Cheers!'.

[173] Expression used before eating, equivalent to 'bon appétit', literally meaning 'I humbly receive'.

'What changes are you talking about? You've been lucky enough not to live in an time when a samurai could cut off your head to test the blade of his sword,' asked Hinata.

His mother still didn't answer. Hinata went on:

'Still,' he went on, 'in the event, the papers for the shoji are changed on New Year's Eve and the last dish of toshi-koshi soba[174] or udon[175] is served at eleven o'clock. Am I right? People still uphold the tradition of not cooking for the next three days and still go to the temple at night.'

'It isn't the same, Hinata, it isn't the same,' his mother replied. 'This new-fangled modernity... that's what I'm talking about.'

'Modernity? But... in what sense? Would you rather have to keep dialling the operator every time you have to make a telephone call?' asked Hinata-san.

'I am not talking about the telephone either, Hinata. I mean values. I mean that we aren't the same, we shall never be the same as the rest of the world. I mean that we have imposed upon ourselves trying to be the same as the others, the rest, the ones that never will be like us. Never, do you hear? Never! And besides,' she concluded, 'the year in this house begins after the second new moon following the winter solstice, and that's that.'

A firecracker boomed in the garden in apparent mockery of her words.

'The doors!' she yelled again amidst the hubbub. 'Close the doors, I said!' she repeated, in an even shriller voice.

'They're closed!'

Through visionary eyes she seemed to have glimpsed the flame within the fire. It wasn't precisely 'modernity' she feared but something different, perhaps represented but

---

[174] Japanese eat buckwheat noodles on an eve crossing from one year to another for a long lasting life.

[175] A type of noodle.

not entirely encompassed by it, a 'something different' exiled from her words that was hard to grasp. But whatever
it was, it made her intensely relive a personal rerun of the
Tokugawa Shogunate, distilled in her question 'Would *you*
go out or wouldn't you?' She might as well have asked 'Are
you an accomplice? Will you too wave that cowardly flag?
Will you make noise your home and everything will get
cheap, shiny and vulgar, like some Chinese toyshop? Will
you bring on an incandescent zenith just where the Sun was
always rising?'

Close the doors, I said!
Close all the doors.

Inside

The tenacity with which the world was brewing behind
closed doors, the urge to restrain time by placing more importance on the curls of sprouting ferns than on events
outside those walls, was there for all to see. There, in the
milky light of the greenhouse, in the mineral steam of the
waters filtering through the lattice of the rocks like an
opium dream. There, where their prehistoric breath nour-
ished the Sumatran orchids brought over from Dejima by a
certain great-grandfather. Some legacies descended like
lightning bolts or crushed like stone, but others were fragile, embroidered or written on the breeze amongst crystals
or on petals... They had to be cherished.

Inside one could sense life carrying on at the same
rhythm as it had for hundreds of years, with the same concern about how to serve the kuromame.[176]

'Perhaps...,' said the cook sweetly to Madame, 'I'm not
sure how you feel about this, Honourable Madame, but
perhaps we could serve them in the traditional fashion, on
a little brochette. Skewered on a couple of pine needles?
Oh!' he sighed rapturously. 'They're so lovely and fresh...!
And right in season.'

His words restored the serenity to her soul and her faith
in the continuity of things. At those times when anguish
and decadence began to seep through the cracks of 'good
habits', there was nothing like sitting and listening to the

---

[176] Sweet black soy beans, consumed at New Year.

cook talking about the china or the produce from the market. It was the closest thing to poetry to be heard there.

'What do you say, Honourable Madame, if we also add some little water chestnuts?' he asked complicitously, as if they were about to run off together and steal them from some forbidden garden. 'Ah,' he went on, smoothing his apron with a sweep of his hands. 'The china! We shall go to the kura this afternoon to choose it. Hmm...,' he continued, 'Those old chawanes that belonged to Honourable Yamana-sama's Honourable grandmother... the ones with the gilt that's slightly worn look so much more elegant. Yes, much more shibui.[177] Or perhaps the Arita-yaki?[178] And for the broth?' he mused aloud, immediately answering himself: 'No. Definitely, the gold lacquer bowls are ideal for autumn but not for winter.'

Aiko's mother-in-law nodded in agreement. She always did. They had an implicit understanding, but she enjoyed listening to him.

Like the rest of the domestic staff the cook's family had been serving the Yamana household for four generations or more. One great-grandfather had even cooked for Hinata-san's father's great-grandfather. They had kept each and every one of the recipes in perfect calligraphy with all the rigour of a notary – including any variations over the years – along with many a hand-written volume containing detailed inventories of every dish to have been served for over two hundred years. With the precision of a watchmaker they knew what had been served on the visit of the Emperor Showa's cousin that Thursday. Or what the Austrian ambassadors had had for dinner on that Tuesday night three years later, when they went to the river to sail

---

[177] Extreme and austere refinement.

[178] Porcelain known in the West as Imari, made in the town of Arita, Saga Prefecture, Japan.

and gaze at the first autumn moon. The same menu would never be served twice, unless requested for some special commemoration. And then it would be copied, down to the very smallest detail.

The servants had been schooled in protocol and customs, and even in each family members' personal tastes. The post of head cook was passed on from father to son rather like a legacy, with honour and pride. They were true aristocrats by now.

On one occasion one of the maids was laying out the vessels for the Hatsugama [179] and had chosen some gilt-trimmed chopsticks. When he saw her, the cook stopped her in her tracks, saying:

'Damé! Damé!'[180] . He asked her how she could dream of putting out gold chopsticks in the tea-house in the garden for the Hatsugama. 'It is in the very poorest of taste!' he added.

The girl stood there petrified, her cold fingers trembling over the marble top of the office table. Having picked out the most elegant chopsticks, she naturally didn't understand why it was 'damé'. The ceremony was extremely formal, after all, and would be attended by some very important guests.

Seeing her confusion and nerves, the cook explained that, being the most elegant, they would use the new plain cedar chopsticks.

'Rikyu-bashi,' he said, 'even if Her Majesty the Empress comes in person. In fact,' he added, 'all the more reason if she does come! Put them in cold water an hour before, tomorrow morning, so that they're easy to handle. The green bamboo ones will be used for serving.'

---

[179] The first tea ceremony of the year, beginning at noon.

[180] Very, very bad!

Aiko liked to curl up in an armchair while she listened to her mother-in-law discussing the menu. She would drift off to sleep, lulled by the words that, weightless and empty of content, lapped against her like waves on the seashore, words that soothed her, like 'sakura salmon petals', short words like hamo[181] or ume,[182] slide-shaped words like hatsu-gama,[183] or rhythmic ones like kurikinton.[184] But what made her happiest was the infinite pleasure of realizing, as she dozed off, that they had lowered their voices to a whisper so as not to waken her. At such times Aiko clung on to the illusion that it may perhaps be possible – if she tried harder – for Hinata's okā-san one day to be like a mother to her too. But the overweening evidence against her speculations meant that those dreams of hers were soon crushed; her mother-in-law always made sure never to get too close. As soon as Aiko began to act a little more like the owner of the house, Madame would make it perfectly clear that she would never be in command of that territory. Like the day – what wounds it reopened! – when the flowers disappeared. She had noticed that a kakejiku[185] was on display in the tokonoma[186]. 'It's pretty, true, but a little sad,' she thought to herself. So she went out into the garden in search of some flowers to brighten it up. She garnered a

---

[181] Conger eel.

[182] Sour plum.

[183] The first tea ceremony of the New Year.

[184] Chestnuts and mashed sweet potatoes consumed on New Year's day.

[185] An art object that hangs on the wall, usually a painting or a piece of calligraphy. It is hung vertically on the inside wall of a tokonoma.

[186] A small raised alcove decorated with hanging scrolls of calligraphy or painting, or ikebana-style flower arrangements or bonsai. It is strictly forbidden to sit within this area.

bouquet and arranged it there artistically, to form an ike-bana.[187] She was no expert, but it looked good. She set it on the right of the kakejiku and stepped back to view it from a distance. 'Perfect,' she said to herself. 'Just what was needed.' Proud of her arrangement, she went into town to run some errands. To her surprise, when she returned at lunchtime, she noticed the arrangement was standing in the kitchen office, on the cabinet below the wall-clock. She picked them up carefully and, carrying her packages in the other hand, went to put the flowers back where she had left them. When night fell, she went back to fetch the pack-ages and discovered, on passing the tokonoma, that the flowers had been removed. She was just about to head back to the office when the butler came in, dressed to the nines, intending to lock up the shoji and turn on the lights. Aiko asked him about the flower arrangement, to which he replied that the Honourable Madame had had them re-moved.

'But… why?' asked Aiko, disconcerted. 'I picked them myself this morning. They were in perfect condition… Why do they have to be removed?' she asked, perplexed.

At that exact instant her mother-in-law walked in and the butler turned to her, saying with a cynical sneer:

'Honourable Madame, the lady here was asking me about the flowers.'

Her mother-in-law ceremoniously rotated towards where they were standing, opposite the softly lit tokonoma. On the wall hung the calligraphy.[188]

'I just found it a little sad…,' Aiko said defensively, slightly unsure of herself.

---

[187] A minimalist strategically placed flower arrangement constructed on three levels.

[188] A reference to the *kakemono*.

The butler looked at Madame out of the corner of his eye, concealing a smile beneath pursed lips, while Madame, her eyes fixed on the kakemono, declared:

'It is a sublime calligraphy by Rosanjin Waka, Master Rosanjin Kitaoji-sama. Wherever he is, there must only be silence.'

'Ah!' Aiko sobbed, transformed all of a sudden into a cockroach. 'I'm sorry. I didn't realize.'

Her mother-in-law left the room without another word. Aiko reeled and lurched forced to forge a sudden alliance with the butler just in order to have something to hold on to. She looked at him and raised her eyebrows – a gesture she would have avoided had she known the quicksands it would leave her in. Not only did she find no support, but he sidestepped her, saying:

'Master Rosanjin is a very famous potter, as you well know. He has also made paintings and produced calligraphy,' he pontificated, making Aiko feel like an ignoramus.

The truth was that she didn't know who Master Rosanjin was and had never heard of him.

'We have had the good fortune,' he added, sharing in something that didn't belong to him, 'to obtain this work by him, which is, as the Honourable Madame says, sublime.'

With these words he bowed long and low, and left.

Aiko stood there rooted to the spot, on her six little legs, staring at the calligraphy on the tokonoma.

'Well, I thought it was a little sad,' she said, her feelers twitching.

The Pickles

For as long as she shared a roof with her mother-in-law, Aiko spent her time trying to be, if not loved, then at least accepted. Or if not accepted, then at least respected. It was hopeless. She never managed either. Nor did she ever pass the famous 'pickle test'.[189] Not for want of trying. Time after time she tried but never succeeded. Not even her husband could tell the difference between the ones she prepared and his okā-san's. There simply wasn't any.

It was not uncommon for Hinata to hear her sobbing about the pickles from behind the screen in the bathroom.

'What are you crying for, Aiko?'

'Can't you see, Hinata?' she answered whimpering, hating herself for not being able to reign in her emotions. 'She'll never say they've turned out right. Never! Never!'

'What hasn't turned out right?'

'The pickles!' and she would burst inconsolably into tears.

When Hinata's mother passed away, Aiko gave the order to clean out the pantry and dispose of all the jars of pickles prepared by her mother-in-law. Her husband didn't notice until several weeks later, when he asked the cook about his mother's jars. The cook explained to him what had happened and offered to relinquish some of the jars which, he confessed, he himself had secretly salvaged and stored in

---

[189] For mothers-in-law the pickles prepared by daughters-in-law always have too much or too little salt for their taste.

his bedroom. Hinata was moved by the gesture, but also took Aiko's decision as a personal, almost mortal affront. She, on the other hand, had not done it to offend him, but because eating something prepared by a dead person in itself seemed to her a dialectic issue impossible to overcome. She even went so far as to think it would have been better for the pickles to have been incinerated along with her mother-in-law. 'I wish she'd have taken them with her to the grave,' thought Aiko, smiling impishly to herself while contemplating her thoughts in horror lest she'd been heard from beyond the grave. For her husband, however, the pickles were the 'last preserve' of his mother.

'You didn't have to eat them, but there was no reason to throw them away, either,' he reproached her indignantly.

'So what then?' Aiko challenged him. 'Leave them to go off on that shelf like one of those children preserved in jars of formaldehyde in the hospital museum?' she asked, fuming.

'I would have eaten them... quite happily!' he retorted, pacing nervously around the kitchen.

'What are you saying?' asked Aiko in horror.

'What does it matter to you? That's... what I don't understand! What need was there to throw them away?' he asked, his voice faltering, as if he'd just found out the world was about to end.

'Sorry, Hinata. It's just that somehow it would be like having part of your mother there. I don't know, like a piece of her. It's macabre!' Aiko answered, carried further and further away by her imagination.

She thought about it for a few seconds until she finally covered her mouth and shrilled: 'I can't even think about such a thing!'

Hinata stopped pacing up and down like a caged bear and looked at her in astonishment.

'I hope my sisters never find out what you've done... *they* would never forgive you!' he said, pointing a threatening finger at her and spitting out his words with such fury one could hardly make out what he was saying.

'You cannot be serious!' yelled Aiko impetuously. 'Because of those bloody pickles! Even from the grave your mother's capable of making us fight about her!'

Aiko immediately regretted what she'd said and ran to him.

'Hinata! Oh, Hinata, please forgive me!' she said, falling to her knees.

Hinata pushed her away from him emphatically. After that, they relapsed into an unbroken silence that lasted for a long time. This time, Hinata thought, Aiko had gone too far – way too far...

Besieged

From that day forward the Chairman slept in his study. Every morning he would fold up the futon and drag it back to the bedroom he once used to share with her, in order to prevent gossip among the staff. He also spent less and less time at home, returning only when Aiko was already sound asleep. She would often wake in the middle of the night, not even knowing what time it was. He was in the habit of disappearing first thing, lugging his futon on his back like a snail and, when she saw the empty space beside her and realized she hadn't even heard him come into the room, she would be overtaken by a profound disquiet.

Sometimes Aiko would think of going to him. She pictured herself groping in the dark and sliding under the quilt. She could see herself holding him but, anticipating his rejection, would think twice, recalling all the things he had said to her and his near morbid relationship with his late mother. In her mind he would caress the jars of pickled cabbage and wrinkled radishes, crying out for her. The formula helped Aiko to keep as cool as a stone under water and, when she sensed his weakness, it made her stronger. She wished this instant strength would dispel her loneliness, but it didn't. Without her mother and husband – her husband's tender side – she was quite alone, tossed on a tempest of emotions. Hanging her head, she wept with all her being until the scent of her pillow carried her away through a field of grain in the March rain.[190]

---

[190] Buckwheat's bran pillows are common in some parts of Japan.

Madame Yamana's death had begun to cast a gloom over her imagined intimacy with her father-in-law within the locked study. The woman whose mere presence had made her feel threatened in life had now taken on panoramic proportions. Wherever she may be, she could see everything, even Aiko's thoughts. There was nowhere she could be safe from the other-worldly 'X-rays' of her mother-in-law: a kami now and forever, her wickedness would know no end.

Aiko continued to defy her perception, trying to persuade herself to maintain a degree of 'rationality'. Yet, frightened though she was, she kept up her visits to her father-in-law's study to 'commune' with him. But one night she was frightened by a shadow outside the window. So she switched off the lights and froze, her chest heaving beneath her yukata. Suddenly something leapt from the bookshelf. A field-mouse? A moth? Whatever it was, it brushed against her hair and she let out a scream. She didn't feel like going back any more; she thought that the best way to keep Madame Yamana at bay would be not to visit certain places for a time. First it was just her father-in-law's study and the library, but her fear spread like an ink-stain to the cobbled central courtyard, where the 'compassionate plum tree' stood. All that had been familiar to her now felt dismal and spectral until the grim shadow fell on the adjoining corridors, the domo opening onto the courtyard and – hardly surprising – the kitchen. How could she ever erase that image of her mother-in-law in the green light of the window clutching the poultry shears? It had been so transformed in the interim that she could no longer clearly recall any of her features, save her black mouth: a gaping darkness that had now spread to become the living image of an ohaguro-bettari.[191]

---

[191] A female figure in Japanese fantasy horror literature who, on turning, reveals a featureless face with a gaping black mouth. It may have been

The only places that seemed to protect her for now were her bedroom and the minka. Most of the time she would spend locked up in her room reading, fixing up her hut, or just sitting like a parrot on a perch, contemplating the changes ushered in by the spring. But while all around her blossomed, inside her something was growing, turning everything into a garden of gloom and shadow.

---

related to the ancient custom, which remained until 1870, of painting the teeth black (de ohaguro: blackening the teeth).

Ever downwards

In late summer preparations for the O-bon Matsuri[192] got under way.

Aiko sat on the committee for the local shrine, responsible among other things for making sure the printed leaflets of prayers, sutras and chants were all in order. To prevent any last-minute arguments the members also made sure that the red lanterns at the entrance were working and that everything was in its place. The families of the dead went to the adjacent cemetery early in the morning. There they would clean the urns containing the remains of their loved ones, leave fresh flowers and incense, and replace their old worn name plates with new ones. Then they would stay and pray and sing for the rest of the day and night, until the end of the Bon Odori.[193]

That year Aiko was particularly exhausted and, for some reason that she couldn't make out, she felt haunted by the intangible presence of her mother-in-law. It was only natural that the last thing she wanted was to light the lanterns all over the house to summon the dead. She went ahead nonetheless, thinking of her own mother and grandparents,

[192] Buddhist Celebration honouring the departed. On this occasion the tomb of the deceased is usually cleaned and the spirits of the dead return home to visit the family altar.

[193] Traditional dance performed to welcome the souls of the dead revisiting Earth.

as well as Hinata's father; the idea of his presence was a comfort to her.

Hakone belonged to the same prefecture as Tokyo, so the O-bon festival was traditionally held in August, while on the west coast it was held in July. Aiko could picture her mother-in-law in another dimension, ranting and raving as ever about the differences in the dates between the solar and lunar calendars. But, surprisingly, according to the brother of her husband's childhood friend, who lived in one of the monasteries on Mount Koya, where he devoted himself to the study of ancient astrological and esoteric knowledge, the difference in dates was in fact more serious than Aiko's mother-in-law could ever have imagined. He explained to her that certain events could not be scattered haphazardly across the calendar, and that rituals have to be performed at a certain conjunction of the Yowatashi Boshi[194] – solely and exclusively within that precise astral window. There were certain ephemerides in the possession of the monks in Koya that took account of deviations of minutes or even seconds with respect to those indicating the "official' astrological course. So a ritual would sometimes be brought forward or put back in order to synchronize it with the 'corresponding cosmic moment'. That, he claimed, was when a 'break' occurred, that would allow a passage between the different dimensions. This happened during the O-bon, for example. He maintained that, taking any date, as, in fact, had happened after the Reform, meant groping blindly through the cosmic order. That could only bring misfortune in its train, or even natural disasters, not to mention personal catastrophes. The most mystic monks refused to do it, remaining faithful to their ideas under all kinds of pressure, be it governmental, social, economic or political.

---

[194] Group of stars – Orion, for example – that passes across the night sky, appearing in the east and setting when the sun rises.

In other ways, though, Aiko's mother-in-law wasn't so far wide of the mark... The thought filled Aiko with a retrospective horror. She would have to backtrack and do things the way they were supposed to be done, even if it went against the grain. She would have to explain to Hinata; perhaps he would listen and, being such an influential man... But how to draw him into an alliance with her and instigate a reorganization that would involve going back on the decision to adopt the new calendar, which had been use for over a hundred years? Hadn't his mother already insisted enough without ever getting her way? It was pragmatic to go on using the solar calendar for administrative matters, but festivities and rituals had to be done in strict accordance with the appropriate auspices. She was quite convinced of that.

Aiko turned her head towards the mirror on her dressing table with the certainty something was watching her. Her mother-in-law's face stared back from it.

'I am you,' she said to herself.

Sick with fright she wondered who had spoken.

From then on she had all the mirrors in the house covered, claiming she was being spied on.

While her cousins and her sister Keiko were in the house for the O-bon, she felt a little calmer, but her fears were rekindled when the guests began to leave. She hadn't slept properly the night before, merely dozing and dreaming as she tossed and turned of legions of spirits hammering on invisible walls. She was certain that the only way to exorcize all these demons and disasters was by doing a volte-face and returning to the old ways. She needed urgently to talk to Hinata.

She grew to detest the dark and the night. It forced her into a sleep in which she could hear everything. 'There's a constant dripping coming from the garden.' 'A clacking of spider legs weaving a web in a corner of the room.' 'A dew on the leaves that torments me.' 'A ceaseless splashing of carp in the pond.'

'I can't sleep for all the noise!' she complained.

She says she can hear the stars scraping the heavens at night!

The Bottom

Her relationship with her husband went from bad to worse. They barely spoke any more, not even to ask to pass the water. She wondered if he was still angry over the pickles or if it was for some other reason... Alone in bed, surrounded by absence, she feared she would wake from a nightmare and not find his reassuring hand. She feared lying there immobile, pearled with sweat, her body electrified, catching glimpses of her mother-in-law in the folds of the gloom. She turned on the light and lit a cigarette just to keep herself company. She wouldn't fall asleep until the room began to fill with the glow of dawn. How she would rejoice at the pale bluish light that rested on the shoji! Then the house would start to come back to life with the soft murmur of maids stowing the sheets in the cupboards of the corridor, the swishing of the gardener's rake sweeping up the October leaves, the fusuma sliding smoothly on its rails. Ah, the old abode back in its morning routine... the aroma of dashi creeping under the doors and wafting through the house... bringing the warmth of childhood mornings and placid winters by the fire of the irori! Only then could she fall serenely asleep in the homely buzzing and lulling of the waking house. If only those moments would last...! But the hours would not pass and her drowsiness would wane. Sometimes slowly like a flame dying on the wick; others abruptly plunging, not outwards but inwards, towards the darkest marrow of her being.

For fear of those abysses Aiko chose not to sleep on the futon again but elsewhere in the house. Dozing when and wherever she could, her sleep patterns began to resemble the nappings of dogs. She would awaken with the clear sensation that Hinata's mother was standing over her, staring at her, and her brooding presence had all the oppressive density of the dark waters of the drowned. Aiko would find it hard to breathe and her heart shook with the very certainty she would die right there and then.

Everyone thought she was acting strangely, and with good reason. What before they had thought of as exaggeration had now, as she persisted in her waywardness, became full-blown 'oddity'. Even her cousins were afraid to visit her. They claimed she couldn't stick to the thread of a conversation, which made it hard for them to understand what she was talking about, and that she would entangle them all in her fantastic ideations about changes in the calendar.

The family doctor – a calm, composed man – went to see her and diagnosed Aiko as suffering from stress, made worse by the heat of the season. He said she had had to bear the deaths of two close relatives in quick succession, but that they already knew. After taking her pulse several times on either wrist and examining her tongue twice, above and below, he finally prescribed her a mix of bitter herbs to help her sleep, as well as a good rest. 'Rest' was all she ever did, she quipped, as she no longer had the strength to walk.

The Lama, who was also present at her husband's express request, guaranteed her that 'True rest comes not from the sleeping but from the awakening,' words that only ended up confusing her once and for all. She had to have some routine tests to rule out anæmia, and the doctor also recommended eating unagi,[195] for among other things she was likely to be suffering from natsubate.[196]

---

[195] Eels.

[196] Summer fatigue.

'Any medication?' asked her husband, to which he replied that 'There are few ills in the East that a change of diet won't cure.' After which Aiko understood that science could do little or nothing for her and that, in the words of that Roman emperor stabbed twenty-four times, whose life she had had to learn all about on her Italian honeymoon: 'Alea iacta est.'[197] Clearly there was no cure for what was happening to her for it was of neither from the East nor the West. Nor even of this world. It came from the Beyond. Of that, she was completely sure.

The cook's assistant went off to search for eels, which had to be transported in barrels from the south. It was still their 'August' there, whereas Gora's had ended. In the kitchen at night the only sound to be heard was of water running non-stop into the barrel where the eels were kept. Aiko could not resist the morbid urge to lean in and inspect the slimy things writhing blindly at the bottom of the barrel. That image came to mind every time she was served them. The cook tried to vary his presentation: he would make them in teppanyaki[198] or in sushi, smoked or barbecued, with or without[199] kabayaki[200] sauce, eastern or western style – eels in uramaki[201] or à la chahan,[202] in tempura[203] or spring onion fritters. Aiko ate so many eels that, if she took to heart the old proverb 'You are what you eat', she would have ended up wriggling about on the floor. Yet the eels

---

[197] 'The die is cast': words attributed to Julius Cæsar by Suetonius.

[198] Cooked on an iron plate.

[199] *Shirayaki*, grilled eels without sauce.

[200] Sweet soy-based sauce.

[201] In a rice roll.

[202] Eels with fried rice.

[203] Coated in a light batter and fried.

did not improve her mood, which turned as black as they were. She felt as if there was nothing left but to climb into the barrel with them.

She was still insomniac and would stay up night after night smoking, until her husband came home. When she heard his footsteps in the corridor, she would sigh with relief. Then he would come in – a perfect stranger to the space and the reality she found herself in – and draw back the shoji directly without so much as a hello. He would open the window to the night air, a freezing gale.

'Aiko, for God's sake!' he would say, raising his voice. 'You'll be the death of us all! It's like a sailors' tavern in here!'

He would go over to her and say goodnight, then, without a word, pick up his snail house, sling it over his shoulder and lug it to his study. She would look at him tenderly and beg him:

'Hinata, please... don't go.'

And he, out of pity, would grant her a 'Very well, I'll and stay' and lie down motionless beside her. Aiko wouldn't dare so much as breathe lest her husband change his mind and leave. She lay there as still as a statue, waiting for some show of affection, but he would fall asleep immediately and start rattling the foundations, grunting and growling like a Himalayan tiger. She would wait a few moments until she was sure he was sound asleep and there was nothing left to be done. She would then be invaded by an immense emptiness and reproach herself for having begged him like that. Her anguish, which had no door or window, would squeeze her chest and throat, suffocating her. A single question echoed a thousand and one times around the walls of her mind: why could he not love her? So, as if he had escaped through the back door into a territory he could not be wrested back from, sheltered by the exile of sleep, he slumbered on... Meanwhile the solitary ship of Aiko's heart slipped its moorings and plunged into the weather-torn night.

'Hinata, Hinata! What are you dreaming?' She shook him till the tears welled in her eyes.

Locked away in his private world, Hinata merely shifted in bed and went back to his snoring.

'Hinata... Hinata...,' she would beg in vain, trying to stifle her sobbing.

Sometimes, in his dreams, he would mutter something.

'What did you say?' she would ask, unable to make it out.

'I said... the English have taken... I don't know... tell him to bring it,' he answered from his dreams.

'Bring it? Bring what?'

'The notebook,' he replied.

'You're talking in your sleep, Hinata!' she would reproach him angrily. Then she would get up, go out into the garden and walk around in circles. She could not bring herself to believe that their love had died just like that, without any warning. She was more willing to deny her own existence than have to accept that love wasn't eternal.

Sometimes she thought she would kill him and then... She would slit his throat with a shard of broken mirror. He would look at her in astonishment and have no time to cry out 'Aiko!' as he choked on his own fluids. Night after night she killed him in her thoughts. Night after night she loved him and loathed him. In her mind she would hold him half-dead in her arms, soaked in his blood and howling with passion, pain and spite, the image of her husband blurring with that of the young man who had long since stripped her of her life, even if she could barely remember him now, he was more of a feeling than an image in himself.

She knew – or rather, she believed with the force of 'certain knowledge' – that her husband arrived home exhausted from spending so much time with another woman, another younger woman... She knew it. She knew he loved her, that he was tangled in her hair. She knew it. That he spoke sweetly to her. That he smothered her in kisses and promises. She wasn't going to let him deny it. She wasn't going to let him tell her she was just imagining things or go on treating her as if she were some raving madwoman.

Sometimes her husband smelt different. She wasn't crazy. She could smell it. Nuzzling up to Hinata's body, she would follow every inch of the trail as he slept. She knew that scent. It was acacias. It was raw flesh... She knew it. She knew it all too well! He had another woman. Another woman in his dreams, another woman in his desires. She knew it! And she would go on knowing it until the images of blood and violence returned. She was going to kill him.

Everyone has left now,
but she has stayed behind dancing
with death

It was cold. It had begun to snow on the higher slopes.

Wrapped in a blanket, Aiko had gone out for a walk in the garden to pacify her demons. The grass crunched beneath her feet. Pillows of black clouds obscured the stars on a moonless night. A reflection on the lawn caught her eye in the dark. She leant to one side, and the glint vanished. To the other, and again it gleamed. So she crouched low to view it close up. Again it vanished. She probed with her fingers, and a clumsy movement brought her hand into contact with a tangle of metal. Some strange wire plant had sprouted from the ground. Aiko let out a cry of terror and leapt backwards, tripping on a rock. She fell to the ground and a stab of pain jarred her right thigh. She could just see the wires in the dark, like... the ribs of an umbrella: broken and buckled, the wooden handle missing, but still with scraps of cloth stuck to them. It was identical to the one her mother had been carrying the day she died.

Her leg burning, she limped and ran to the nearest shelter she could find. A bolt of lightning lit up the bamboo, then came a deafening rumble that made her scream again. Groping her way in terror through the undergrowth, she managed to make it as far as the old azumaya,[204] soaked to

---

[204] Wooden pergola with no walls, the roof being supported on four posts, used for guests to rest in as they walk through a large garden.

the skin by a sudden deluge. She slowed to a trance-like walk, repeating to herself: 'It can't be true. It cannot be true. Wake up!' she cried and slapped herself hard in the face.

It couldn't be a coincidence; someone must have put it there. By the time she had caught her breath, she was completely disoriented. For a few moments she didn't know who she was. With bewildered eyes she looked around for some point of reference, something to snap her back to reality. But she had no idea where she was.

She never found out what happened next, but the magic of writing means that authors know more than their characters imagine, and can testify to what goes on when everyone's asleep. So, though Aiko never remembered, at some point she could make out her minka rising up motionless like a hill amidst the blackness of the foliage. She ran to it, went inside and sat there, sobbing and trembling by the irori. Sometime later – impossible to tell how long, for her mind was a blank – overcome with fatigue and tears, she either passed out or fell asleep. Then, as so often before, she dreamed she was flying amidst the frozen roof-tops of the houses, naked and wearing the broken crown of an umbrella, thinking to herself 'It's torn to shreds! I'm going to fall! But it doesn't matter anymore…' And yet she floated on. She realized her flight did not depend on the umbrella, which was all in tatters, but on the rise and fall of her breathing and, ultimately, on her own will. She could see the river down below, all lit up with paper lanterns, drifting away as they do at the end of the O-Bon so that the spirits of the dead could find their way back and depart this world.

She was chilled to the bone and her fingers had started to freeze up. In the middle of the dream she remembered she had already dreamed it before. She knew exactly what would happen next: she would see the little crib rocking on the water and want to descend to rescue her little boy, and the wind would be very strong and it would be so cold… Then the crib would drift away.

'Son of mine!' she shouted, a tortured cry that came from within and woke her.

She opened her eyes: it was already dawn. Exhausted, her lips blue with cold, she got up. She felt a sharp pain in her leg and noticed that the fabric of her camisole was all bloody and stuck to the skin of her thigh. Her movement tore away the clotted blood and reopened the wound. She cleaned herself as best as she could with the unbloodied part of the garment and, barefoot, left the minka. She raced to where she thought she had seen the umbrella the night before. She scrabbled and searched through the frosty white leaves and grass, but to no avail. In the distance, amid the fog, the gardener was pruning the hedges. She ran to him.

'Utamaro-san! Utamaro-san!' she called. 'Have you seen an umbrella lying around?' she asked.

'Oh, Madame Yamana! Good morning!' he replied decorously. 'Well... I'm afraid I haven't, I haven't...'

Before he could finish, she was off to the main house and into the kitchen to interrogate the staff.

'An umbrella? A red umbrella?' she asked breathlessly. 'But... how can it be? Has no one seen a red umbrella lying in the middle of the garden? You, Kaoru-san!' she asked one of the maids, who looked back at her in fright. 'Where did you put the umbrella that was in the middle of the garden? Where is the umbrella?' she insisted.

The house staff began to file off to the kitchen with all the curiosity of Kobe cattle.

'What are you gawping at?' she roared. 'Help me look! It has to be somewhere!'

She hurried over to the rubbish containers in the yard at the side and felt a stab of pain where she had wounded herself. When she touched it, she noticed it was bleeding again. She could put no weight on her foot and had to limp and hop the rest of the way. Then she set about delving in the rubbish in the hope she would find that damned umbrella.

'It has to be here, it must be, surely...,' she said, like someone searching for evidence of a conspiracy.

In that case it would be better for everyone if it never appeared.

Coming out of his office, her husband spotted her but couldn't tell for sure.

'Aiko?' he called out. 'Aiko?' he repeated, moving closer, but she seemed to be in a world of her own and didn't hear him.

She went on talking to herself, saying that it had to be in there, spilling the bags of chicken giblets and vegetable peel everywhere. The stench was unbearable. Oblivious to it all, she went on digging through feathers and bones.

'What are you doing? Aiko?' Hinata insisted. 'Aiko!' he shouted, taking her by the arm.

Feeling someone touch her, she let out a cry and, not realizing it was her husband, fled at full pelt to her room as fast as her good leg would carry her.

'You're bleeding!' shouted Hinata. 'Aiko! What's happened to you?'

He ran after her, but Aiko bolted the shoji shut, leaving a trail of blood behind her.

Her husband called insistently at the door. Then he went round the back of the house and tried to climb in through a window, but that too was closed. He decided it would be best to phone the doctor immediately and let her rest in the meantime. Aiko's problem looked more serious than a lack of eels in her diet.

She didn't get up all day. Her husband ordered the staff to take her something to eat in her room, but she didn't touch the food. The procession of trays continued throughout the day, laid on the floor outside her door, until the servants picked up the last one at ten o'clock at night exactly where they had left it, along with a packet of bandages and disinfectant that were also untouched.

Yamana Hinata-sama, the Chairman

'Suddenly, I saw her, as if... for the first time. I saw her. The shadows under her eyes were more prominent in the pallor of her face. It reminded me of the scene in the Sagi Musume,[205] the one where the heron dies... You must remember it, Yoshida sensei,'[206] said Hinata to the doctor. 'Her eyes were lost in spirals of blue smoke,' he continued, as if thinking aloud, 'since when did she take up smoking? I could barely recognize her. She'd stopped being who she was and become an apparition wandering through the shadows of the house. It wasn't so much a change of character but of her very nature. I still remember that night. It may have been the last gala reception we attended together, less than a year ago – for Ambassador Urusume's anniversary. I pushed so hard for her to come with me that in the end she caved in and agreed. Her fragility...,' he stammered. 'You know? She'd lost so much weight, and she was already slim when I met her. She was always ethereal but she had become almost ghostly...'

'She wore her black tomesode,[207] the one with the embroidered peonies I'd given her one anniversary. It was splendid! She looked breathtakingly beautiful. She complained a couple of times about the weight of the kimono, something she'd never done before; she used to wear it

---

[205] Kabuki theatre play.

[206] 'Master': an honorific used for doctors and teachers.

[207] A formal kimono that married women wear.

with the dignity of an empress. The reception dragged on, so we slipped out at the start of the shamisen concert, stealthily, like a couple of deer. That was something we used to do in the past, when we were younger. I felt oddly moved, as if enfolded in a cloud of renewed vitality. Silly, isn't it. At that stage in life!' he smiled mirthlessly. 'When we got home, Erizawa-san was sitting waiting for her as usual to help her undress and put away the kimono in the boxes. I had the hare-brained scheme – a bad one as it turned out – of sitting on the dresser and contemplating the whole process out of curiosity. I had never seen it before and perhaps... Hmmm... Oh, I have to confess,' he said in an intimate tone, 'I found it quite erotic: the idea of staying there, watching her, while Erizawa-san – who's a charming young woman – slowly undressed her. I imagine you understand me perfectly. Well, perhaps I'd had a little to drink as well... But, sensei, nothing could have been wider of the mark than my eroticism that night.'

The doctor listened attentively.

'As Erizawa-san gradually removed one layer of the kimono after another, peeling her like an onion, my wife was reduced to practically nothing; she vanished along with the dress. Later on, Erizawa-san finished up her duties and went to bed, bidding us goodnight and drawing the shoji behind her. Aiko – this skinny little slip of thing – lay down beside me and started to search for me with her hands, and I began to feel strange... as if I were outside the situation. At that moment, as I heard her bones creak with her every move, I realized I'd been doing nothing but feeding fantasies all night. It felt as if all her bones were loose beneath her skin. When there was no longer any way to avoid her, I told her with all the tenderness I could muster right then: "Darling, sorry, but I have something really urgent to do tomorrow. You've made such an effort this evening! My poor dear, you must be tired... Don't force yourself any more, I'll leave you alone so you can rest." That's what I said to her. I got up and walked out, leaving her and her creaking bones alone on the futon. How could I have been such a swine? She looked at me but didn't say a word. I know I should have simply stayed and embraced her, but I couldn't. I got up and walked out... smiling like a fool. I left without another word. I despised myself for that because I realized it had been an act of cowardice. I couldn't stand the idea of exploring the bone-house of her body. The very thought of it stirred the certainty of my own death in the pit of my soul.'

Yoshida sensei lit a cigarette and reclined in his easy chair.

'Just a few days ago I found her in a state I'd rather not to recall, but I can't get that image out of my head. Barefoot in the middle of a winter cold enough to crack stone, her hair all of a tangle, digging through the rubbish. Her clothes were in tatters from head to toe, and soaked in blood. What a sight! Like something had taken possession of her! I called her by her name. "Aiko?" I said. "What are you doing?" She appeared not to hear me. I took her by the arm, and at that moment she let out a scream that froze the blood in my veins. She looked at me as if I were some mythological beast that had escaped from a dark temple and ran off in fright without a word. I ran after her, but she bolted the door behind her, blocking my way. No matter how longed I knocked on the door, she wouldn't open it. There was no sense in kicking down the door. "Go away!" she shouted. But how could I just go away and leave her in that state? At that moment I wasn't sure whether she needed a doctor or an exorcist, but the rationalist education I received from my father steered me towards science. So I decided to call you, Doctor Yoshida. I wanted you to come and at least look at her leg. You know what happened next; she refused to open the door to you. From behind the screen she growled that no doctor could cure her and that you should leave... So. You might also recall that you told me we should wait, and that you asked me to call you in the afternoon to see how she was getting on. So I felt like an orphan, sensei. I must confess I dreaded the moment you left me alone with her. Again I thought perhaps she was in the grip of some evil spirit and I felt fear – dread. It was no ordinary emotion, nothing like I'd felt before; rather, it was a clammy apprehension – something almost supernatural. It had never happened to me, and I wondered again if she might be possessed. You know me, I usually have no difficulty mastering my fears. It's obvious. Otherwise how could I do what I do? You're my friend and confidant: you know my work and you know it isn't easy... But I didn't know what to do at those moments. It was something that came to me from another world. She remained locked in the room the whole day, and then several more. Do you remember?'

'Yes, of course I remember,' Dr Yoshida replied, leaning forward. '...so tell me, is she eating better?'

'She eats very little,' answered Hinata.

'Is she sleeping?'

'I've heard her wandering about the house a good deal at night. It keeps me awake because I don't know what she's about. It makes me nervous,' replied Hinata. 'It must have been a gradual change I didn't notice, a change that probably started when she got back from our honeymoon and found she wasn't pregnant. That handicap may have developed shortly after her mother died. They were speculations. They didn't speak about the matter. He suggested that she see the family gynæcologist – the same one that had assisted his mother in her births – but she always let it slide for one reason or another. "Yes, yes," she'd say but then wouldn't go.'

'Hmm... I see,' remarked the doctor. 'You know her better than I do, but I can't guarantee that's the problem. It's our obligation as men of science to doubt, you know, to put theories to the test. But let's start from the premise that you're right. First, why do you believe that she's the one who's sterile and not you? Second, why did you decide not to be tested too?'

An icy wave washed over Hinata.

'Heavens...!' he replied falteringly. 'Well, I don't know what to say to you. It never occurred to me, you know.'

'Why not?' asked the sensei in a deliberately nonchalant tone.

'It's something we all ruled out, stupidly enough,' said Hinata.

Yoshida sensei looked at him quizzically. Catching his look, Hinata tried to justify his words.

'It's just that it's never happened in our family. You know my grandfather...,' he said, getting back into his stride.

'Yes, yours has certainly been a prolific family, but that doesn't... Well, anyway. What I mean is that, while genetics are very important, they aren't the be-all-and-end-all. It's all a bit of a lottery. Our genes aren't exact replicas of our parents',' he added. 'There are many other factors that intervene. So,' he went on, 'effectively you haven't done anything to find out what the problem is.'

'No, I haven't done anything like that, sensei. But do you really think I...?'

'Well,' he replied, 'it isn't a question of "thinking..."' he laughed uncomfortably. 'It's something that has to be ruled out, and the fact is that you could be the one that's sterile.'

The doctor saw the anxiety in Hinata's face and added:

'I simply mean that anything's possible. It isn't the end of the world, Hinata. Do you understand?'

'But... even with no precedents in the family?' he asked, trying to play down any prejudgment about his sterility.

Yoshida sensei nodded gently, compassionately. Hinata understood and, taking a deep breath, replied:

'Oh! What are you saying? That... that is something I can't...,' he muttered. 'Dying without an heir would be like a crime against the ancestors of this house. You know that, don't you?' he asked.

'Let's wait and see. First of all, it's something that doesn't depend on you, Hinata. It's nature's way, do you see?' said the doctor. 'It's absurd for you to be ashamed about something like that, something that can be sorted out. Look, it's still not too late.'

Hinata started to weep.

'All this time,' he sobbed, 'I've been trying to reassure myself that it was all my wife's fault... I mean,' he corrected himself, 'I thought it had to be my wife's fault, not mine. What a calamity! This is terrible, Yoshida sensei! I didn't have the nerve to stop my mother or my sisters!'

'You weren't to know, Hinata. I'm not trying to justify you, but don't get yourself all worked up. For one thing, we still don't know. That's why I'm recommending you have some tests done, even if it's just for your peace of mind. You know, just to rule it out.'

'I see...'

'Besides, there's always the option of adopting, it wouldn't be the first time or the last.'

'I can't think clearly, Yoshida sensei. All this time I've kept inside... please forgive me.'

'Well, the fact is you've been through so much of late... I think you've also been under a lot of stress and have had the worst of it being the one in charge of the house. You know how we were brought up... But people snap, Hinata-san. They snap. It happens all the time. I see it every day in my surgery: important people, politicians, intellectuals, governors, but the same happens to bureaucrats, teachers... You wouldn't believe the number of suicides committed in this country, not each year but each day! This one can't sleep, that one's depressed, the other has palpitations or recurring nightmares that are so bad they're afraid to go to sleep at night, Hinata! And then there are those who'd like to sleep for ever. So many demands, so much pressure. Then come the drastic and dramatic decisions. Anyway, let's put it to one side for now,' the doctor said cautiously.

There certainly were great expectations when it came to Hinata's paternity. Who wouldn't have them, being the first-born and the last member of the line? In his home, when they sat down at the table, he was the first to be served after his father. Then came his sisters in order of age, the youngest last – the poor hiyameshi-san.[208] His mother still kept up the ancient tradition of bringing him up so strictly that her own cousins had often accused her – only half in jest – of preparing her son for life as a warrior or a criminal. How many times did they catch her with the *Bushidō: The Soul of Japan*,[209] by Nitobe Inazō,[210] by her night-table at the side of her futon? It was a book she read intensively. Indeed, it is safe to say it was her favourite. He had no idea why, when there were so many interesting women's novels, she fought her way through such a dense, male-oriented canon, so chock-full of codes of ethics and written specifically for samurai. Perhaps it was the ideas her father had filled her head with. He had been a tough, gruff man on whom life had bestowed only daughters, and he had never been able to come to terms with his misfortune. So, to even up the score, he decided to treat them as if they were boys, even waking them up at four in the morning to take them hawking with his peregrine falcons. Meanwhile, their mother stayed at home frightened, sobbing, living in dread

---

[208] 'Lady of the Cold Rice': a term referring to younger brothers, who get their rice last, by which time it has gone cold.

[209] *The Way of the Warrior*.

[210] 1862–1933: an agricultural economist, author, educator, diplomat, politician during the pre-War period.

of the day he would returned one of her daughters to her with an eye missing. In the winter he would force them to bathe in water so cold that they had first to break the ice on the surface. They were forbidden to play with dolls and instead had to spend their afternoons perfecting their aim with the bow and arrow or revising their daily lessons in geography, history, arithmetic and astronomy. It became impossible to tell whether he wanted to turn them into soldiers or whether deep down he just wanted to vent the frustration of his boyless fatherhood on them.

No doubt Hinata's mother to some degree took after him, whom she idolized. After he died from falling into a deer trap he himself had set, she spent her life paying him a homage that surely went beyond anything he might have merited.

It was the same in all families: people hoped for a boy. Girls, on the other hand, had to be 'accommodated' and found a husband only for them to vanish with their in-laws. It was different with boys. Boys would follow in their father's footsteps, along a clearly drawn path. Their clan was in a way the very path that family history would take, flowing into descendancy like a river flowing into the sea. Therefore, it seemed quite natural for everyone to hope for a son, a young man to bear the noble name of his honourable father: Yamana. Continuing the line was a very serious responsibility. No one could ever imagine that one day his ancestors would end up drifting around the world with no one to take care of them with the proper rituals.

He simply presumed that belonging to a family whose name dated back to the Muromachi Period would be a great honour for Aiko and that she would understand the responsibility this entailed. That, of course, may have been the nub of the problem: Aiko had had the misfortune of being caught up in a world that had been stacked against her for more than a thousand years.

He had been introduced to several girls, daughters of his parents' friends every one. They came from families like the Toyotomis or the Urakimis or the Sakumas, who also had a kamon[211] similar to their own. They thought it might bring them luck and that there might be some design of destiny in it.

'That girl isn't in our class, Hinata,' his sisters had warned him. 'Besides, she laughs too much. She'll be trouble.' To which Hinata had sarcastically replied: 'She'll learn. You'll see. Didn't the chōnin[212] learn through the Shingaku?'[213] 'What is inherited is not stolen. You know that, don't you, Hinata? It isn't a matter of learning; it's just that she's made of different stuff. She'll bring shame on our family,' they insisted. 'You'll see.'

And so it was. She never learned, even if she could recite all of Confucius by heart. She never learned to hold her tongue because she was only wrapped up in herself. She never for one moment considered the commitment entailed either by his or his family's public image. 'She never learns because she holds too much water,' his aunt told him, alluding to Aiko's tendency to get emotional. Too much water? Precisely! It was that lack of inhibition that he'd fallen in love with; she was different! It had to be her and no other: light as a cloud and a little reckless, whose laughter

---

[211] Coats-of-arms of the various clans that existed during Japan's feudal period, linked to the history and philosophy of the ancestors. They began in the Heian period (794-1192). Later, in the Kamakura era (1192-1333), the Kamon was printed on the flags and banners carried by the samurai.

[212] Literally: 'Men of the cities', a name by which traders and craftsmen from the lowest castes were known.

[213] A philosophy or school of thought disseminated in the mid-eighteenth century, aiming to provide an ethical and cultural education for the chōnin. It borrowed elements from ancient religions, Buddhism and above all, Confusionism.

filled the room with bubbles and drove away the shadows that had haunted the bedrooms all those years since his father's death, the shadows of that house shunned even by the turtle doves nesting in springtime.

His mother called him selfish. How could it cross his mind that one could think 'al fresco'? Since when could one do whatever one fancied without taking into account matters of family, of the tradition and society into which one had been born?

'You know perfectly well you can have your affairs outside, with whomever you like,' she told him. 'But why bring a stranger into the heart of this family for the sake of it?'

Hinata innocently awaited a second look from his mother after her initial uncertainty, a look she never permitted herself. He realized then that he didn't fully know her, or rather, that he had kept battling against all the evidence and arguments echoing around the centuries-old walls and the portraits of his forebears. He was certain his mother had not found it at all easy to accept his decision, but he never imagined her resolve would, with the passing of the years, become more and more severe. There was no doubt she would have fought tooth and nail to preserve her dignity beneath the roof of the traditions of her line so that, by the end of her life, leaks would have begun to appear. To Hinata's mother Aiko represented a species foreign to her domain, a kind of alien invader in its most undiscovered and obscure dimensions, which led her little by little to cultivate a muzzled dread that prevented her from coming any closer. Perhaps aware her end was near, and even aware of the damage her words could do should they filter out beyond the house, that day when she had clashed with his wife in the kitchen she hadn't been able to take any more and she had let her know. She, who had always been so mindful of harmony as the keystone of human cohabitation, had acted out of reflex from her frustration and, most of all, from her fear – fear of that person whose insouciance made her feel morally beleaguered. So, in a gesture of self-immolation, she packed a small suitcase and left.

'I can't go on living in this house,' she secretly told the cook, who watched her leave with the expression of a whipped dog. 'Don't worry. Everything will be fine. You'll see, everything will be fine.'

All the same, knowing that this would compromise the good name of the house, she made it understood to the rest of the domestic staff and to those in the village who knew her, that she had to oversee certain repairs to her grandfather's estate. She made out that it would be complicated to come back every night to sleep and would therefore be staying there. In so doing she also implicitly trusted in the loyal discretion of the cook and his assistant, who had both been in the kitchen at the time and had witnessed her anger. What she didn't notice, however, was the delivery boys, who had arrived with the duck eggs and had squatted down at the back door when they had heard her yelling.

For a time his mother still came to visit them. She did so for the sake of public image, because it was unlike her and most strange – despite her explanations about repairing the house by the river – that she wasn't living with them. Besides, it was obvious that the only thing going on in that house on the river was an incessant scratching and scraping at walls that, already painted, she had decided to repaint. It stood to reason that no one needed to be there all day, watching the decorator rolling his roller up and down the wall or rinsing his brushes. So she would turn up, casual as the day was long, merely to silence the gossips, tidy the cupboards and tick off an inventory the length of her arm, making sure all was in order. Naturally it would be, as she was the only one who had the keys.

When summer came, she had all the shoji[214] changed for yoshizu[215] and had the tatami covered with ajiro[216] wicker to keep the rooms cool. She even took care of the ornaments in the tokonoma when the season passed from summer to autumn. But the day came when her visits stopped completely.

As for Hinata-san, his natural ability to navigate elegantly between two currents had deserted him, and he no longer had the patience to attempt yet another reconciliation between the two parties, as anyway it was hopeless. But on the other hand, something wasn't right with his wife. The cook claimed she curdled the sauce whenever she entered the kitchen.

The few times he had slept at Aiko's side – defeated more by exhaustion than anything else – when he had awoken, almost at daybreak, she hadn't been there. It happened not just once but several times. At first he would go back to sleep, thinking she had got up to go to the bathroom, but later, when he opened his eyes again and saw she hadn't returned, he would set about looking for her. Where could she be? He would search every inch of the bathrooms and kitchen. Searching for the sake of searching, he would even look behind the curtains. He knew she couldn't be in there, but he would look all the same. He wondered the first time if she might have walked out on him without so much as leaving a note, but a second later he saw her flit by the window like a ghost. On another such night – there were so many – Hinata found himself crossing the courtyard towards the water tank, torch in hand, having already explored the garden. Then, passing his father's

---

[214] Paper screens.

[215] Wicker screens.

[216] A hand woven rattan mat.

study, he heard a murmuring coming from within. The room had been closed off after his father's death, and no one had ever been allowed to enter. Had he not recognized Aiko's voice, he would have thought it was burglars. He automatically thought she must be on the phone to her sister, but why would she ring her from in there when there were so many telephones in the house? How had she got in? Why? What for? He looked at his watch – which never left his wrist, not even in bed – and saw that it was... four in the morning? Four! The cocks were starting to crow. He decided – good politician that he was – not to mention the matter. If she was up to something, he'd find out all the details before he acted, as was his style.

For several nights Hinata went on secretly following Aiko to the study, slipping away like a kuroko[217] through the shadows of the stage. She would creep in on tiptoe, turn on a light and remain there for hours. Meanwhile, he would merely wait before, perishing with cold or devoured by mosquitoes, going back to his study, where for some time now he had been spending his nights. He would toss and turn sleeplessly until, sick and tired, he got up again. Then he would go back to the courtyard and from there to the kitchen. He often thought of bursting into the study and surprising her: 'Aiko! What are you doing in here at this hour?' But he always managed to contain himself. His chance would come soon enough.

He had heard his father tell of a curious state that sometimes took hold of people and made them walk when they were asleep. An extremely inquisitive man, his father always knew things that others didn't. But the story in the psychiatry books came to life when he heard of a neighbour

---

[217] Literally, 'black man': an assistant on stage during a Kabuki theatre performance, who dresses all in black in order to remain 'invisible' to the audience.

of his at the summer-house by the sea who, fast asleep, would get up in the middle of the night and prepare a meal. She would cook till sunrise, filling the corridors with all manner of dishes, and then go back to bed. The following morning, she wouldn't remember a thing. On more than one occasion, the maid had slipped on the warabi,[218] until one day she ended up breaking her hip. To prevent further accidents, without having to leave his wife under lock and key, her husband decided to weave an intricate web of strings to halt her in her tracks before she could leave the bedroom. But in the morning they found the corridors laden with food, set out on tiny pieces of china, like a Greek mosaic. They came across the string on a chair, carefully wound up into a ball. Not even he, in his waking hours, could have unravelled it so perfectly.

---

[218] A gelatinous dessert.

The Lama

Overcome with worry, Hinata opened his heart to the Lama. They had been friends since childhood and he confided to him that one day, after his mother's death, he'd felt a real curiosity about his wife's nocturnal wanderings, so he was lead to the window of his father's study, which had been left half-open. To his surprise the lights went out at that exact moment and he thought he heard her cry out. Then the shoji of the entrance had slid open. He ran to the door and made out a shadow slipping quickly towards the house. Hinata-san had waited a few moments, breathless, before returning. He didn't want to confront her just yet.

After some time, to cap his confusion, he realized that Aiko's mysterious interlocutor – if he could be called that – was his late father, a man she had had never seen in her life.

'Hinata, Hinata...,' his friend the Lama consoled him. 'People speak to the ancestors, ask them for favours, tell them their sorrows... It's perfectly normal.'

But Hinata could tell the difference: it lay not in Aiko's words but in her tone.

'They sound more like the actions of someone out of their mind. In spite of what you say, it's very strange. She seems to have a relationship with my father that not even I had.'

'He's more like an imaginary friend,' the monk replied. 'We've all had one. In fact, I still do. Do you not think it possible to have imaginary friends?'

Hinata thought for a moment then replied:

'To tell you the truth, I've so often been accused of having "imaginary enemies" that... All right, maybe it is possible, yes.'

'Hmm...,' mused the Lama. 'Perhaps Aiko should go and see my brother, or maybe write to him. I'm sure she'll find a remedy. At least she'll have someone to talk to about these strange things that are happening to her, because my brother is a little peculiar too, you know. You've met him.'

'All right,' said Hinata in resignation. 'Drop by the house whenever you like and pick up the donation. I'll leave a cheque for Kondo-kun.'[219]

---

[219] Generally used to call men after his either last or first name by an older person than him on a higher position.

Awakening

It was the first day of the fourth lunar month, and the Minami[220] was blowing. A ray of sunshine filtering through the half-open shoji fell across her face and woke her.

'What day is it?' asked Aiko, crawling to the window.

She drew back the screen with effort and, sitting on the floor, gazed out into the garden. It all looked so green and brilliant again, as if it had come back to life, as if just washed with soap and water. As she took in the miracle of the blossoming utsugi[221] swaying carefree in the breeze, she felt suddenly transported to that little plastic bubble with Alpine cottages inside it that she used to play with as a girl: when she shook it, she would watch in glee as an instant snowfall blanketed the tiny landscape within.

She closed her eyes and breathed in the warm air of mountain cedars.

'What day is it?' she asked again.

Erizawa-san, coming in with a breakfast tray, was surprised to see her up.

'Honourable Madame! You've drawn the shoji!' she said.

She hastily put down the tray and ran to set the table.

'Would you like to get up for breakfast?'

---

[220] A south wind.

[221] The *Deutzia scabra* grows in the mountains, and flowers between May and June with double white flowers in clusters resembling snowflakes (yuki), which is why they are sometimes called *yukimi-os*. They reflect the brightness of the nights.

'Well I don't know...,' replied Aiko hesitantly. 'Did I use to get up before?'

'Not always...,' Erizawa-san answered. 'How are you feeling today?'

'What day is it?' Aiko asked again.

Several months had passed.

'Where have I been all this time?'

'You were lost, Honourable Madame, but now you're back! Come,' said Erizawa fondly, 'eat. Eat before it gets cold.'

Everyone in the house rejoiced when they saw her come out of her room. She felt as if her soul was whole again.

As if in dreamland, she could remember hearing someone say that the soul can be driven from the body by a fright. Afterwards it might float about in a kind of limbo, who knows where... But a shaman was needed to guide it back to the body, with chants and drum beats, known only to him. How did these things happen? She had no idea, and she was in no state to explain it or waste any more time on the matter. In that instant, like a bear emerging from its cave in the spring, her accumulated hunger was so fierce that all she could think of was eating. Everything looked juicy and succulent to her.

The days passed serenely, days of being reunited with her notebooks and belongings, days of rediscovering the intimate joy of old forgotten friends. She began to frequent the nearby onsen with her cousin Miura-san. There they'd stay until their fingertips looked like prunes and reminded them it was time to get out of the water. Then they'd sit and sip tea and eat wagashi[222] all the colours of the rainbow.

'We should go to Tokyo, you know, spend a few days there, get out of town... Don't you think?'

---

[222] Seasonal sweets to accompany tea.

'We'll have moss growing on us if we don't get out of here,' Aiko replied. 'Shall we have some more wagashi? I don't know why I'm so hungry. Mmm... the jelly ones, or the...'

Her cousin laughed out loud.

'What are you laughing at?'

'Nothing,' she answered, 'I was just remembering that theory you told me about the soul returning to the body, and I was wondering... if it really is yours that's come back or whether its place has been taken by the soul of a sumo wrestler.'

They both burst out laughing.

'At any rate, I hope he didn't get mine in return,' said Aiko. 'He'll break it on the high heels!' she laughed.

'Come on, let's go home. I'll fix you some soup, then I'll challenge you to a tournament,' she joked.

The way to Tokyo by train was straightforward enough, but her husband wouldn't hear of it.

'By train? To Tokyo? Alone?' he asked. 'It's a madcap scheme!' he said. 'I don't want you travelling by public transport alone.'

Aiko tried to persuade him that the street was just as public as any transport and that she hadn't been living on a magnolia petal.

'I've gone by train all my life, Hinata. It's what everyone does,' she said.

They were troubled times, however, and the Chairman felt more comfortable if she went by private car, like all his colleagues' wives. But Aiko still couldn't see what difference it made.

The Chairman got his doorman to spread the word in the neighbourhood that he was in need of a chauffeur, and eventually Tanaka Hikaru-san appeared, recommended by a neighbour whose mother had a small inn nearby.

'Mr Tanaka has been driving tourists to Sōnzan and Togednai in the van. I think he'll like it, being someone responsible. We really look on him as a member of the family. Unfortunately, with the economic crisis it's getting hard to pay his wages all year round. If you'll return him to me in autumn, I'd be most grateful.'

This was the gist of Mrs Fujiwara's words to the Chairman's doorman, Mr Kobayashi, and he was careful to pass them on as accurately as possible.

'Hmm…,' murmured the Chairman, rubbing his chin. 'So he wants him back in autumn?'

'That's what he said, Honourable Yamana-sama. He said autumn because it's the season this area's become famous for. Because of the maple trees,' he added.

'Have you been taking classes to improve your memory?'

'Oh, Honourable Chairman, my memory hasn't been so good of late!' he replied.

The Chairman smiled at him like someone listening to a child and added:

'Tell him to get in touch with my assistant, Kondo-kun,' and he nodded to his chauffeur to open the car door.

The boy had apparently made a good impression on him.

'He's still very young and inexperienced,' the Chairman remarked, 'but it's better like that. He'll be quick to learn our ways.'

Keiko-san

It was sheer coincidence that Aiko's sister was living in Odaiba at the time. She'd spent the last two years drifting in every direction about Japan, only to end up in Sapporo out of love for someone else's man who never returned her love as she would have wished.

'The fact is your sister's a little slow on the uptake,' her mother had once said, having lost all hope of her daughter coming to her senses.

But life hadn't turned out easy for Keiko. As a little girl she'd had to leave school after her father's gambling debts had left the family in ruin. Then she missed a year's studies, which, due to differences in the curricula, ended up being two. When she returned to classes at a state-subsidized school, Keiko-san was the eldest of the students and, an early developer, she was far taller than the others. She'd sit at a desk at the back and, although an average student, her classmates treated her like a half-wit. To make matters worse, she had started a tempestuous pre-adolescence that had covered her porcelain skin in burning red spots, which she tried to remove in the mirror but only managed to make things worse.

She sometimes seemed to have become enmired, but would then suddenly explode. She simmered in her solitude, brewing these explosions, which would come quite out of the blue, set off by the least little thing. Her mood was generally taciturn, her temperament quiet. Nothing amusing appeared to make her laugh. It was as if she came from another country where they spoke a different language. On other occasions she would laugh at things others couldn't make out. It was no surprise she was left out: she was too different from the others – too 'strange'. It may have been precisely this history of rejection that led Keiko to fall in love with the first man to tell her she was pretty. Had he not already been married, he would have tied the knot. His words were enough to make her decide she would follow him to the grave and, if possible, beyond it. So, from one day to the next, she upped and left, in pursuit of his inconstant wanderings. She spent nomadic years moving from one town to the next, doing whatever work she could find, driven by that fever of lethal love for her swallow-man, a man who had never laid a finger on her, not even in his dreams. Keiko didn't mind sleeping in stations or waiting for him in the rain for hours. Such was her devotion that it seemed to be directed more towards some miraculous saint than a man of flesh and blood: wherever he went, there she would be. Keiko pursued him constantly, anytime, anywhere. To find him she devised strategies of such complexity that an actual case of international espionage could easily have been inferred. But her tear-smudged twenty-page letters and her throat-cutting love poems – not to mention her surprise appearances just where and when she was least expected – drove the poor man, fearing the worst, to resort to threats against her. In his despair he told her he was leaving Sapporo that very afternoon and that she had better stop following him and his family or he would be forced to call the police.

In a fleeting moment of clarity Keiko realized he meant it. It almost certainly wasn't pride – for she had barely any shred of that left – but perhaps a flash of intuition that led her to picture herself lying shivering in the rottenness of a Hokkaido cell, dying of a broken heart. So she gathered up her few ragged possessions and left, not without first putting in writing the coercive reason for her departure on the pavement outside the guesthouse where he was lodging, along with all kinds of insults. She took the first train to Tokyo, her humiliation hidden away and rolled into a ball in the dark mire of her soul. She covered it up with the haughty certainty that 'There are men who always deny the love they feel for a woman' and that he was definitely one of those men. Nevertheless, she was sure he wouldn't have a moment's peace and that the memory of her would haunt him to the end of his days. No one would dare contradict her out of pity, but it was pathetic to hear her talk about it and she provoked an urge to tell her just to be quiet and stop talking such drivel.

But it so happened that, fifty years later, Keiko died – death still apparently being an inevitable mishap – and the object of her love survived her. It was one of life's ironies that the poor man ended up living in the precise place where Keiko had daubed her insults in red. Although ever fainter, he was forced to look at them every day when he left the house, and no matter how hard they tried to get rid of them, scrubbing the pavement time and again with turps, the kanji just went on bleeding, even half a century later. And so it was that he never knew a moment's peace. The memory of Keiko haunted him to his dying day.

Jachi-san

It was only to be expected that Keiko should be lost for a long time. More blinkered than usual, she seemed to be surrounded by a thick personal fog, from which she would emerge ever so slowly... even to say something as simple as 'hello'. By this stage her feet couldn't recognize anywhere that wasn't the inhospitable outline of her imaginary lover's footprints. As she had difficulty recognizing other people's feelings, she thought this might be the moment to embark upon a new stage in her relationship with her sister. Now that their mother was no longer around, they had no one but each other. Aiko said yes to everything just to break the trance, but she felt apprehensive. She had long suspected something in Keiko's head didn't work properly. Terrified by the idea of her taking refuge in her house in Hakone, Aiko pre-empted her, encouraging her to look for an apartment and offering to pay the rent.

To tell the truth, her only intention in her journeys to Tokyo, apart from to shake out the cobwebs, was to catch up with her old friend Suzuki-san, who went by the moniker of 'Jachi' – the little bee. Though they hadn't seen much of each other these last few years, they had stayed in touch by phone. Jachi had given Aiko all her support, putting her mother's things in order after her death, taking care of far more than just a good friend needed to. From then on, as agreed with Keiko, Aiko would only attend to her okā-san's spiritual matters. She therefore moved her remains from the cemetery in Tokyo to the one in Gora shortly after her passing.

Jachi-san had been widowed young, having married a Frenchman much older than herself. His parents had always held him to be an eccentric, and his family, who lived in the middle of the countryside in the vineyards of the Languedoc, predictably found it peculiar that he should marry an Asian. The only relationship they recognized with Asia was the one France had with its colonies, and it wasn't the done thing to marry colonists. Nor did they appear to have a clear grasp of territorial distinctions between China, Indonesia or Japan.

Jachi and her brand new husband moved to a petit hôtel in Saint-Germain-des-Prés, where they spent many a happy year together. They would visit Kyoto more and more frequently, until her husband ended up falling in love with the city and wanted to stay there till the day he died. Jachi-san never remarried and spent the rest of her days remembering her Jacques as if he were still alive. She lived alone in an old machiya[223] in the upper part of the city, from where one could see the mysterious Inari Jinja's[224] endless ghostly succession of Torii.[225] That house, which looked like a vision from sixteenth century etchings of the Floating World,[226] had been a gift from her husband. Its verandahs were lit with paper lanterns, and its labyrinthine rooms opened onto secret little gardens and natural ponds where carp lazed among water plants. The house was hidden behind a wall crowned with Chinese tiles and jasmines. It gave

---

[223] Traditional wooden houses in Kyoto.

[224] Temple of the Inari pantheon. One of their main goddesses is Ameno-uzume-no-mikoto, the protector of actors and the art of Kabuki. The temple is guarded by stone sculptures of foxes.

[225] Traditional stone arches found in sanctuaries, marking the border between the sacred and the profane. They consist of two columns crossed by two parallel beams usually painted crimson.

[226] Kyoto in the time of the printers of the ukiyo-e.

the impression of being an old okiya,[227] and on several occasions maiko[228] had even entered it, confused by its resemblance to the one around the corner. That 'style' – in the broadest sense of the word – was typical of Kyoto: nothing was what it seemed and, just like the maiko, anyone could find themselves utterly confused.

Jachi-san, on the other hand, spent almost all her time in Tokyo. She had a little apartment in the Roppongi district, one of the most prestigious areas of the city. There she would hold cultural soirées, where the guests tended to be artists, theatre performers, musicians and writers, as well as other rather eclectic characters. Though they had known each other since they were girls, Aiko often felt as though she were looking at a complete stranger. It even made her slightly uncomfortable, as if she were speaking to someone with a squint who, their eyes focusing independently on two places at once, made her doubt where she was standing.

One day, without prior notice, she took her to the apartment of a friend, one Hiyoshi-san, a well-known otoko geisha.[229] She did this as if it were the most natural thing in the world, only revealing her intentions as they were about to arrive at their appointment, twenty storeys up, in the lift. Aiko forced her to stop the elevator and get out. So they descended the stairs to the sixteenth floor.

'A lover?' she said in annoyance.

Jachi-san let out a raucous laugh.

'Don't get angry, Aiko-san! I wasn't being serious.'

Aiko raised her eyebrows.

'We've come all this way for you to introduce me to a lover? What kind of nonsense is this?'

---

[227] Houses where geishas live.

[228] An apprentice geisha.

[229] A male geisha.

'You remind me sometimes of the writer, Kaibara Ekiken-san. Have I never lent any of you his books?'

'No.'

'He's written several volumes on the comportment of women and bringing up children. Well, you understand me...,' she continued, 'a moralist in the Neo-Confucian vein.'

'Oh, Jachi-san! Don't talk to me about Kaibara. What is it you're suggesting?'

'I just want to introduce you to a friend of mine,' she replied.

'Who is he?'

'He isn't a "lover",' she said to calm her, 'he's a Taikomochi. Does that word mean anything to you?'

'There you go with the riddles again!' she complained.

'No, no, it isn't a riddle.'

'I really don't know... Well? How do you spell it? Can you write it in kanji for me?'

'Hmm... *C'était quoi? Je ne me souviens pas,*' she said in French, the language in which she thought, reckoned and swore. 'Oh, like this!' she said, writing in the air with her finger.

'Like the one who holds the drum?' asked Aiko.

Jachi-san explained that Taikomochi were no less than the original geishas of Japan, who entertained the daimyo.[230] Their role had gradually altered. First, it was the dance and the tea ceremony... and over the years they came to change their name, calling themselves otokogeisha,[231] because that was what they did: tell stories.'

'Tales,' she added. 'They would even go into battle with their lords!'

'I would never have imagined it,' said Aiko with surprise.

---

[230] Feudal lords.

[231] Storytellers.

'No, of course not. They're things they just don't teach you in school.' They both giggled like schoolgirls, with their hands over their mouths.

'You might say that nowadays they view themselves as "friends", though they tend to charge a pretty penny for their "friendship". Anyway, I thought it would do you good to meet one.'

Aiko burst out laughing.

'You've gone completely crazy! Let's go and have lunch and stop fooling around!' she said.

'But I'm serious! This friend of mine isn't just anyone.'

'Now, tell me, why do you think I'd need to pay for "friendship"?' asked Aiko.

'Well...,' Jachi answered, thoughtfully. 'One reason might be... because interesting people are very busy!'

'Goodness me!' she laughed. 'Now, that *is* a good argument.'

'Well?' asked her friend.

'I don't know, I don't know... Maybe just going to your gatherings will be enough for me. Besides, these luxuries must be very costly for a woman.'

'Yes, they are,' she confirmed.

'And what would I get for, say... a hundred-thousand-yen night?' asked Aiko.

Jachi-san laughed.

'Aaah... you're thinking about it! Well I imagine you'd go for dinner or drinks, or maybe out to a sumo tournament. You know... women don't go out alone.' Aiko listened in silence. 'What do you think a woman can do when her husband's always away or constantly entertaining his colleagues? Stay at home making pickles?' asked Jachi.

'Don't talk to me about pickles!'

'What's wrong with pickles?' she laughed.

'It's a long story... let's get back to what you were telling me.'

'Well, there isn't much more to say. Actually,' Jachi-san clarified, 'it wasn't exactly a lover I meant. Sorry if I offended you. I did it to *épater le bourgeois*, as we say in Paris. I knew you'd be shocked,' she whispered mischievously, 'but it wasn't my intention to offend. Really. I mean it. I'm sorry.'

Aiko breathed a sigh of relief.

'You didn't offend me, don't worry. You just surprised me. And then some!'

'He's more of a close friend,' she went on, 'closer than any you could meet at my gatherings. You know: a discreet shoulder to cry on, a good advisor who's been around and knows the ropes, someone really close who's there for you, who'll go for a walk with you… A man who can anticipate your needs and, why not, your desires.'

'Oh!' breathed Aiko in ecstasy. 'He sounds ideal, but… how much of it is true friendship?'

'Hmm… that's very hard to say at this stage, Aiko,' replied 'the little bee', glancing at her wrist-watch. 'We're going to be late! Come on, two more floors! If you don't like him, well then… we'll just leave and it's business as usual.'

'Actually, I'm not sure I understand the concept, but all right,' said Aiko. 'No obligations. If I don't like him, business as usual,' she repeated.

The Meeting

The young man her friend introduced was indeed very charismatic. He 'couldn't play the shamisen or dance with two fans,' as he said himself with a chuckle, but he'd finished his theatre studies at the National Conservatory of Kabuki Arts[232] and Noh or Nogaku Theatre,[233] and this had taught him great expressiveness and a feel for the stage. Aiko saw in the young Hiyoshi-san an extension of herself, someone whom she would have liked to be. They appreciated the same things and picked up on details that others overlooked. In time they fell to discussing the problems of life, subjects that, considered taboo, weren't generally brought up. The effect that these conversations had on Aiko was entirely liberating.

'Gohatto…,'[234] he mused. 'Funny how culture works, isn't it? There are no end of things that have been reinterpreted and condemned today, but that were accepted in their original context. And vice versa, of course. The perception of what is or isn't gohatto, with some rare exceptions, changes more often than one might want to think.'

'What you're saying gives me a peculiar feeling…,' said Aiko.

'Peculiar? In what way?' asked Hiyoshi-san.

---

[232] Dance and theatre performance linked to the Buddhist religion.

[233] Japanese lyric drama.

[234] Taboo.

'I always supposed that what's gohatto goes back to the dawn of time, to something handed down from somewhere... supreme.'

'That, my dear, is precisely the idea: you're on the right track. Insofar as you're starting to feel that, you're fulfilling the expectations that lie behind social rules.'

'I feel like I'm a bunraku.[235] We don't even question these things... How is that possible?'

'It's difficult. All the more so when it's something for which there have been no words... just silences made eloquent by looks, for instance. That's where the power of those kinds of rules lies. There are things that words daren't touch and that, perhaps precisely because of that, carry tremendous weight... Do you see what I mean? They're imprinted on the body.'

Aiko listened, open-mouthed. At that moment all she could take in was more down to intuition than reason. She was lost in intangible territory, but it didn't matter; she was enjoying it.

'Are you an intellectual?' she asked naively.

Hiyoshi let out a loud laugh.

'You're very sweet,' he replied. 'Sorry... am I confusing you?'

He accompanied every phrase with a perfect gesture that lent his words profound drama. She was mesmerized by the way he expressed. It mattered not a jot what he said, but how he said it, and it was this difference that made her want to agree even with something she might reject in principle, just to preserve the magic of being swept away and to keep the conversation flowing.

In the world she inhabited – there in her mountain home as she was wont to call it – some things were taken as read.

---

[235] A puppet.

One avoided speaking about transcendent matters, for example, as they sparked conflict and opened yawning chasms of opinion, they were not generally spoken or discussed but, as Hiyoshi-san mentioned, made eloquent in their most subtle ways. It was quite common and even reasonable, since everything possible had to be done to preserve harmony, which is the only thing that allows people to live together. But feelings will out.

'So, otoko geisha...,' said Aiko, finishing off her rice wine 'I've never met an otoko geisha before.'

'Well, for a start... that's my masu...'[236] He smiled as he picked up Aiko's cup.

'Oh! I am sorry,' she laughed. 'I think I've had too much to drink. I was asking you about...'

'About my profession?' he interrupted. 'You know the saying about "the cycle", don't you?'

'The cycle?' Aiko repeated, uncertain what he was referring to.

'It goes more or less like this,' he replied. 'Taikomochi agete suideno taikomochi.' Or, in other words, a man who spends his time and money on taikomochi will be ruined. His wife will throw him out and he'll be left with no option but to become a taikomochi himself. Which was exactly what happened to me,' he added with a laugh.

'That saying must surely be from the ancient capital, Edo,' said Jachi. 'In the Edo Period it was believed that the Edokko[237] were reduced to living in poverty by their love of entertainment. The Kyotoites,[238] by their love of dresses, and those from Osaka by their love of food.'

---

[236] A small square wooden container formerly used for measuring out rice and later for drinking sake.

[237] People who were born and raised in Edo, old Tokyo.

[238] From Kyoto.

'Well, I can see nothing's changed in all these years,' chuckled Aiko.

Laughter rang out in the little room.

Aiko had started to feel hungry, again.

'Aiko, I declare you an honorary citizen of Osaka!' said Jachi, laughing. 'Let's go to the teppanyakki across the road. It'll be my treat!'

As the days went by, she grew closer to her new friend. She confided to him her most intimate secrets and asked his advice on more than one occasion. Whenever their conversation took a melancholy turn, he would try to cheer her up by telling her stories he knew she'd love to hear. He also recommended she read a certain collection of storybooks, thinking they'd amuse her.

'They're called Seisuishou,'[239] he explained. 'They were compiled around 1600. Maybe I can find some commentaries or essays to lend you.'

'That's very kind of you. Were they written by courtesans, like Sei Shonagon?'[240]

'They were written by Anarakuan-san,' he replied, 'so, you've read Sei Shonagon, have you?' he asked in surprise. 'How curious!' he smiled.

Aiko told him about her incursions into her father-in-law's library and her curiosity about the Floating World and the geishas after getting to know the ukiyo-e.[241]

'That was when I realized I knew hardly anything about my own country and its customs,' she said.

'Don't worry,' he reassured her. 'That's true of most people. Our history and literature are so very rich... Take theatre

---

[239] Translated as 'The laughter that banishes sleep.'

[240] An author and courtesan who wrote *The Pillow Book* around the year 1000, describing events in the Imperial Palace.

[241] Engravings or prints made mostly in the Edo period.

plays, for example. You've studied the dramatic arts, so you know they started in the sixth century! What was happening in the West at that time? They were living in caves. And to make matters worse, after studying all you can imagine about Japanese history, literature and language, you inevitably end up tying yourself in cultural knots over...'

'...China,' they chimed in unison and burst out laughing.

'Exactly,' he said, 'but... Heavens, you do surprise me!'

'That's because my father-in-law thought just the same, so I've been told,' Aiko answered. 'That all things Japanese lead to Chinese culture.'

'That's right, very true. We, Japanese don't like to admit it...'

'Not at all. We're too proud of our heritage,' laughed Aiko.

'Then we shouldn't be ignorant of it...'

'What I've told you was from my father-in-law's harvest. It isn't mine, I have to acknowledge,' she insisted modestly. 'He knew an awful lot about Taoism and Confucianism.'

'I appreciate your humility,' he replied, 'and yet you surprise me. It doesn't matter if knowledge is "borrowed"; it always is, in a way... That's something I've always wondered: where is knowledge found? Is it something given that one simply discovers? It's a mystery, isn't it? But the fact is that, of all the information the world presents to us, one tends to pay attention to certain things rather than others.'

'Tell me more about yourself,' she implored.

'For my part...,' he continued, 'they call on me to entertain at traditional banquets and royal galas, I teach a few courses at cultural centres in Osaka and Kobe, and I also write articles in periodicals. Look,' he said, handing her a copy of the Sunday newspaper lying on the table, 'I wrote a short one here... There isn't much else really. Then there's my work, of course. I describe it as "personalized",' he added.

Their lunches would often go on until the Kabuki shows began and then would come the cocktails and rendez-vous with friends, always punctuated by witty japes from Jachi, who was invariably the life and soul of the party.

'You must go to Kyoto. It's a whole different world! Has Jachi-san never told you about it? Tell her to take you to her house, up in the heights of the city. Tell her to introduce you to her "sect",' her friend said jokingly.

One of the leading lights in those days was Tamasaburo Bando, a very young Kabuki Master. Her new friends professed boundless admiration for this artist, and Aiko wanted very much to meet him.

Overhearing her remark, someone interrupted: 'What? You mean you haven't met him yet? Hiyoshi-san, you have to introduce her!'

'Do you know him?' Aiko asked her friend.

'Listen, come to his dressing room with me after the show next week, darling, and I'll introduce you to him,' chimed a camp young man in a flowery shirt.

Aiko felt as if she were dreaming. So it was that she had the privilege of attending, yet again, the presentation of Sagi Musume,[242] this time in the company of Jachi and Hiyoshi-san.

'My husband used to say I looked like the heron,' she whispered.

---

[242] *The Heron Maiden*, a dance classic.

Hiyoshi-san looked at her admiringly.

'Only...,' Aiko went on, 'in the scene where the heron dies.'

'Well now!' her friend said, 'that *is* encouraging!'

Keiko-san and her demons

'On the record' Aiko slept at her sister's apartment for many months, while actually staying at her friend Jachi's. So it was that one night, her husband, back from his trip earlier than expected, surprised her when he called her at Keiko's house and she wasn't there. It wasn't that Aiko was lying; no, she was just being thrifty with the truth.

'I'm telling you he's called,' said her sister, urging her to return immediately. 'Get yourself here right now, he's calling back in half an hour!' she exclaimed. 'Don't force me to make up any more stories, please!' she begged.

'What stories? You can perfectly well tell him I've just popped out to the... chemist's' Aiko replied.

'But he said he'd call you back in half an hour. Will you be able to make it on time?' she asked.

'I'll try,' she replied testily.

Aiko said goodbye to her friends and took a taxi, her chauffeur being away until the following day.

'It's unbelievable,' thought Keiko after hanging up on her sister. 'I have to tell her over and over again because she just doesn't understand but me I never learn either she's always used me as cover for her nights out but that's it this time it's over I'm sick of it all my life she's used me making me think this would be a special time for the two of us but no she doesn't give a damn she lands me in some really tight spots but I don't forget I haven't forgotten everything she put me through all those years ago on our holidays... she said the same thing to me back then I remember it well she said that those holidays were all about me her dear sister and that she would have other opportunities in the future but it wasn't true they weren't my holidays the first chance she got she hooked up with that guy at the bar the one with the amazing Abyssinian eyes left me on my own she did yes on my own and I had to get back to the ryokan in the middle of the night and risk getting a double telling-off from mother one for running off and another for leaving her there with those guys smoking and drinking beer out of the can and those girls who were so drunk they were cross-eyed... sitting on the laps of those guys smoking and drinking and grabbing them hard by their hair while the girls laughed what kind of holiday was that and that Chairman that Hinata-san how could he think of it a man of the world like him what was he thinking about when he chose that place walking around gawping at her only thinking of buying kimonos for my stupid sister so expensive I couldn't have earned that much in three years and on top of that when I got back jumping over the frozen stones the hanao from my geta snapped... and I knew then and there seeing as that brings the worst of luck I knew something terrible was about to happen... and I think that must also have been why I've been so unlucky my whole life I've never had any luck with men because I'm ugly no man with amazing Abyssinian eyes has ever desired me and I don't have water reflections in my hair like my sister who spent her time dancing happily like the morning light in the apple orchards my skin's like the surface of the moon not as soft and smooth as the inside of oyster valves and I... I was frightened and didn't know what would become of her and at the same time I was thinking I'd feel free forever free of her beauty and her perfect mouth if anything happened to her and I'd have to look after my mother forever and she'd lull me with her words You're my baby girl and now we're alone just the two of us for each other no she has no right but she'll never change and here I am… I feel so incredibly alone,' she said to herself and burst into tears.

'What's the matter, Wata-chan?[243] Why are you crying?' asked Aiko, stepping out of the bathroom with a towel wrapped around her head like a turban.

'Sorry,' said Keiko-san, blowing her nose into a paper tissue, 'I just got a bit worked up. I'm very tired.'

'Well it's all right now,' Aiko consoled her. I'm here. You can stop worrying now, right?'

'Yes, all right,' replied Keiko-san with a grim smile and disappeared behind the kitchen noren.[244]

'And then on top of that she speaks to me as if nothing had happened and says What's the matter Wata-chan what does she think the matter is can't she see what the hell she doesn't see a thing she lives in her bubble she goes out on the town with those theatre types and leaves me to cover up for her and palm her husband off with explanations when she knows perfectly well I'm terrified of him,' she thought, blowing her nose again. 'He's no fool… and now it's night time and she's all relaxed watching TV in her pink cotton pyjamas and waiting for her husband to call while I… I'm a bag of nerves all my clothes are creased and I haven't had time to iron them for thinking about it all while she's out having fun I have to stay here by the phone chewing my nails and scratching my arms and picking the scabs till they bleed thinking that one day the Chairman will suspect something and have her followed then he definitely won't like what he finds out and will have her killed tired of her mischief because… well I'm tired too I've never meant anything to her I was always invisible when mum died and

---

[243] Wata from Watanabe, Keiko's full name being Keiko Watanabe. First names are sometimes shortened and '-chan' added as an affectionate way of addressing a girl.

[244] A dividing curtain made of two or more short cloths.

I had to take care of everything in the house by myself because Princess Aiko was exhausted,' she sneered. 'And me I was exhausted too maybe she thought it was easy for me I loved Okā-san too and it was really hard having to open all her drawers and remove her belongings the bathroom cabinet her medicine boxes interrupted by that death such an absurd death to this day I wonder if it could have been prevented if Aiko hadn't got that silly snobby idea into her head of the damned golf umbrella if she'd taken her usual oil-paper umbrella with the bamboo rods maybe she wouldn't have gone as far as she did in search of who knows what she wouldn't have relied on it just as I shouldn't have relied on Aiko... of course anything she said to my mother she'd go and do as she was told she was always her favourite yet it wasn't her but me... I was the one who had to throw away her little slippers and her little chequered apron.'

Great tears began to roll down her face.

'And that wasn't all I had to take care of damn it! lots of other things I'll never tell her about like her son and that business with the photos the shameless hussy I'll never tell her there are many things she doesn't know or have any idea about and I'll never ever tell her and that idiot who drove me crazy with all those promises of marriage that he never kept only to end up threatening to call the police! I hate them! I hate them so much!,' shrieked Keiko to herself, stifling her sobbing.

Aiko came into the kitchen at that moment, interrupting her sister's tempestuous ruminations. She saw her sitting there, looking like an orphaned child. Her fists clenched, her eyes red, her gaze boring into the knife drawer. She crouched down beside her and took her tense fists in her hands.

'Are you all right?' she asked her, passing her a tissue. 'Shall I make you a cup of tea?'

270

'I'm doing just fine,' answered Keiko, clearing her throat, 'thank you. Don't trouble yourself, little sister. You're always looking out for me.'

'It's no trouble. You deserve it more than anyone,' replied Aiko, putting the water on to boil.

❖

Her husband had gone away on business and wouldn't be back for at least a week. Aiko seized her chance to go to Kyoto and spend a few days with her friend Jachi, who had stayed behind to take care of some family matters.

It was night-time when they arrived. They went to the house and put their overnight cases in one of the rooms, then set out for a bar whose terrace overlooked the Ta-kase-gawa.[245] Jachi met up with an old friend who was a well-known engraver. Something about his outfit made him look like a castaway. He had long grey hair tied in a ponytail and old, round glasses that magnified his appearance of helplessness.

'The best thing that can happen to you' she explained to her, 'is to be in with the local artists. This place has a secret life that Tokyoites would never dream of. Isn't that right, chéri?' she asked her friend, who nodded with a smile.

Aiko didn't want to go with them, as she felt she would be in the way and preferred to leave them alone. She was hopeful that Jachi might fall in love again. She knew the friends from the bar and decided to stop by for a few moments.

'Go back to the house when you get bored,' said Jachi, pointing her fan at her. 'You know the address. I'll leave the key under the stone chimera in the garden. Make yourself at home.'

---

[245] A canal in the Gion area of Kyoto.

The friends made room for her and immediately offered her something to drink. She meant to stay just another half an hour, then order a taxi and spend the night at Jachi's.

An hour must have passed when, glancing towards the bar, Aiko froze. There stood Hiyoshi-san with a woman who, while very beautiful, might have been his mother. Aiko tried to act naturally, as if she had seen nothing, and started pulling on her coat to leave. But Hiyoshi saw her and came over.

'What a surprise, Yamana-sama, seeing you here! Where did you come from? Where are you going?' he asked seductively.

'Well, I was just on my way home,' replied Aiko nervously.

'Home? In Gora?' he asked.

'Where else?'

Hiyoshi-san took her by the arm and, as he did so, Aiko had a sudden flashback to what had happened twenty years ago in that bar by the beach.

'Come,' he said, holding her softly but firmly.

'Please let go of me,' replied Aiko.

'You're going home to Gora at this hour? Are you sure? I have an apartment here. You can stay if you like,' Hiyoshi said intimately. 'It's no trouble.'

'No,' she answered. 'You're very kind, please let me go!'

Hiyoshi couldn't understand what was going on. Why was she reacting like this?

'I could make us tea... or something,' he insisted, as the woman he'd been flirting with tugged at his other hand as if to separate him from Aiko. 'In fact, I could do with a coffee myself,' he said, rubbing his face to wake himself up. 'Wait for me, please,' he added, leaving her alone and disappearing behind the noren painted with white chrysanthemums.

She waited a few moments for him to return. She felt foolish. She tried to work out what to do but couldn't think straight. All she wanted to do was to break down and cry.

She felt hurt and couldn't understand why. Was she jealous? Her reaction was to go to the counter and order a taxi. Hyoshi-san appeared behind her and, almost brushing her neck with his lips, asked her:

'What's the matter? Aren't you happy to see me? Why the bad mood?' Aiko didn't answer. 'What's wrong?' he insisted.

He guessed that maybe he'd gone too far and that this was Aiko's way of letting him know in no uncertain terms. Was he just a toy to her and she despised being seen there with him? Perhaps... when all was said and done, she *was* just another client. What had he been thinking, getting himself involved like this?

'Hyoshi-san,' said Aiko, 'perhaps it was a mistake coming here.'

He stood there in silence, waiting for her to go on, but Aiko pushed herself forcefully away from the counter and said no more. Hiyoshi felt attacked and confused. All was lost. He responded with sarcasm:

'A mistake? I'm sorry, but what are you talking about? I never asked you to come. Or did I? Did I ask you and I don't remember?' he laughed.

Aiko pulled a sour face.

'I'm sorry,' repeated Hiyoshi apologetically, 'I'm very drunk. I'm not normally like this.'

Making for the exit, Aiko stopped for a moment and looked at him. He looked so handsome and so unabashed in the light of the paper lantern. Maybe she was in deeper than she wanted to be.

'But where will you go at this time of the night?' he asked, all stiffness again. 'Would you like to go to a hotel?'

'I'd like to go home,' she replied.

Hiyoshi-san clicked his tongue. He'd ruined it. He seemed to have got everything back to front and didn't dare try to clear things up lest he made matters worse. Yet he felt attacked for no reason and tried to control the situation for the sake of his wounded pride. He could see she was upset at finding him there, under those circumstances... Things were always clear with his clients but not, apparently, with her.

'Clients?' asked Aiko, confused.

Unable to grasp why she would ask such an obvious question at this stage in the game, Hyoshi-san stared at her and answered:

'I thought we both had a contract. A contract, even a tacit one...,' he faltered, 'is still a contract.'

Even if he'd given her unlimited credit – which effectively he had, not having seen a cent yet – they clearly had accounts to settle.

Hyoshi-san had had no intention of saying it, but he was in his cups and it had been the first thing that came to mind.

'A contract?' she asked. 'I thought what we had was a friendship, not a contract.'

'Friendship? Oh, yes! Of course!' Hiyoshi-san replied sarcastically. 'Yamana-sama, please do excuse me,' he said, addressing her in keigo.[246]

'But... aren't we friends, you and I?' she asked in a last-ditch attempt to clarify things.

'Yamana-sama...,'[247] the boy stammered.

Aiko could see humiliation looming and tried to head it off:

'I see...'

Having said this, she picked up her bag and coat and strode swiftly towards the exit across the whirlpool that yawned at her feet. He stopped her and asked her:

---

[246] The ultimate level of formality, Hiyoshi-san's attitude is clearly ironic.

[247] Hiyoshi switches from a familiar tone, calling her by her name, to using Yamana and the suffix -sama, which would be the more correct expression when speaking to a customer. He thus puts a considerable distance between them with his way of expressing himself.

'Didn't Suzuki-san mention anything?'

Yes, she had indeed mentioned it. She had been perfectly clear and had talked a blue streak about Hiyoshi-san's work, but for some reason the social custom of keeping everything wrapped in ambiguity led her to make the mistake.

'Forgive me, Yamana-sama. Besides, I never expected to find you here. As you can see, I'm working. But I can arrange things and leave here with you.'

'And how much will charge me for that?' she asked him, regretting her words.

Aiko knew she should have left as soon as the conversation had begun. Why had she stayed? It was enough. She made for the door, ignoring Hiyoshi-san. He called her name a couple of times, but a new fire took hold inside her.

'Go back to your client,' she told him, looking over her shoulder, 'she's waiting for you.'

He turned in the same direction as Aiko's gaze. The woman was sitting at the bar, her elbows resting on the counter behind her. When Hiyoshi turned back, Aiko had disappeared.

She walked and walked through the icy night to the door of the Centre Hotel, which was locked. She rang the bell. The old night-watchman opened the door, rubbing the sleep from his eyes. She asked him if he'd be so kind as to call her a taxi.

'A taxi? At this time of the night?' the man asked, scratching his head. 'You'll be lucky to find one, miss,' he grumbled.

Aiko waited until the old man finally came out and said:

'It's on its way.'

Aiko stared at him blankly.

'*The taxi.* It's coming.'

Ten minutes later a car pulled up outside the hotel. The driver opened the back door and she got in. Then he shut and locked the door. Aiko was overcome with sudden panic at finding herself alone with a man, shut inside a vehicle she couldn't leave by her own means, in the middle of the deserted night.

'To Gora, please' she ordered the driver.

'Excuse me?'

'To Gora, please,' she repeated.

'Gora?' the driver asked, astonished.

'If you'd be so kind,' Aiko replied.

'Gora... in Hakone Machi?' he inquired.

'Yes.'

'But... do you know where that is...? It's nearly three hundred miles from here,' the driver explained.

'Yes, of course,' Aiko answered. 'I know where it is, I live there.'

'In Kanagawa,' he insisted.

'Yes, precisely!' replied Aiko, losing her patience. 'Gora in Hakone Machi, Kanagawa Prefecture. Can you take me there or not?' she asked impatiently.

'Hmm...,' the taxi driver hesitated, 'but we'll be getting there at dawn.'

'I don't mind. If you're willing to take me, then let's get going,' replied Aiko.

The taxi driver settled into his seat, rubbed his hands, cleared his throat and they pulled out.

'Hmm... Hakone Machi... Hakone Machi...,' he repeated to himself.

Aiko was shaking. She prayed that he knew the way. The scenes from that night flashed across her mind. She wondered whether everything would be forgotten by tomorrow, just as Jachi used to say: 'It doesn't matter if you get drunk and fall over in the middle of the bar. It doesn't matter if you sleep with a man you've just met in the onsen or tell your boss he's a total fool. No one "remembers" anything in the morning, and it isn't because they've forgotten.'

Half an hour had passed since they'd set off and Aiko's stomach was churning with nerves. Everything had suddenly become a nightmare.

'Stop the car!' Aiko said urgently. 'I have to go to the toilet.'

'The toilet? Here? That's impossible!' said the driver. 'We're in the middle of the motorway. There's no toilet around here, Ma'am, and it's at least two miles to the next service station.'

'Stop the car! Now, please!' she begged. 'It's an emergency.'

'The driver looked in his mirror, hesitated a moment and finally pulled over onto the hard shoulder. The motorway was deserted.

'Let me out, please!' she begged.

The driver unlocked the door and she headed out as fast as she could to some tall grass. It was cold. She ran across the field and hid behind some bushes. Crouching there, doubled up from the shooting pain in her belly, she began to weep.

'Are you all right?' shouted the taxi driver from the hard shoulder.

'Yes!' answered Aiko, wiping her nose and tears on her coat sleeve. 'I'm perfectly fine!'

It was daybreak by the time they reached Gora.

She was amazed to realize she had never held the keys to her house. She had insisted so much on holding the keys to the kura, the inside rooms and the wardrobes... but never the keys to outside. It was the doorman who opened and closed the gate, and everyone had always been in the garden by the door to greet her.

'How odd...!' she thought.

Aiko managed to steal in like a thief through the bamboo canes growing at the back of the garden then, entering the haven of home, she crossed the living room with its scent of wood and tatami.

'Ah... home, sweet home!' she breathed deep.

Her futon was laid out on the floor. Even when she decided to stay over in Tokyo, they always turned her bed, every night, in case she changed her mind and decided to come back. She went into the bathroom and threw her clothes into the laundry basket. She sat on the shower stool, soaped herself, rinsed herself and sank back in the overflowing cedar bath tub, where she lay for a long time. Then, worried in case she fell asleep in the water and utterly defeated by exhaustion, she went to her room and fell into bed.

Although the relationship with her husband had changed so much in recent years, Aiko suddenly felt a profound desire to feel his arms around her. She realized that, whatever happened, Hinata was still her iyashi.[248]

'My eyes, having seen it all,
turned to the white chrysanthemums.'

---

[248] Like her comforting relief.

Hinata had with him a package for the president of the Port Authority. It was from his son-in-law, who lived in Paris and contained a jewel designed especially by a Fabergé jeweller for his parents' anniversary. And it had to be sent by special delivery in the coming month as the sender had planned. He thought Tanaka-kun might do him the great favour.

'I have to speak to him to explain the importance of the gift and how it's to be delivered,' he told his wife. 'Tell him I'll call him.

Aiko nodded. She'd tell the boy as soon she had the opportunity, the following Tuesday. A few days later she received a call from Hiyoshi-san, despite all such contact being strictly forbidden. Her husband, as one might imagine, wouldn't take kindly to her friendship with a man who wasn't one of her cousins and Hiyoshi-san was wary of writing to her, not knowing whose hands the letter might fall into.

The weather had been stormy in the mountains and some telephone lines were down, which meant the reception was poor. Aiko could only catch isolated words but could make no sense of them.

'You can't call here,' she told him, lowering her voice. 'Please, tell me what I owe you for the work you did on my dress,' she went on, making it sound as if she were talking to her dressmaker.

Hiyoshi-san refused to take her money, but at Aiko's insistence – and to be over and done with it – he replied that she could make a 'gesture' to him if she so desired. She told him she would pay her debts and, almost as if trying to humiliate him, she informed him she was in no way prepared at that time to travel to Kyoto, where Hiyoshi-san was. The latter, seeing Aiko's annoyance, suggested she could give the money to a friend who worked at the Four Seasons Hotel in Tokyo. He would arrange for him to pick it up on Tuesday afternoon. Aiko still needed to know who to give the money to. She thought it would perhaps be best to put a stop to this business once and for all and to put this phase of her life behind her.

'Who should I leave the money with and where?' she asked again.

'Write, please (...) -san leave the envelope with (...). Aiko, can you hear me?' his voice was breaking up.

'I can't hear you very well. What did you say?' she asked, moving the receiver away from her ear as it kept bursting with unexpected high-pitched noises.

'Hotel Four Seasons (...) Ke (...) ro Hikaru-sama.

'Who, sorry? What was the surname?'

Aiko heard a click. They'd been cut off. She took an envelope from her husband's desk and started to write the first name. She'd call back later to find out the surname. She was feeling nervous. Just then her husband walked into the study. A cold sweat ran down her back. She picked up the half-written envelope and put it in her bag.

'What are you doing?' he asked.

'Nothing, dear husband,' she replied, taking a glove from her bag, 'I'd just lost a glove and... what a scatter-brain! I'd left it in your study! Come on, let's have lunch.'

Knowing that Hinata-san was such a worldly man, it was hard to believe he would buy a single word of the glove story.

On the Tuesday morning she went to wait for her chauffeur as usual. The scent of the wisteria warm in the sun drifted to her from the front gate.

Her husband came out into the garden and greeted her.
'Hello.'

'Hello,' she answered.

He sat next to her on the bench. The day was cold.

'How lovely!' Aiko whispered, closing her eyes.

'It won't last,' replied Hinata. 'There's a storm forecast for this afternoon. Don't be too long, and watch out for mudslides on the mountain,' he warned.

'Don't worry, I won't be back late.'

'Ah, Aiko!' he added, making her start. 'Before I forget, remind Tanaka-kun about that business I mentioned to you. Find out if he's willing to do me that favour for the Port Authority President's son. I'll call him as soon as I have a minute.'

'I don't remember... what favour?'

'The one I told you about, Chairman Utamaro's jewel. Tell him I need him to do me a favour and that I'll call him,' he said, getting up from the bench. 'It's complicated to explain. I need to speak to him personally.'

'Very well, I'll tell him,' answered Aiko with a smile.

Sitting opposite the row of persimmon trees, she noticed how she balanced the little lizard skin handbag on her knees just the way her mother used to, despite there still being an hour to go before her appointment. Dark clouds heralded a storm in the distance. Her husband might be right: she oughtn't to be late back. Tanaka-san appeared at the gate and they greeted each other.

'Oh, Tanaka-kun,' said Aiko, 'before I forget! My husband needs you to do him a favour, but he'd like to speak to you personally because he has to give you precise instructions. He's very busy this week. Anyway, he told me he'd call you. All right?' asked Madame.

Tanaka hesitated, then nodded politely.

'Of course, Yamana-sama, anything I can do to help.'

They got into the car and drove away from Hakone. At that hour there were long queues on the way into Tokyo, and Aiko wanted to come back to Gora on the same day. By leaving early she could drop in at the depachika [249] in Mitsukoshi, [250] go to the hairdresser's, have lunch with Jachi and finally head for the hotel. There she would hand over that damned envelope containing the cheque – if, that was, she had been able to get in touch with Hiyoshi-san by then to find out the addressee's full name. So far she hadn't been able to contact him all morning.

'Tanaka-kun, if you'd be so kind,' she said, 'come and pick me up from the Four Seasons Hotel at half past three. I'll be waiting at the door. We'll return home today. Then remember to take the car back so that they can take care of the upholstery.'

'Yes, Madame Yamana,' he replied, 'I'll be there at half past three.'

It was twenty past three before Aiko reached the hotel in a taxi, ready to hand over the envelope, although she still hadn't been able to get hold of Hiyoshi-san. She headed for the reception and asked the concierge if he knew anyone by that name.

'Yes,' he replied, 'Kentaro-san. Kentaro Hikaru-san is the assistant to the public relations manager, but I'm afraid he isn't in today.'

Aiko asked him to please pass on the envelope she had for him, and the concierge agreed.

'Of course, Madame! I'll give it to him tomorrow morning, as soon as I see him.'

She looked for it in her bag, but... she couldn't find it.

'What... I put it in here! Did I take it out afterwards?' she wondered.

She couldn't remember.

---

[249] The 'delicatessen' in the basement of shopping centres, usually called the first or second basement.

[250] A prestigious shopping centre.

'Yamana-sama,' she heard. It was Hiyoshi-san's voice. When she turned around, she saw him standing there, impeccably dressed in a pearl grey Chinese jacket.

'Heavens above, you surprised me!' said Aiko.

'Yamana-sama… How are you?' asked Hiyoshi-san.

'I'm fine. And you?' she said coldly. 'You're looking well, too… I mean, I've survived,' she answered with a smile.

'I've survived too, as you can see,' her friend replied, 'and I've been waiting for you.'

'Look, Hiyoshi,' Aiko explained uncomfortably, 'I can't be seen here with you. I came with the intention of handing the money to your friend, but there's been a mishap and I haven't brought it with me. I don't know what could have happened or where I might have left it…,' said Aiko anxiously.

'Don't worry,' he tried to calm her. 'At least, not about me. Is it possible that you've dropped it?'

'I don't know. What a mess! I'd left a note inside!'

'I hope it isn't a note that might compromise you…'

'I had a cheque for you,' she said. 'We'll have to set up another meeting. Well, how very annoying!' she went on, feeling lost and a strong urge to cry.

Hiyoshi watched her, overcome with sympathy.

'I came all the way here for the sole purpose of…,' said Aiko. 'The only thing I hope is that I didn't drop it in the garden at home…'

'I hope you didn't!' he replied. 'Have you had lunch yet?'

'Yes, of course. I've just seen Jachi but… I have to go now. Please, let me call you this week so we can arrange another meeting. I promise my debts shan't go unpaid.'

'Yamana-sama, please, don't worry about that. I'd like us to talk,' he insisted. 'There are some things I need to say to you. If you would kindly listen to me'

'We'll have to leave it for another time,' she replied nervously. 'I'm sorry about everything that's happened but I have to be going now. You'll get your cheque, don't worry,' she repeated.

'It was all a misunderstanding...'

'No. It was I who misunderstood that what we had, I mean "our friendship"... Anyway.' Aiko was on the verge of saying something she didn't want to.

'You live and learn. Right?' she added. 'Can I give you a lift anywhere?' she asked, heading for the door.

She was anxious to leave the hotel lobby, but at the same time wished that moment would never end.

'I'm going to Ginza,' he replied.

'Let's go to Ginza, then,' said Aiko.

'Taxi?' the hotel doorman asked Hiyoshi-san.

'Yes, thank you,' Aiko replied.

'I've missed you' he said, as they were getting into the taxi.

'The lady and gentleman are going to Ginza,' the door-man told the taxi driver.

'Please, Hiyoshi...,' Aiko begged.

'It's true. I had to tell you because it's true,' he answered. 'I don't understand what happened that night. I lie awake trying to figure it out.'

'Rest easy, dear. It was my fault. I don't know what happened either... but I'm certain it was my fault.'

'Please... don't blame yourself. It was my fault... but I don't want to leave things like this. You matter to me. I know this may not be the time or the place, but there's something I have to tell you.'

Aiko looked at him and waited for him to continue.

'First, it was all a misunderstanding. I misunderstood. Second... it's about your son. I've dreamed about him.'

'You've dreamed about what?'

'Your son.'

'What do you mean you've dreamed about my son?' asked Aiko. 'You've never even seen him!'

'Remember that bad dream you told me you used to have? The one where he was swept away by the river?'

As Hiyoshi described the dream, Aiko wished she had never told him. How could she have confided something to him that might put her in danger? Now here he was, exposing her at her most vulnerable, talking about things she had told him in the tenderest intimacy.

'Yes' she said, amazed at his memory for detail.

'You've had it several times, haven't you?'

'I'm wondering why you're bringing this up.'

'Answer me, please. It's important.'

'Just as I told you before, it's a dream that's plagued me all my life.' Aiko lowered her gaze. 'But I don't want to talk about it anymore! Why do you have to bring these things up now? Forget it, will you? I never mentioned it.'

Hiyoshi-san forged on.

'Well, I dreamt I was by the river and I saw the whole scene in my dream.'

Aiko turned to him with a stern look.

'But... how?'

'I don't know. I just have to tell you. That's why I called you. It was a very powerful feeling and I was afraid. I don't want to be responsible for what might happen if I don't tell you.'

'What might happen? What is it that might happen? Honestly, coming all the way here to tell me about a dream...'

'Don't be so hard on me. I came here to tell you about the dream and because I missed you.'

'Fine, you've told me about your dream. Now please put it out of your mind and don't bring the subject up ever again.'

'How can you ask me to forget it? Besides, I haven't finished yet...'

'Well?'

'You'll see, "A dream that keeps coming back is a messenger that doesn't wish to be heard." That's what an Ainu shaman I once met told me, but I'll tell you that story another day.' He went on with great concentration: 'The challenge is... well, let's say that... what if you finally listened to that message?'

'What would I have to do, in your opinion?' asked Aiko ironically.

'Go and find him,' he replied, searching for Aiko's eyes.

She remained silent.

'Go and find him,' he repeated.

Aiko shook her head and pondered.

'I've thought about it at times,' she said, gazing out of the window, 'but I'm afraid... Afraid of the meeting. Afraid we'll be just strangers to each other. You...,' she stuttered, searching for his eyes once again. 'Goodness me, you couldn't understand it. You can't imagine what it means to a mother to look on her son as if she were a stranger.'

'You will be... strangers to each other. So what? You'll come to know each other in time. Besides, what's the alternative?' he went on. 'I know all this really isn't any of my business, but I'm very fond of you,' he said, searching for her eyes again, and this time Aiko met his gaze.

'I really am very fond of you. You don't believe me... Do you?'

'It isn't that, Hiyoshi, it's just that it's easy to say it. It's easy because you're not in my position. I... I knew it. I knew it the minute I got to the station where my mother and sister were waiting. I knew I might be making the biggest mistake of my life, but the die was cast: "Alea iacta est", as a Roman emperor once said. Do you know the story of Julius Cæsar?'

Hiyoshi gently changed the subject:

'You once mentioned to me that your husband used to say you looked like the heron in the Kabuki play, *Sagi Musume*. Do you remember? You said he identified you with the scene where the heron dies.

'Yes...'

'I've been putting two and two together.'

'That's right. That's what my husband used to say to me. But... where is all this leading?'

'It's leading to the fact that that isn't your real story.'

Aiko looked at Hiyoshi in bewilderment. He went on:

'It isn't that story, but the story of *Kumagai Jinya*,[251] a play you know very well. You have lived, shall we say... with your "head shaven".'[252]

'Heavens, I...,' she murmured, almost speechless from the stabbing blow the truth of Hiyoshi's words had dealt her.

He remained silent.

'How can you understand,' she went on, 'that although somewhere inside me I was so strongly aware that I was making perhaps... the biggest mistake of my life, it all seemed so easy afterwards...? As if I were turning a page, forever...'

'Pages may turn but they don't stop being part of your book,' Hiyoshi broke in, 'so every morning you brushed your bald pate, in the emptiness, until you ended up truly believing you had hair. Over the years your reality began to seep into your dreams, just like the girl in the story of the well, who went out every night counting to nine.'[253]

Aiko shuddered.

'You're frightening me,' she said. 'For some reason... I've spent a long time thinking about that girl too. At home we have an abandoned cistern where...'

---

[251] *The Battlefield of Kumagi* tells the story of General Kumagi, who finds himself at a crossroads between love and duty. By opting for the latter, he has to cut off his son's head and replace it with the head of his lord's son. The work is a meditation on remorse and pain, as well as profound desolation.

[252] A mark of mourning.

[253] An ancient legend.

Aiko stopped and stared into space as if seeing something invisible to Hiyoshi.

'Never mind...,' she said.

Hiyoshi looked at her.

'So?' he asked.

'So it was' replied Aiko. 'But at those moments when one has to make a decision that...' Aiko's eyes clouded

'You have to go. I've told you before, this isn't the first time we've had this conversation.'

Aiko put a finger to Hiyoshi-san's lips.

'Hush...,' she said, trying to cleave to the magic of the moment. 'I know... In fact, sometimes I think you've given me the strength I needed to face that. Should I call him "that"?' she went on. 'It's something I would never have considered before. You... you've gradually transformed me into an overflowing fountain. I've watched things grow inside me that I never knew I had.'

'Go and find him and be at peace. Otherwise his ghost will never leave you be, and you would never forgive yourself if anything happened. Don't deny yourself this opportunity to embrace your life, your story. Part of who you are, Aiko.'

'You're right,' she replied. 'I think I should go to the land of dragons...'

'Where do you think you've been living all this time?'

'You talk like my friend the Lama... The dragons watch over the entrance to temples.'

'No, it's not that they "watch over" the entrance. They're there to warn the pilgrim that that is the point where the illusions of the self have to be transcended, because there's no other way to enter.'

Aiko remained silent. She suddenly felt as if her heart had been laid bare before the elements. She was possessed by a profound ambiguity. Was there also the possibility she might forget about it all? leave it all behind? ...that would be difficult. After hearing her friend's words, something was changing... Then she remembered that conversation with the blind fortune teller who sold lucky charms at the local shrine. She had told her that inside every person were two warriors in constant battle.

'And which one will win?' Aiko had asked.

'That depends,' she had replied.

'Depends? Depends on what?'

'On which of them you decide to feed.'

They had nearly reached Ginza. Aiko gathered all her strength, looked at Hiroshi-san and said in a quiver:

'No one has ever known my heart the way you do.'

'I thought so too. But that night when we saw each other in the bar in Kyoto I thought that... I hadn't been able to see...'

Aiko interrupted him.

'Don't worry, you know "we have to look a hundred times before we see for the first." You said that once. Isn't it so? Words you said were "trite", words from a "romantic novel". Now look: how true they turned out to be,' Aiko whispered with a forlorn smile. 'I wasn't able to see what lay hidden behind my own dragons...'

Hiyoshi-san hugged her and she kissed him tenderly, suffused by a deep feeling of calm.

They were coming to their destination. There was so much left to say...

'I'll call you,' he said.

'Yes. Please, make sure you do. Say you're my dressmaker's assistant,' she replied, smiling.

'I will,' he answered. 'Please, take care.'

'I promise.'

Hiyoshi got out of the taxi and it pulled away. Aiko felt lighter than she ever had before. Suddenly, as they waited at a traffic lights, someone began to bang on the window, making her jump in her seat. It was Tanaka, her chauffeur! Goodness! She'd forgotten all about him!

❖

It was a bright morning. Aiko was talking to the gardener about the new bulbs, when she suddenly remembered: 'The envelope with the money! Where could it have got to?' She called Tanaka's house to ask him if it had fallen out in the car. The boy who answered the phone told her that Tanaka had popped out and that he would leave him a message.

That same day, Aiko received a call from her sister, telling her that her Aunt Michi-san had died in the hospital in Okinawa and that her body was being taken to Sato. The time had come. She would set off the following day.

That night, she dreamed again of the river, the cradle and the boy being swept away on the current as she desperately tried to reach him. But the waters stopped flowing and she began to descend gently to where her son was. She could feel the warmth of his body radiating from the sheet that covered him. She approached to take him in her arms and then she woke up. Aiko started to weep. She went to draw the screen and let in some fresh air, but accidentally woke Hinata, who was sharing their bed again. Half asleep, he asked her what had happened. Aiko sat beside him on the futon and said:

'I need to talk to you. There's something you need to know.'

'Can't it wait till the morning. Leave it till then, won't you?' he begged.

She leaned over him, stroked his hair and kissed him.

'Very well, my love, very well.'

The Call

Since that fateful night when he'd torn the envelope that Madame Yamana had left in the back seat of the car, Tanaka had been confined to his bed with fever. This may have been the result of the afternoon he'd lost the car and searched for it desperately in the cold city wind, only to find he'd taken a wrong turn on leaving the restaurant. That and another nervous episode he'd had when Madame had informed him the Chairman wished to speak to him in person to 'ask him a favour'. Night after night he flailed in his futon, fighting the waves of fever until morning found him exhausted. His friend Oshima shouldered the task of nursing him. When he finally managed to get Tanaka to sleep, he would tidy up the astonishing disarray of bowls, cloths, pans and colanders in the tiny kitchen. His illness lasted a week, just as the doctor from the hospital had said it would. On the eighth day, still weak from his time in bed, he was able to get up and eat and no longer had a fever.

Madame had called when Tanaka was in the bathroom.

'I'll talk to her and give her back the torn envelope along with my resignation this afternoon.'

'All right,' said Oshima. 'It's what you've got to do.'

The telephone rang again in the other room.

'That must be her.'

Oshima ran to answer. He spoke for a few moments and then said:

'it's your father, Tana-chan. He wants to talk to you.'

Here were dragons

The celadon colour of the paint hadn't changed. But where it had cracked, little wounds of rust had opened up that the sea spray relentlessly bled.

Behind the counter a young woman in a kerchief and chequered apron served green tea in waxed paper cups, as if she were in her own home. On the display cabinet, colourful cream cakes and yokan[254] waited to be removed from their cellophane wrappers. The girl was talking to the passengers about people they knew, children who had moved to another town, husband's work, weather... no end of everyday matters, in short. She had a warm smile that revealed a gold tooth in the corner of her mouth. Aiko would have liked to have had something to talk to her about, a story in common, something they could marvel and rejoice at, just to be lulled in the woolly scarf of her breath of sugar and tea.

She felt as if she were suddenly back in the old house of her childhood, exploring the nooks and crannies of a secret wardrobe her memory kept in the attic. She walked slowly over to the starboard deck and leant on the rail. In the distance a siren bellowed from the throat of a ship passing in the opposite direction, trailing gulls in its wake, and she was seized by nostalgia for all things small and simple... Almost painfully, she recalled the time spent in the little back garden of her aunt's house, when the air was bright... as

---

[254] A sweet made of azuki beans.

she sat by the line on which t-shirts hung drying in the sun and swaying in the breeze. Then the horizon blurred and trembled, filling with glints and gleams. She thought of the times she had wanted to die and revisited the shock that it caused her as a young girl to find out that her father's brother had taken his own life. She imagined the scene lit by cold, buzzing neon lights that chilled her heart with a dull sensation she couldn't quite explain. 'It was to avoid the shame,' she had been told. Perhaps they thought those words would clarify everything, that in a single stroke they would erase the horror of the image of the hand holding the dagger, pointing unflinchingly at the pale belly – a hand she never saw, yet which harried her day and night all through her childhood, and would still return from time to time to tug at her sheets throughout her teenage years. 'To avoid the shame,' she had been told... 'He has walked through the Gate of Honour,' they said. But what kind of gate is it that dashes a human being's chances of repairing the error of his ways? The answers she had been given could never account for his death, so she had had to squeeze herself and her nightmares into the 'how-it-is' of things. She was overcome by the bitter certainty that her beloved country had fallen into the trap of overvaluing the dignifying power of death over life. She breathed deeply as someone behind her called her by her name.

'Yamana-sama?' Her heart leapt.

'Hiyoshi-san?' she murmured.

As she turned, she saw her young chauffeur standing before her. Tanaka's deer eyes gazed back at her in surprise.

'Yamana-sama?' he repeated, amazed to see it really was her.

Aiko barely recognized him, caught up as she was in the webs of her thoughts

'It's me, Tanaka, your chauffeur!' he said.

'Tanaka-kun!' she reacted. 'What are you doing here?'

The boy apologized for not having returned her call immediately. He said that he'd been ill and the fever... and to please forgive him for not taking the car to the garage when he was supposed to and only managing to yesterday. But realizing he had no excuse, all he could do was bow deeply in regret. Aiko was moved. Tanaka-kun was a loyal and honourable person. She told him not to worry, that it didn't matter, that the delay wasn't so important, and that she hoped he was better because relapses could lead to complications.

She asked him where he was heading.

'To Sato,' he replied.

Aiko stared at him in astonishment and, perceiving the confusion in her face, Tanaka assumed that little island was not part of her mental geography. He humbly explained the story his grandmother had told him, that Sato 'had languished in obscurity because, in the days when the navigation charts were drawn – so, so long ago – dragons populated the edges of the maps and for that reason Sato lay hidden beneath the fang...'

'...of a dragon' they chorused in unison.

'I see you know the story,' Tanaka, smiled.

'The left one,' Aiko clarified. 'The left fang! But... what brings you to such a mysterious island? A paper for university, maybe?'

'Well, you see...,' Tanaka murmured, lowering his gaze, 'my mother's died. I'm attending her funeral.'

Aiko was broken-hearted. Why hadn't he said so in the first place?

She asked the young man about his mother and his family, whether he had any brothers and sisters. She realized she knew nothing about him. She had never thought to ask him anything about his life. Tanaka replied that he still had his father and that his grandmother had died a little over three years ago.

'It was back during that really harsh winter. Do you remember?' he asked.

'Yes, yes,' Aiko replied. 'How could I forget? So many elderly people suffered that winter. Even my own mother... but, what happened to your grandmother?'

Tanaka explained to her that she had apparently been carried away by the wind because, being very tiny, almost the height of a child, the umbrella she was carrying was so large that...

Aiko didn't let him finish. In a broken voice, she managed to speak his name: 'Hikaru...?'

The boy gazed at her, his deer's eyes red from fighting back the tears. Aiko saw him without being able to believe it. He looked so much like her... How was it possible she had never noticed? Frozen to the spot, it felt like the ground was opening beneath her. She groped at the wall behind her and managed to lean back to stop herself from falling.

'Are you all right?' asked Tanaka Hikaru.

'Yes... yes, thank you,' Aiko gasped. 'I'm having a bit of a dizzy spell.'

'Maybe because we've come into the bay and the sea is completely calm here,' said the boy, offering her his arm.

Then, they walked to a bench on the deck and sat there, the way old friends do, as the ferry slipped serenely towards the sunset.

The tuna season had begun.

In the tea-houses, by the yellow bamboo bushes, the spring waters awaited the new tea. Soon the rivers would open and the boats would go out fishing for ayu, bearing the cormorants on their backs. The fishermen would wait in silence by the bonfires beneath a clear cerulean sky for night to fall, while the moon descended, round as a pink grapefruit, over the sea at the other end of the island.

Aiko looked once again into the eyes of her son, now lit by the gossamer light of the bay.

'Hikaru…,' she murmured, seeing again his little feet… his milky mouth at her breast. So many years had passed… She asked herself – as she had that morning on waking and seeing the utsugi flowering in the garden – where she had been all that time, what absences had possessed her, what forces had spun her round and round and flung her so very very far from herself? Her throat tightened and Tanaka's face began to blur. Aiko had to turn away and let the wind dry her eyes to conceal her weeping.

Tanaka looked at her, perplexed. She had never called him by that name; he had always been Tanaka-kun to her. He realized at the same time that he hadn't asked Madame why she was travelling, so timidly he ventured:

'Erm… Forgive me, Yamana-sama, and… what about you? What brings you here?'

Aiko hesitated. How to say it? How to explain the sleepless nights, the nightmares? How to talk to him of that insatiable search that, Ulysses-like, led her back to her port of departure. How to speak of all these things without explaining who she was, when she wasn't sure herself? So, raising a smile above the obstinate knot in her throat, she replied:

'I've come to find what has long been hidden beneath the dragon's fang.'

Tanaka raised his eyebrows and smiled at the apparent ambiguity of her reply.

'It's just that sometimes,' she went on, '"we have to look a hundred times before we see for the first.'

'How true,' answered Tanaka, without fully understanding what she was talking about.

It was something his old friend Ito-san always used to say. A common saying. So common, indeed, that it reflected its own meaning back on itself. A saying that was on everyone's lips but was seldom heeded. Then, thinking how hard it was to find accommodation on the island, he added:

'Forgive me, Madame, but… do you have somewhere to stay? It's just that all we have is a little travellers' inn. Well, just so you know, if you can't find anywhere to lodge… our little house is humble but please do consider it your home.

At that moment the ferry reached the port of Sato.

The End

Made in the USA
Middletown, DE
01 August 2020